T0315917

Everyday Mutinies:
Funding Lesbian Activism

Everyday Mutinies: Funding Lesbian Activism has been co-published simultaneously as *Journal of Lesbian Studies*, Volume 5, Number 3 2001.

Everyday Mutinies: Funding Lesbian Activism

Nanette K. Gartrell, MD
Esther D. Rothblum, PhD
Editors

Everyday Mutinies: Funding Lesbian Activism has been co-published simultaneously as *Journal of Lesbian Studies*, Volume 5, Number 3 2001.

Routledge
Taylor & Francis Group

NEW YORK AND LONDON

First published by
The Haworth Press, Inc.
10 Alice Street
Binghamton, N Y 13904-1580

This edition published 2011 by Routledge

Routledge
Taylor & Francis Group
711 Third Avenue
New York, NY 10017

Routledge
Taylor & Francis Group
2 Park Square, Milton Park
Abingdon, Oxon OX14 4RN

Everyday Mutinies: Funding Lesbian Activism has been co-published simultaneously as *Journal of Lesbian Studies*, Volume 5, Number 3 2001.

The development, preparation, and publication of this work has been undertaken with great care. However, the publisher, employees, editors, and agents of The Haworth Press and all imprints of The Haworth Press, Inc., including The Haworth Medical Press® and The Pharmaceutical Products Press®, are not responsible for any errors contained herein or for consequences that may ensue from use of materials or information contained in this work. Opinions expressed by the author(s) are not necessarily those of The Haworth Press, Inc.

Cover design by Jennifer M. Gaska

Library of Congress Cataloging-in-Publication Data

Everyday mutinies : funding lesbian activism / Nanette K. Gartrell, Esther D. Rothblum, editors.
    p. cm.
    "Co-published simultaneously as Journal of lesbian studies, volume 5, number 3 2001."
    Includes bibliographical references and index.
    ISBN 1-56023-258-7 (alk. paper) – ISBN 1-56023-259-5 (alk. paper)
    1. Lesbians–United States–Political activity. 2. Fund raising–United States. 3. Gay rights–United States. I. Gartrell, Nanette. II. Rothblum, Esther D.
HQ75.6.U5 E84 2001
305.48′9664–dc21

2001039490

Everday Mutinies:
Funding Lesbian Activism

CONTENTS

ABOUT THE EDITORS

Nanette K. Gartrell, MD, was the first out lesbian physician on the Harvard Medical School faculty. She is currently Associate Clinical Professor of Psychiatry at the University of California, San Francisco, and has a private psychotherapy practice in that city. She has been documenting sexual abuse by physicians since 1982 and conducting a longitudinal study of lesbian families since 1986. She is the editor of *Bringing Ethics Alive: Feminist Ethics for Psychotherapy Practice* (Harrington Park Press). In 1999, Dr. Gartrell received the LAVA award for Lesbians of Action, Vision, and Achievement.

Esther D. Rothblum, PhD, is Professor of Psychology at the University of Vermont, and Editor of the *Journal of Lesbian Studies*. She is a past president of the Society for the Psychological Study of Lesbian, Gay, and Bisexual Issues-Division 44 of the American Psychological Association. Dr. Rothblum has edited 23 books, including *Lesbian Friendships* and *Boston Marriages: Romantic but Asexual Relationships Among Lesbians.*

Foreword

Who are the women who struggled to form lesbian communities and how did they fund their activism? In this volume, two dozen lesbians tell the stories of their activism, with an emphasis on how they support themselves and fund their political activities. Less than 0.3% of all philanthropic dollars are awarded to lesbian and gay projects each year (and how much of that goes to gay men versus lesbians?). Consequently, lesbian activists must find alternative ways of supporting their work.

We defined a lesbian activist as a woman who supports the lesbian community via her time or money. The contributors to this volume include lesbians in the arts, politics, philanthropy, publishing, and the corporate world. When we think of lesbian activists, we may not immediately picture a scientist, a cartoonist, a photographer, a tennis player, or an employee at the Internal Revenue Service. Yet each activist in her own way enhances our lives, identities, and communities.

The lesbians featured here became activists via widely diverging paths, but each one swam *contra la corriente* (against the current), as Ángela Pattatucci-Aragón, the first author in this series, describes it. Pursuing their own visions rather than following mainstream goals, the authors faced enormous obstacles in funding their dreams. It has taken enormous creativity and resourcefulness to succeed.

Alison Bechdel, author of the *Dykes to Watch Out For* cartoon strip, states: "Just being a dyke in the early eighties fulfilled your activism requirement. Even if you weren't out, lesbianism was a revolutionary act." Why did some lesbians remain activists even while others entered more mainstream paths, eschewing political action for money, status, or a more comfortable or quieter life, or through lack of energy, or due to becoming heterosexual?

[Haworth co-indexing entry note]: "Foreword." Gartrell, Nanette K., and Esther D. Rothblum. Co-published simultaneously in *Journal of Lesbian Studies* (Harrington Park Press, an imprint of The Haworth Press, Inc.) Vol. 5, Number 3, 2001, pp. xxi-xxiii; and: *Everyday Mutinies: Funding Lesbian Activism* (ed: Nanette K. Gartrell, and Esther D. Rothblum) Harrington Park Press, an imprint of The Haworth Press, Inc., 2001, pp. xiii-xv. Single or multiple copies of this article are available for a fee from The Haworth Document Delivery Service [1-800-342-9678, 9:00 a.m. - 5:00 p.m. (EST). E-mail address: getinfo@haworthpressinc.com].

xiii

Clearly, what motivates lesbians to pursue activism is love of their work. Barbara Grier, publisher of the lesbian Naiad Press, writes: "I've always been lucky in my life in that I've always loved what I was doing." Lesbian photographer Joan Biren states, "The stuff that kept me going was that people loved the work." Lesbian poet and writer Elana Dykewomon maintains that "Nothing beats knowing you've touched other women's lives, and that the ideas you were part of will survive long after you've been forgotten–except maybe seeing that you have the power to create more freedom for yourself and others."

It takes tremendous perseverance and creativity for activists to make ends meet. The lesbians in this volume shared information, bartered for services, used up their savings, even "liberated" equipment from their place of work. Del Martin and Phyllis Lyon, publishers of the lesbian periodical *The Ladder,* describe a fundraising auction in 1962: "People donated things they wanted to clean out of their closets, many of which were white elephants that no one wanted. So bids were made for someone else as a joke, and the same junk items would show up at the next auction. Each auction brought in $1,000 or more." As soon as *The Ladder* had enough money to make ends meet, extra funds were donated to a lesbian mother fighting a custody case.

Activism raises issues of income and social class. Jewelle Gomez grew up on welfare and later on found herself in the role of giving out money as administrator with the New York State Council on the Arts. Tee Corinne describes how lesbian artists have favored blue collar jobs because "these jobs free the mind and often pay better wages than other traditional women's jobs." Elana Dykewomon writes: "We have always been undercapitalized–we don't have enough money; we don't take money seriously and we hold suspect those who do take money seriously. Very few lesbian activists think in terms of million dollar projects (urban cooperative housing, a lesbian technical institute) while men routinely finance shopping malls and trucking fleets."

Yet some lesbian activists do have access to money. Kate Kendell and Ruth Herring are leaders of the National Center for Lesbian Rights, which has a one million dollar budget. Léonie Walker was born into a wealthy family, and is co-chair of the 3.4 million dollar endowment campaign of the Astraea Lesbian Action Foundation. There are even "out" lesbians in the corporate world– Kathy Levinson, former president and Chief Operating Officer of E*TRADE Group, Inc., established the Lesbian Equity Foundation of Silicon Valley.

In a recent essay entitled "Losing ground: Where do feminists go when their gathering places vanish?" Lisa Weil writes (2000, p. 8): "We were grounding thought, emotion, vision, desire, making them visible, communicable, palpable. Those of us who weren't writing poems or essays or fiction, making films or art or videos or music, were founding journals, coffeehouses, bookstores, performance spaces, hosting fairs and conferences and festivals. We were creating spaces where the dream could become real. Giving it a place to land, thus showing it was never just a dream to begin with. We were taking what exists–despite our having been told it didn't, or if did it didn't matter–and making it *be*."

What is the future of lesbian activism? As the current generation of activists ages and retires, lesbian filmmaker Dee Mosbacher expresses concern about aging activists lacking health insurance or the resources to retire. Lesbian social worker Caitlin Ryan writes, "Our communities are changing and evolving faster than we can identify and document those changes." And Sherry Thomas, leader in the Lambda Legal Defense and Education Fund, urges current lesbian activists to model and teach the next generation of lesbian fundraisers. In sum, as Nanette Gartrell states in her chapter, we hope to model strategies for "those who are long on determination, but short on resources."

Nanette K. Gartrell
Esther D. Rothblum

REFERENCE

Weil, L. (2000). Losing ground: Where do feminists go when their gathering places vanish? *The Women's Review of Books, XVII*, 8-10.

Acknowledgments

We gratefully acknowledge the work of Dr. Mary Eichbauer, consulting editor on this volume, and of Amalia Deck.

Contra la Corriente
(Against the Current)

Ángela Pattatucci-Aragón

SUMMARY. The experiences of a Latina Lesbian behavioral scientist at the National Institutes of Health, the largest biomedical research facility in the world, are chronicled. She broke ground in directing the first

Ángela Pattatucci-Aragón, PhD, is Visiting Professor of women's studies and psychology at the University of Louisville. She conducted her doctoral dissertation research in behavior genetics at Indiana University. This was followed by postdoctoral training in epidemiology and adolescent sexuality at the National Cancer Institute, where she gained international recognition for her work in human sexual orientation–in particular Lesbian sexuality. Hailing from Puerto Rico, she returned home to conduct HIV intervention and prevention research, and served two years as Professor of epidemiology and experimental psychology at the Ponce School of Medicine on the southern part of the island. She then moved north to the University of Puerto Rico-Rio Piedras, where she served as Professor of psychology and sociology, and also as Coordinator of evaluation and assessment of Puerto Statewide Systemic Initiative (SSI), University of Puerto Rico. The SSI program, aimed at all public school students in Puerto Rico, is an intervention designed to increase student knowledge and skills in science and mathematics. Dr. Pattatucci-Aragón is a member of the Latin American Studies Association and the Society for Women in Philosophy, and has received numerous awards. She has a broad range of publications, including a book entitled *Women in science: Meeting career challenges*, which has been used as a textbook in undergraduate and graduate courses.

Address correspondence to: Ángela Pattatucci-Aragón, AIDS & AIDS-Related Research, Division of Clinical & Population-Based Studies, Center for Scientific Review, National Institutes of Health, 6701 Rockledge Drive, Bethesda, MD 20892.

[Haworth co-indexing entry note]: "Contra la Corriente (Against the Current)." Pattatucci-Aragón, Ángela. Co-published simultaneously in *Journal of Lesbian Studies* (Harrington Park Press, an imprint of The Haworth Press, Inc.) Vol. 5, Number 3, 2001, pp. 1-13; and: *Everyday Mutinies: Funding Lesbian Activism* (ed: Nanette K. Gartrell, and Esther D. Rothblum) Harrington Park Press, an imprint of The Haworth Press, Inc., 2001, pp. 1-13. Single or multiple copies of this article are available for a fee from The Haworth Document Delivery Service [1-800-342-9678, 9:00 a.m. - 5:00 p.m. (EST). E-mail address: getinfo@ haworthpressinc.com].

federally funded major clinical study focused on Lesbian sexuality and health. *[Article copies available for a fee from The Haworth Document Delivery Service: 1-800-342-9678. E-mail address: <getinfo@haworthpressinc.com> Website: <http://www.HaworthPress.com> © 2001 by The Haworth Press, Inc. All rights reserved.]*

KEYWORDS. Lesbian, lesbian activism, fundraising

It is a regular occurrence for scientific discoveries to be reported in the news media. However, they typically are used as "fillers" in the deep recesses of newspapers and, while they may be interesting in a quirky sense, more often than not they lack relevance to our everyday lives. Once in awhile, though, a scientific study comes along at precisely the right moment in history, within the context of a truculent political climate, that literally rocks the social status quo by challenging basic and long-held assumptions about what we are as human beings. Rather than a filler, that scientific study is featured on the front pages of the world's major newspapers, is reported on all of the television news networks from New York to Bejing to Sydney to Río de Janeiro, dominates talk radio discussions around the world, and remains a major topic of debate on the Internet. Instead of attenuating the pugnacious political climate, it intensifies it. Everyone has an opinion; many are extreme.

With scientists portrayed as eccentric, spectacle-wearing, socially inept nerds with a single-minded focus on obscure matters that have little connection to the real world, what scientific topic could possibly cause such a social upheaval? There are few, to be sure, but probably only one in 1993. That was the topic of homosexuality.

I was a member of a government-sponsored research group at the National Institutes of Health (NIH) in Bethesda, Maryland, the world's largest biomedical research facility, that had been quietly studying natural variations in human sexuality. I say "quietly" because that all changed on 16 July 1993, when our group published findings suggesting not only that sexual orientation has a heritable component, something that had been speculated by scientists for over a century, but also that we had molecularly localized heritability of male homosexuality in a specific study sample consisting of Gay brothers to a small region on the human X chromosome. The speculation was over and in its place shock, followed by outrage among political and religious conservatives, followed by misgivings and criticism within Lesbian, Gay, Bisexual, and Transgendered (LGBT) communities.

Ángela Pattatucci-Aragón

It was not the first time that science had investigated this topic. In fact, historically it was a mere blip on the screen of 150 years of science trying to "explain" human sexual variability and an even longer history of trying to control it. Our article, "A Linkage Between DNA Markers on the X Chromosome and Male Sexual Orientation," published in *Science*–the technical journal of the American Association for the Advancement of Science–came on the heels of several previous studies all suggesting that human sexual orientation has a biological or genetic component. Unlike the studies of earlier decades, these new investigations, ours being one among several, examined non-clinical samples of women and men in the context of homosexuality and bisexuality being viewed as normal variations of human behavior. This paradigm shift among a small group of scientists contrasted with a strong conservative political climate that fostered an ongoing paranoia surrounding the AIDS epidemic. Conservatives so tightly linked homosexuality with AIDS that the two were considered synonymous in many circles. Much as mosquitos represent the vector by which many tropical diseases are transmitted, Gay people were viewed as the "vector" for AIDS transmission. Conservatives were therefore more than willing to fund investigations that treated us as a pathology–modern Typhoid Marys–that had to be contained, controlled and eventually eradicated. However, funding projects that viewed us as normal human beings was unthinkable. That is, until we quietly convinced the federal government to approve funding support for our study.

Contrary to how the media sensationalized the modest 16-page article, our group did not discover a "gay gene." Rather, we identified a discrete region on the human X chromosome containing in excess of 100 genes, one (or more) of which is somehow associated with the pairs of Gay brothers in the sample that we studied. While it is possible that this yet-unidentified gene or genes within this region contributed in some way to the development of a homosexual orientation in these men, it is equally plausible that what we identified is associated with a more general trait, such as *resiliency under stress,* that is shared by these brothers but is not necessarily unique to homosexuals. At this point, there is not enough information to say one way or the other.

While our study represented a major step forward in understanding human sexual variability, it was not earth shattering by scientific standards. We merely applied well-established scientific techniques to a research question that prior to our investigation the technology was inadequate to address. The media circus surrounding the publication of our findings can therefore best be understood in terms of its political rather than its scientific ramifications. Religious and political conservatives had shifted from concentrating on outside adversaries after the fall of communism in the Soviet bloc, the arrest of Manuel Noriega, and the brief skirmish with Saddam Hussein in the Gulf War, to focusing on the enemy within. Homosexuality was identified as America's nemesis. Queers became the country's scapegoat, with what seemed like all social, economic and spiritual problems somehow connected to our existence–the AIDS epidemic being at the top of the list. It was in the context of this conservative backlash on us that our newly elected President, Bill Clinton, announced that he was lifting the long-standing ban on homosexuals serving in the military. His instructions to the Pentagon to establish a new policy on homosexuality by 15 July 1993 launched a heated debate in the U.S. Congress that literally stalled consideration of all other important government business. Our article was published just one day after this deadline, which went unmet due to the Congressional debate, and many political pundits speculated that the President had orchestrated the entire thing to advance his "liberal agenda."

However, nothing could be further from the truth. In reality, our clinical proto-col underwent rigorous scientific peer review and examination by the highest ranking officials at both the NIH and the U.S. Department of Health and Hu-man Services prior to its approval during the Republican-led *George Bush* ad-ministration! Moreover, scientific journal articles are submitted to editors several months to a year prior to actual publication and also undergo stringent peer review. Thus, the juxtaposition of our article with the Gays in the military dispute was by coincidence rather than by design. In fact, we were concerned about the opposite–that publication of our article would be delayed because of the debate. However, in the end, saner minds prevailed and the article was pub-lished according to the regular established procedures of the journal without regard to the ongoing political vitriol.

Why did I go against the current (*contra la corriente*) and become involved in sexual orientation research in the first place? Why did I ignore friends, col-leagues, and mentors that collectively advised that it would be a career-ending move? I had already gained an international reputation as a geneticist while in graduate school and everyone had great expectations for me to become a "su-perstar" in the field. The logical and safe course would have been to stay on that path. My choice to pursue a career in behavioral research therefore seemed abrupt to onlookers–as if I had "quit" and taken this major step down. In real-ity, I was pursuing a dream.

While the reasons behind my going against the current are many, it really boils down to a personality trait that has been with me all of my life. I do not like people telling me what I can and cannot do. In this instance, upon entering graduate school at Indiana University–Bloomington, the only Latina in the en-tire program, I had a brief meeting with the chairperson of the department of biology. I enthusiastically expressed a strong desire to conduct research that would bridge across the departments of psychology and biology, sharing that I saw the intersection of these two fields as a challenging new research frontier. His response was sternly disapproving, indicating that if I wanted to pursue that line of inquiry *after* I left Indiana University that would be fine, but as long as I was part of his program I would be conducting biological research. Un-daunted, after passing my comprehensive exams that admitted me to doctoral candidacy, I clandestinely arranged with the psychology department to sit in on a full complement of courses and seminars in developmental and social psychology. Thus, my decision to join a biobehavioral project focused on hu-man sexuality research was not the radical move that most people perceived it to be, but actually represented the culmination of my original goal and the next logical step in my career–the integration of my graduate studies in psychology and biology.

My colleague Dean Hamer and I shared a number of commonalities that facilitated our collaboration. For example, we are both creative people that thrive on challenge. Each of us was also bored with our previous work and thus ready for a change. However, beyond that our circumstances were radically different. Dean is a tenured scientist at the NIH, the Chief of a laboratory section, and had a well-established research track record. Although he certainly weathered a lot of incredulous remarks from colleagues when he changed his research direction, Dean still had a safety net. He had established himself in an obscure but scientifically respectable area in yeast genetics, branching into the risky area of human sexuality research under the protection of being a tenured scientist. Even if the project turned out to be a total failure, he still had his tenured position and could simply switch to a different focus. Conversely, I had no safety net. I was a postdoctoral research associate trying to establish her career and eventually secure a job on a risky area of research. For me, it was do or die.

Human sexual orientation is variable. This is the first sentence of our 1993 article. To me, this is self-evident. We need only to look at the immense variability within our own local Lesbian communities to acknowledge this. Whether our genes make a contribution to some of this variability is an open and interesting question. However, for me it was not nearly as compelling as other related areas of inquiry such as how individuals experience their gender and sexuality, how gender and sexual orientation intersect in individuals, how gender and sexuality evolve in individuals over time, and a myriad of Lesbian health issues. Thus, while the men's arm of the study was focused almost exclusively on genetics, the women's arm that I directed was much broader in scope.

A detailed account of the challenges that were faced in getting the research protocol approved by the NIH hierarchy has been written elsewhere (see Hamer & Copeland, 1994). Suffice it to say that numerous roadblocks were encountered–for example, being required to address human subjects' concerns that bordered on the ridiculous–and we faced even greater obstacles to maintaining the protocol after the initial sanction was obtained. However, the challenges to securing approval for the women's arm of the study were significantly greater. The prejudice and ignorance were at a much higher level. No matter how cogent our argument, the oversight committee reviewers could not seem to grasp the importance of studying Lesbians–particularly Lesbian health issues. The questions that they raised were nonsensical. Why bother in the first place? What is it that is unique about Lesbians that will not be learned by studying Gay men?

The male study had the AIDS epidemic at its core and reviewers easily recognized the potential value for a research focus on Gay men. Additionally, it is heterosexual men in general that have the greatest discomfort with male homosexuals, so it stands to reason that a scientific infrastructure dominated by heterosexual males might want to find out what is going on so that they could eventually control it. Furthermore, there is the psychological distance factor. Most men, including those that are scientists, do not have a clue of what makes *heterosexual* women tick. Therefore, understanding Lesbians would seem a remote possibility at best. Consequently, there was little enthusiasm for the women's arm of the protocol, but the male arm was viewed with great promise. Even if we did not find what we proposed to look for with respect to AIDS and Kaposi's Sarcoma, everyone was confident that meaningful information would nonetheless be derived because the protocol was considered comprehensive.

Curiously, the women's arm of study was much more comprehensive than that proposed for men, but the optimistic attitude of the oversight committee did not extend to women. We faced obstacle after obstacle in attempting to persuade the review committee that studying sexual variability in women, and more importantly Lesbian health, was a worthwhile thing to do–that there were unique things that needed to be addressed, not the least of which was the issue of parenting, including insemination and childbearing. Cancer was another area in which I had a great deal of interest. However, at that time there was little supporting literature on Lesbians and cancer that could be used to justify conducting such a study. Of course in my mind, this alone represented a compelling reason for initiating research in this area, but it did little to sway the obstinacy of the oversight committee. This, despite the fact that our group was unique, perhaps the only one in the world at the time, that had the resources, infrastructure and access to a vast Lesbian population to get the investigation up and running. Most baffling to me was the fact that the approved study protocol focused on men was just as speculative as the one proposed for women! I was left with the impression that the committee considered *any* research focused on women to be inherently speculative and fraught with potential complications.

Although we eventually obtained selective approval to collect a limited amount of information on the heritability of sexual orientation in women, mainly because this was seen as a logical complement to the male study, we never actually succeeded in convincing the oversight committee that studying Lesbian health is a worthwhile thing to do. Fortunately, the NIH moves at a slow pace and once turned down, you are given an opportunity to address the committee's concerns and resubmit your request at their next meeting. Therefore, we responded to the oversight committee's criticisms and returned round after round to present our case again. In the meantime, I was gathering the data. Our group had a yearly budget and we simply allocated part of it to conducting the women's arm of the study under the sincere belief that we would eventually gain approval to investigate Lesbian health issues. Regrettably, as the initial excitement surrounding the study began to wane and in its place came extreme pressure from conservative leaders in Congress and public figures to stop the research entirely, it became painfully apparent that the oversight committee would never approve the protocol for studying Lesbian health. In the short term, I collected a massive amount of data anyway. However, in the long term it eventually marked the end of my time as a research scientist at the NIH, and in turn spelled the end of Lesbian research at the NIH.

While things have gotten progressively better over the years, one could still say that *any* woman entering a scientific field is going against the current (see Pattatucci, 1998). However, the situation can be orders of magnitude worse for Lesbians. In addition to the sexism encountered by most women in science, Lesbians must contend with heterosexism, where the worst aspersions at times come from "threatened" women in supervisory positions–ones that might have initially been considered allies and role models. Couple this with being a member of a minority group and one can have a sense of the suffocating environment that I was in. I was on this vast NIH campus, with thousands of researchers and staff but no support outside of the small six-member research group to which I belonged.

I have arrived at the conclusion through my life experiences that Lesbians are viewed by the world as lacking authenticity. We are seen as "incomplete" women, much like an unfinished painting on a canvas by a deceased artist, stuck in an inescapable limbo that becomes its existence, its reality, and everything interesting about the work–the levels of meaning in its depiction, its tone, hue, texture, lines, depth, and contour–are all relegated insignificant. Nothing matters except the fact that the painting, or the woman in our case, is an "unfinished work." People always wonder what we could have been, instead of celebrating what we are. This summarizes the basic reaction that I received from colleagues at the NIH. Most were amicable but there was always an undercurrent of disappointment and discomfort with me. I was the out Lesbian conducting research on Lesbians–an inauthentic woman conducting inauthentic research. In its best light, my work was *cute*. I was like the young daughter in "girl training" that greets her father at the door with the proclamation that she helped cook dinner with mommy. No one believes that she actually contributed to the success of the meal–she's just there and cute. Similarly, the research that I conducted, no matter how carefully crafted, meticulous and precise, and no matter how impressive the data were, was always viewed at the level of being *cute* and never really taken seriously. Part of the condescending attitudes that I faced was connected to my being a behavioral scientist in an environment consisting of hard core biochemists and molecular biologists that believed that the term "behavioral science" is an oxymoron. However, the major aspect was that, despite making a major contribution to the study by characterizing the samples of men and women that informed the genetic analysis that my colleague Dean Hamer conducted, I was still a Lesbian with an interest in studying Lesbians. I was *cute*.

While my experience at the NIH as a Latina Lesbian behavioral scientist was characterized by devaluation and marginalization, I completely underestimated the profound impact of me being an out Lesbian–the only member of the team that was public about her sexual orientation–would have on how the study was perceived. At the NIH I was surrounded by attitudes that I was insignificant and had pretty much grown to think of myself in those terms. However, our 1993 article that garnered the deluge of media attention and had Gay men in the Washington, DC, area running around proudly wearing T-shirts displaying the logo, "Xq28–Thanks for the Genes Mom!", intersected with the Congressional debate over Gays in the military that resulted in the infamous *don't ask, don't tell* policy. This resulted in more public scrutiny surrounding our study than would otherwise have occurred. I was completely blind-sided by being thrust literally overnight under the international media microscope and their almost exclusive focus on the problematic nature of my Lesbian status relative to the research study. Equally disconcerting was the sudden attention that the NIH hierarchy and other U.S. government agencies directed toward me. There seemed to be grave concern and preoccupation at the NIH over what I, their token Latina Lesbian, might say to the press. (We all have "hot blood," you know, and therefore are unpredictable.) Thus, I was ordered by one of those "threatened" woman supervisors to say nothing (under a warning of dire consequences if I did not comply). On 16 July 1993, the day that our article was officially released to the public and the media flurry began, there was a Congressional request for my curriculum vita. All of this made me decidedly uncomfortable and created a growing sense of disillusionment.

I was unprepared in many other respects as well. For example, my phone number and street address were published in the telephone directory. This meant that I came home nightly to an answering machine loaded with calls from "concerned citizens" and a mailbox full of letters containing similar vituperations. My colleague Dean Hamer received the bulk of the positive press and I the negative. While he was viewed as a legitimate scientist, I was an activist with an agenda–all because I was an out Lesbian. When the pendulum swung from initial excitement to disdain in LGBT communities, particularly in academia, I again was the focus of castigation. Many seemed to view me as a Lesbian turncoat, and the sting of becoming a pariah in the community that I loved was deep and long-lasting. I found myself in the curious position of being held responsible for what *others* were writing about the study, as if I actually had some overarching control over what the news media chooses to present. I learned that the quickest way to stop conversation at social gather-

ings was to tell people what I did. Complete silence usually followed that statement, with people subsequently excusing themselves to visit the lavatory or to
tend to other priorities. Prejudicial assumptions were also held by my NIH
peers. For example, after delivering a presentation on the progress of my research to our laboratory division at the National Cancer Institute, I received
several "compliments" indicating pleasant surprise that my seminar was at a
high professional level, contrasting with the unbridled stream of activist dia-
tribe that had been expected. I was obviously offended. However, most astounding is the fact that these colleagues felt perfectly comfortable sharing
their prejudices with me!

Being a government scientist and not just proudly out to my circle of friends
and co-workers, but also out internationally through a frenzy of incessant media attention, was a major thorn in the side of government policy makers. The
federal government was telling Lesbians and Gay men that a requirement for
serving in the U.S. military is staying deeply hidden in the closet. Conversely, I
was identified in media interviews as a government employee who was
proudly out and emphatically advocating that the most important thing that
any LGBT person could do is to come out of hiding and be public about their
sexual orientation! I represented a contradiction in federal government policy
and this did not bode well for me and my future.

Several months after the 1993 study was published and the suffocating in-
tensity of the media attention had subsided, I arrived at work to the shock of
being informed that Senator Jesse Helms was attacking me on the U.S. Senate
floor. It seems that his staff researched the LGBT media and once per year
Senator Helms would have an aide publicly catalog through a list of the most
egregious examples of LGBT "perversity" and/or uses of public funds to support the "Gay agenda." As an out Lesbian government employee publicly advocating a course of action by LGBT individuals that was contrary to U.S.
government policy, I was a prime target for his wrath. Especially problematic
was a photograph published in a well-known LGBT periodical that Senator
Helms alleged set a corrupting example because it depicted me opening a
black leather biker jacket to reveal the word "DYKE" written in large bold letters across my chest (it was a T-shirt, not skin). Everything from the validity of
my academic credentials and my credibility as a researcher to my appropriate-
ness as a government employee were questioned. While no direct connection
to this event can be made, it was not long after that I was informed that my employment contract at the NIH would not be renewed. This, despite the fact that
I was eligible for five years of support and had only used two of them.

The severity of the reproach coming from all sides had cumulatively taken
its toll. I returned to Puerto Rico, vowing never to set foot on U.S. mainland
soil again. My hope was that I would be able to analyze all of the data that I had

collected while continuing to gather more, cross-cultural, data there. Unfortunately, I encountered essentially the same attitudes that I had experienced at the NIH. In other words, Lesbian health research was *cute*, but not really a worthwhile thing to do. Some of the reactions were of a passive-aggressive nature. For example, I was the first behavioral scientist appointed to the faculty at the Ponce School of Medicine (PSM) on the southern part of the island. Shortly after I began my duties there, the Dean of Research called me to his office for a meeting and asked me what sort of research program I was planning to initiate at PSM. Much like my similar interview in graduate school, I enthusiastically responded by outlining the compelling reasons for studying sexual orientation in women from a number of different perspectives, indicating that I had a large amount of data that I wanted to analyze and publish, while at the same time instituting a new study on the island that would allow me to conduct cross-cultural comparisons with my existing data, and hopefully also expand into some new directions as well. The Dean just glared at me and finally responded by repeating his initial question as if we were starting again from scratch. Thus, without stating so explicitly, he sent a clear and very strong message that there would be no support for me to study Lesbian health. This meant that I had not only zero hope of securing internal funding, but also no prospect for obtaining external federal funds if I chose to pursue this line of inquiry, because there is a component in the evaluation process that requires institutional support for the project. Nevertheless, I continued to interview families and collect data at my own expense and on my own time. However, this left me with little opportunity to analyze the data because in order to survive I had to engage in projects that were of interest to the institution. After a few years at PSM, I moved to the University of Puerto Rico at Río Piedras (UPR) on the northern part of the island, but received no better reception there than I had at PSM for Lesbian Health research and my situation remained essentially the same.

Like many women, I had spent my professional career in the academic ghetto as a contract employee–positions that are inherently unstable and demand a great deal of effort with little professional respect. We are the underclass that the university tries to hide, the academic migrant workers, maids, and laundresses that toil so that the privileged can direct their attention to matters of social importance. Thus, when our governor, Pedro Rosselló, announced in 1998 that he was "trimming" forty million dollars from the UPR operating budget, I was again faced with the looming prospect that my contract might not be renewed. However, this time I was not alone. Instead I was in the company of many other professionals on the island all scrambling to find new positions in an environment of great uncertainty surrounding this massive budget cut. Fortunately, I am fluent in English and was able to expand my search to the U.S. mainland. I eventually landed a one-year visiting professor position at the University of Louisville teaching in the Women's Studies program. This meant breaking my promise never to return to the U.S. mainland, but promises are always easier to keep when they do not involve putting food on the table.

I now have come full circle and am back working at the NIH as a Scientific Review Administrator, where I direct the scientific review of AIDS and AIDS-Related Research grant applications with a behavioral science focus submitted to the NIH for funding consideration. While composing this article, I initiated a search on the NIH Computer Retrieval of Information on Scientific Projects (CRISP) system, which lists data on all funded projects from 1986 to present. Searching with *Lesbian* as a keyword, which scans for Lesbian in the title as well as the abstract, yielded 18 funded applications. Of these, 8 were focused on sexually transmitted infections (including HIV) in which the major focus is on men. The remaining 10 applications were split, with five focused on both sexes and five focused exclusively on women. Of the five focused exclusively on women, four were focused exclusively on Lesbians. They break down as follows: two predoctoral National Research Service Awards (F31), one postdoctoral National Research Service Award (F32), and one R01 (regular research grant). The R01 is currently in its funding cycle, which means that it was recently awarded. The NIH is much more charitable in the predoctoral and postdoctoral projects that it funds. Thus, it is not surprising that there are representatives from these groups. However, it is particularly disturbing that only one regular (R01) grant has been funded in the past fifteen years that is specifically focused on Lesbian health. This must change.

I am currently in a position where I advise applicants and am invited to universities and conferences to deliver seminars on how to successfully approach the grant writing and review process. As NIH staff, I can also advocate for the importance of Lesbian health research with others at the NIH and, at least sometimes, be taken seriously. This in turn enables me to direct potential applicants interested in obtaining federal funding to study Lesbian health to NIH program personnel that can share specific program foci and goals that may ultimately assist the applicants in developing a successful strategy for a grant application. Although just one funded R01 application focused on Lesbian health in the past fifteen years is a dismal record, viewed differently this grant has opened a door for the rest of you to walk through. I therefore encourage those interested in conducting research on Lesbian health to take full advantage of the vast NIH resources that are available to all researchers, to use those resources to develop project proposals, and to submit them to the NIH for funding consideration.

As for me, I am currently collaborating with several individuals to analyze and publish the large data set that I collected in Puerto Rico and in the U.S. on sexual orientation in women and Lesbian health. As usual, this is not part of my official NIH duties and therefore must be completed on my own time. Thus, my life continues *contra la corriente*.

SOURCES AND FURTHER READING

Pattatucci, Á.M., 1998. *Women in Science: Meeting Career Challenges.* Thousand Oaks, CA: Sage Publications, Inc.

Pattatucci, Á.M., 1998. Biopsychosocial Interactions and the Development of Sexual Orientation. In: Patterson, C., and D'Augelli, A. (Eds.), *Lesbian, Gay, and Bisexual Identities in Families: Psychological Perspectives.* New York: Oxford University Press.

Pattatucci, Á.M., and Hamer, D.H., 1995. The Genetics of Sexual Orientation: From Fruit Flies to Humans. In: P. Abramson, S. Pinkerton, eds., *Sexual Nature/Sexual Culture.* Chicago: University of Chicago Press.

Hamer, D.H., and Copeland, P., 1994. *The Science of Desire: The Search for the Gay Gene and The Biology of Behavior.* New York: Simon & Schuster.

Ordinary Insurrections:
Alison Bechdel Interviewed by Marny Hall

Alison Bechdel
Marny Hall

SUMMARY. Lesbian cartoonist Alison Bechdel published her first *Dykes to Watch Out For* comic strip almost twenty years ago. During a phone interview with Marny Hall, Bechdel describes the ways in which her politics and her art have intersected and evolved over the years. Bechdel also discusses the harsh realities of subcultural economics, as well as the strategies she has relied upon to support herself and her art. *[Article copies available for a fee from The Haworth Document Delivery Service: 1-800-342-9678. E-mail address: <getinfo@haworthpressinc.com> Website: <http://www.HaworthPress.com> © 2001 by The Haworth Press, Inc. All rights reserved.]*

KEYWORDS. Lesbian, lesbian activism, fundraising

Alison Bechdel has been drawing the comic strip *Dykes to Watch Out For* since 1983. Nine collections of her award-winning cartoons, including the most recent *Post-Dykes to Watch Out For*, have been published by Firebrand Books. Her strip appears biweekly in 70 publications in the US and Canada.

Marny Hall, psychotherapist and author, lives and works in the San Francisco Bay Area. Her books include *The Lavender Couch, Sexualities, The Lesbian Love Companion*, and, with Kimeron Hardin, *Queer Blues*.

Address correspondence to: Alison Bechdel, P.O. Box 215, Jonesville, VT 05466 or Marny Hall, 4112 24th Street, San Francisco, CA 94114.

[Haworth co-indexing entry note]: "Ordinary Insurrections: Alison Bechdel Interviewed by Marny Hall." Bechdel, Alison, and Marny Hall. Co-published simultaneously in *Journal of Lesbian Studies* (Harrington Park Press, an imprint of The Haworth Press, Inc.) Vol. 5, Number 3, 2001, pp. 15-21; and: *Everyday Mutinies: Funding Lesbian Activism* (ed: Nanette K. Gartrell, and Esther D. Rothblum) Harrington Park Press, an imprint of The Haworth Press, Inc., 2001, pp. 15-21. Single or multiple copies of this article are available for a fee from The Haworth Document Delivery Service [1-800-342-9678, 9:00 a.m. - 5:00 p.m. (EST). E-mail address: getinfo@haworthpressinc.com].

For one glorious moment, we existed. The L-word echoed from sea to shining sea. It was drawled on verandahs in Virginia, barked in Bronx tenements, declaimed from pulpits in Skokie. One of our own had made the big time. But no sooner than it had begun, the flurry subsided. The TV show was canceled. Our 15-minute prance on the national stage was over. (In a recent interview in *People* magazine, even Ellen DeGeneres herself said she was tired of being defined as a lesbian.) Today, we are as passé as hippies flashing peace signs or last season's sitcom. We *are* last season's sitcom: retro without a trace of trendiness.

Invisibility is nothing new. After decades of deletion from family wills and political agendas, of exclusion from social policy and media coverage, we should be used to it. But this latest erasure, the been-there-done-that yawn, is particularly ignominious. Yet, just as we are about to take up permanent residence in Hasbian Nation, we are rescued, improbably enough, by a posse of scrappy, irreverent, idealistic, cynical, larger-than-life cartoon characters.

The characters are the stars of *Dykes to Watch Out For*. Many of us have been following the strip, on and off, for years. But now, browsing in a lesbian bookstore or thumbing through the pages of a gay newspaper, we are riveted by it. A new transfusion of inky blood pumps into our veins, a new swagger surges into our step. It turns out that we do exist after all. We have the subversive pen of Alison Bechdel to thank (or curse) for this vexatious, last-minute resurrection.

Bechdel is an unlikely messiah. When I call her at her home in Vermont, I imagine her surrounded by what Sydney, one of her postmodernesque characters, might refer to as "indeterminacy" and what anyone else would call clutter: books bristling with post-its, computer printouts, photos, newspaper clippings, half-finished cartoon strips, tokens from admiring fans, and perhaps a half-eaten bagel or package of trail mix.

I explain that I'm calling to talk about the ways in which lesbian activists support themselves and their work. Self-effacing anti-hero that she is, Alison immediately balks at the activist label. Back in the old days, it was a little easier to assume the activist mantle, she tells me: "Just being a dyke in the early eighties fulfilled your activism requirement. Even if you weren't out, lesbianism was a revolutionary act."

In fact, when she first began her cartoon strip in the eighties, she considered it pro-dyke propaganda. But after what Bechdel refers to as "the Ellenization factor," it takes more than mere depiction of lesbian lifestyles to make a political point. Bechdel's mission was fuzzy for awhile. After the passage of the Vermont civil union bill, however, it acquired fresh momentum. She says she felt a sense of legitimation that she didn't even know she was missing.

Alison Bechdel
Photo by Alan Jakubek. Used by permission.

"I'm feeling more lately like I can write about anything and that I can do this through my lesbian characters. I want a lesbian perspective to be considered a human perspective. I don't like the word *universal,* but for lack of a better term–a universal perspective. Why shouldn't it be? And I think that's one of the possible benefits of all this assimilation and mainstreaming that's been going on. That in all of the banality and schlock that our subculture seems to be disintegrating into, there's also a chance for a really astute lesbian perspective to reach a broader audience. I was looking up at CNN at the gym a couple of months ago and there was Kate Clinton talking about Hillary Clinton's run for the Senate. I don't think that would have happened without the assimilation that has been going on."

Her more recent cartoons reflect this renewed sense of legitimacy and purpose. After years of depicting a dyke-only world, straight characters—even white males–have been integrated into DTWOF. But, these characters exist in a lesbian world and are subject to lesbian narrative requirements. In other words, instead of featuring the mainstreaming of lesbians, Alison depicts the

Marny Hall
Photo by Nanette K. Gartrell. Used by permission.

dyke-streaming of heterosexuals. It is a revolutionary act: a bloodless coup where all the hostages are eager to be taken.

But, I realize as we talk, this is the end . . . or rather the latest installment in Alison's life/work. What about the beginning? I ask how she got started. It was more or less an accident, a matter of being at the right place at the right time, Alison tells me:

"When I graduated from college I was clueless. I had no ambition, no direction. It didn't occur to me to have a career, to start looking for some kind of job that was going to eventually pay me a lot of money. I don't know why. I don't know if it was a generational thing or just a personality trait. So it left me free to do whatever the hell I wanted, after I paid the rent of course."

She discovered that what she wanted to do was create cartoons for and about dykes. The first were published in 1983 in *Womanews,* a New York-based feminist newspaper. The only compensation was the pleasure of seeing her work in print and the very positive response from her readers. How, I asked, had she paid the rent?

"At first, I had some menial office jobs and then I worked in the warehouse of a food bank. Then I worked part time as a production manager at a gay and lesbian newspaper. Meanwhile, I had approached Boston's *Gay Community News* and the *Philadelphia Gay News.* They gave me ten or fifteen dollars for my cartoons."

Around this time in her life, Alison tells me that she had a pivotal dream: "I was living in New York City at the time and I dreamed I was trying to get on the subway. Instead of a token, I had a cartoon drawn on a piece of paper. That got me through the turnstile." I ask how the dream influenced her.

"It was a pretty powerful image and it stuck with me, but it wasn't until five or six years later that I actually had the courage to quit my day job. It was a very scary thing to do, although I was only thirty so I didn't have a whole lot of financial obligations. It wasn't like I had a family or a mortgage or anything. Still it felt like this frightening kind of commitment, like you would feel marrying somebody."

Alison's comments remind me of an episode in her latest collection: *Post Dykes to Watch Out For.* Academically ambitious Sydney realizes that she is married to her work. Her primary partner, Mo, must accept second-fiddle status.

Alison reads my mind. "I'm a workaholic," she says. "I admit it. And in a way my work is unusual because it really is my life, you know. I mean it's not autobiographical, but it is about life, the kind of life that I lead. And so, in a way I never stop working."

Even with all the hard work, she wouldn't have been able to support herself unless certain factors had fallen into place. "I started doing my comic strip at a time when the gay and lesbian press was just beginning to really take off–when these newspapers were starting all over the country. It was fortuitous because there were the vehicles to carry my work."

Alison adds that her novelist friends have a much harder time supporting themselves. "Comic strips are more economically viable, which is pretty sad in general but lucky for me," she says. "Partly this is because they are so accessible. I mean, a lot more people read *Garfield* than Dostoevsky. But also comic strips are a form of serial fiction. If you know what you're doing, your work promotes itself by creating a continuing demand for narrative resolution."

My own addiction proves her point. Whenever my new *Lesbian Connection* comes in the mail, I always flip to the cartoons. I am dying to know what new hell Sydney is perpetrating on long-suffering Mo.

"But publishing cartoons in newspapers isn't enough. Another critical part of the formula," Alison continues, "is the publication of collections of the cartoons in book form. When I had three books under my belt, the royalty income enabled me to risk quitting my day job. Plus there's a synergy between the strips and the books, to use a tiresome, but apt bit of media jargon. The newspaper strips create a market for the collections and vice versa."

As we're talking, I have a flashback. "It seems once, a long time ago, somebody gave me a Mo T-shirt."

"Oh yes, I also had this little business . . . I forgot. Another way that I subsidized my cartoons for many years was by selling merchandise with my characters on it."

"At gay and lesbian bookstores?"

"Also by mail order and at women's festivals. For years I had a booth at Michigan. But I'm not a very skillful business person. Ultimately I abandoned the whole proceedings, but it did keep me from having to go and work a shift at McDonald's."

"Okay, so you made enough money from cartoon syndication and royalties, mugs and T-shirts. Anything else?"

"I also do public speaking."

"So over the years your celebrity status has become a way of supporting yourself as well?"

"I feel like a prostitute half the time." Alison hesitates. "Well, not really, but I'm a cartoonist, not a performer. Trading on my minor celebrity to get speaking gigs feels like selling myself. That doesn't stop me from doing it, though, because I need the money. I have a slide lecture I take to colleges. But even though I know I'm providing an interesting talk and an important point of view for the students, I feel like I should be home drawing."

The sell-out: It is one of the ongoing themes in Alison's work. It is what all her main characters, in one way or another, are wrestling with: How to keep the counterculture alive in a corporate world; how to be true to feminist principles and still be receptive to postfeminist theory.

I want to reassure Alison, to protest that she's not selling out, that—whether speaking to college students or drawing cartoons—she is contributing just as much as her real-life heroes: those grass roots organizers, the legislators, and the lawyers who got the Vermont bill passed. I stifle my impulse to persuade her. I realize that if Alison weren't riddled with self-doubts, she wouldn't be able to reflect our own parallel dilemmas with such wisdom and wit. If she didn't have a bad case of assimilation anxiety herself, she wouldn't be able to teach us how to survive in the belly of the beast, how to salvage the positive things that the dominant culture has to offer, and how to convert them to dyke-fodder.

And she does just that. There is plenty of evidence. When I first called to set up the interview, we had a casual conversation about the impact of her work. I asked if readers contacted her very often. She read me an e-mail she had just gotten from a student thanking her for her strip. The young dyke wrote that "the kind of community that's shown in Madwimmin books" had inspired her to start a gay-straight alliance in her high school. Such a supportive group, she was sure, would help others like herself come out.

Although Alison is reluctant to take credit for providing such inspiration, she is eager to give it. She feels she is deeply indebted to the lesbian community. Make that "communities," plural. She gets her ideas from contact with friends and strangers. "There is even a message board on the Internet about my characters," she tells me. She loves it. "The greatest pleasure and honor of what I do is that people really are engaged with the story I'm telling. The encouragement is what enables me to continue–both the critical encouragement and the financial reimbursement."

What about the reimbursement, I inquire. Does she still have to hustle?

"Yeah, I'm always hustling pretty hard. I make a modest living and that's it. I think there's a perception in the lesbian community that I make a lot of money. Even informed activists don't understand the reality of subcultural economics. People come up to me and solicit me for donations for things, like I'm some big benefactor. Man, give *ME* some money!"

Or better yet, buy her books. And don't overlook the very first *Dykes to Watch Out For*. It is as funny, as subversive as it was when it was originally published in the mid-eighties. One of the strips, entitled "The Seven Ages of Lesbians," shows all our incarnations–from baby dyke to progressive yuppie, from first-wave politico to old school bar dyke (who asks the cutie on the next barstool, "Wanna see me tie this maraschino cherry stem into a knot using only my tongue?"). The last scene shows the tireless activist dyke, leaping over the U.S. Army depot barricades and egging on her confederates. Inscribed next to this frame is Alison's editorial comment: "Last scene of all, which ends this strange eventful herstory, is renewed hope and young idealism."

That about sums it up.

JEB (Joan E. Biren):
Lesbian Photographer, Video Producer, Activist

Joan E. Biren
Gayle E. Pitman

SUMMARY. This article is based on a telephone interview between Joan E. Biren and Gayle Pitman. During the interview, Joan, a lesbian-feminist photographer and video producer, talked about the effect the women's movement had on her career choice, the barriers and oppression she endures as a result of working for social change, and the personal characteristics and coping strategies she utilizes as she attempts

JEB (Joan E. Biren), an internationally recognized documentary artist, is the author of two books of photographs: *Eye to Eye: Portraits of Lesbians* (1979) and *Making a Way: Lesbians Out Front* (1987). As the video producer for the 1993 March on Washington for Lesbian, Gay and Bi Equal Rights and Liberation, JEB was responsible for the giant screens on the Mall and the official video, *A Simple Matter of Justice*. JEB's videos have been broadcast on public television and her photographs are in the permanent collections of the Library of Congress, Harvard University, and the Academy of Arts in Berlin, Germany. JEB is president of Moonforce Media, a non-profit video production company. She recently completed a video on women organizers and is currently at work on *No Secret Anymore: The Times of Del Martin and Phyllis Lyon*.

Gayle E. Pitman is Assistant Professor of Psychology at Sacramento City College. Her professional interests include lesbian body image, feminist therapy, multicultural issues, and the influence of oppression and minority status on mental health.

Address correspondence to: JEB, Moonforce Media, P.O. Box 2934, Washington, DC 20003 (E-mail: jebmedia@hotmail.com).

[Haworth co-indexing entry note]: "JEB (Joan E. Biren): Lesbian Photographer, Video Producer, Activist." Biren, Joan E., and Gayle E. Pitman. Co-published simultaneously in *Journal of Lesbian Studies* (Harrington Park Press, an imprint of The Haworth Press, Inc.) Vol. 5, Number 3, 2001, pp. 23-31; and: *Everyday Mutinies: Funding Lesbian Activism* (ed: Nanette K. Gartrell, and Esther D. Rothblum) Harrington Park Press, an imprint of The Haworth Press, Inc., 2001, pp. 23-31. Single or multiple copies of this article are available for a fee from The Haworth Document Delivery Service [1-800-342-9678, 9:00 a.m. - 5:00 p.m. (EST). E-mail address: getinfo@haworthpressinc.com].

23

to overcome these barriers. Joan's story offers an inspiring portrait of a woman who, in the face of adversity, stays true to her feminist politics and integrates lesbianism, feminism, and activism in her everyday life. *[Article copies available for a fee from The Haworth Document Delivery Service: 1-800-342-9678. E-mail address: <getinfo@haworthpressinc.com> Website: <http://www.HaworthPress.com> © 2001 by The Haworth Press, Inc. All rights reserved.]*

KEYWORDS. Lesbian, lesbian activism, fundraising

JEB (Joan E. Biren) is a freelance photographer/documentary artist and the president of Moonforce Media, a non-profit film and video production/distribution company that specializes in serving the LGBT communities. She is one of the first lesbian photographers to document authentic images of "out" lesbians. I (Gayle) had the opportunity to interview Joan over the phone one afternoon. As I spoke with Joan, despite the fact that I have never met her in person, I began to envision a woman with great determination, focus, creativity and ingenuity, and a pioneering spirit. In many ways, these personal strengths seem to be what has sustained her life's work in the face of struggle and adversity.

Joan started out not in photography or media, but in politics. She graduated magna cum laude from Mount Holyoke with a B.A. in political science, and then got an M.A. equivalent in politics and sociology at Nuffield College, Oxford University. Joan became radicalized first by the Black civil rights movement and the anti-Vietnam War movement, and then by the feminist/women's liberation movement. Joan came out as a lesbian in 1964 during her sophomore year in college, and her thought at the time was, "that's the end of my career in electoral politics." In the early 1970s, Joan became involved with the Furies, an early lesbian-feminist-separatist collective, which rose to national visibility through their publications and their activism. Joan described how her involvement in the Furies caused her to re-evaluate her politics, her values, and her life choices:

> It was a tough collective, in the sense that part of what we were trying to do was reinvent everything, including all of our own values and skills. I decided that I had to do something that I was totally not trained to do by the patriarchy, and that's when I taught myself photography.

Other than a correspondence course, Joan was entirely self-taught in photography, learning primarily through trial and error. The same was true two decades later when she shifted from photography to video; she taught herself and

Joan E. Biren
Photo by Leigh Mosley. Used by permission.

never attended any classes. In the context of groundbreaking lesbian-feminist activism, women activists didn't expect mainstream support for their efforts. In fact, taking classes and receiving training from an "expert" was, in addition to being expensive, viewed as supporting and upholding patriarchal values.

As Joan started out in her new endeavor, she set two goals that were consistent with her lesbian-feminist consciousness and activism. The first was to be

Gayle E. Pitman
Photo by Amy Tackett. Used by permission.

an out lesbian photographer, a bold move in that, before Joan, few photographers had publicly identified themselves as lesbian. In the early stages of her career, Joan did some research on the women photographers who preceded her. This allowed Joan to feel more grounded and secured a foundation for her work. Equally important was becoming part of a network with other lesbian photographers as they became visible to each other. Today many of these photographers form the core of a virtual community for lesbian visual artists from around the world who communicate via an Internet mailing list.

When Joan started making photographs in the early 1970s, there were no images that represented lesbian lives and experiences authentically. Joan's second goal was to document lesbian lives, identities, relationships, and activism as accurately and as widely as possible.

> I think media can play a big part in bringing about social change, partly through educating, but mostly through showing things in a way that helps people imagine that they can be different. When I was showing pictures of lesbians being out, that made people see that it was possible. When you show people that they have a history, you are empowering them to imagine and demand a better future. When you reflect people back to themselves in all their diversity, they can visualize and begin to create inclusive communities.

As our discussion progressed, Joan described how she tries to fight oppression in her work and in her daily life:

> Today we have bigger and bigger media conglomerates offering fewer and fewer points of view. Those who have a vested interest in keeping power impose their values on everyone else. When we don't resist and challenge those values, we uphold the privilege of rich over poor, men over women, whites over people of color, straights over queers, youth over age, buff or thin over fat, Christian over other faiths, and so on. People acquiescing to "norms" that define almost everyone out of "normalcy" help to maintain the status quo. That's why I have always tried to make the invisible visible: to make sure that we are not excluding certain parts of our community because we think that by appearing "just like everyone else" we can win our rights more easily. I am a self-employed person, in part, because I didn't want to conform my appearance to get or keep a regular job. I look very butch–that's me, that's how I'm comfortable inside myself.

Joan's still and video work had a tremendous effect on how lesbians view themselves and how others perceive them. Her videos, particularly *Tools for Caring,* have also influenced social and public policy regarding LGBT issues. Unfortunately, social change is often accompanied by oppression and backlash, phenomena that Joan experiences on a daily basis.

Choosing to step outside of the patriarchy, as many lesbian-feminist activists can attest, comes with a number of ramifications. At the beginning of the interview, Joan shared two events that had occurred within the previous two days, each of which underscored the everyday stresses Joan faces as a lesbian-feminist activist.

The first "hassle" that Joan described occurred when she was scheduled to do a program for LGBT employees at the Department of Commerce for Pride month. The day before the program, Joan received a phone call from the Department asking if they could preview her video before she did the program, because, as Joan put it, "it might have dirty pictures in it." Despite the fact that Joan's images and videos are not explicitly sexual, the Department was concerned about the content of her work. Joan's reaction was as follows:

> This is the kind of ridiculous stuff you get into because the work is lesbian. If I was giving a talk on mulching your garden, I don't think they'd be so uptight.

Homophobia and censorship have limited the public's access to Joan's work and the work of other lesbians in the media industry, restricting lesbian visibility and excluding certain types of images and experiences. Yet homophobia and oppression have been limiting in other ways, most notably in terms of money and funding.

The second event that occurred was as follows: Joan had been contacted by a university professor who was publishing a book about feminism in the 1970s, and she asked if Joan would donate some of her images to be published in the book. The professor's plea was that she was untenured and she was operating on a limited budget. Joan's reaction was as follows:

> Don't tell me about limited budgets. Twenty years of film, darkroom supplies, cameras, salary and everything else were paid by nobody. I never had a budget supplied by anyone until I got into video. And from 1971 to today, I have regularly been asked to give my photographs away for free.

As Joan talked about financial issues, it became clear that lack of funding has severely limited the work that she does. Joan made money by taking pictures on spec in the hope that she would be able to sell them. However, "if I had to rely on selling my pictures, I could never have survived. Period." Although demand for her photographs has increased over the years due to the upsurge in interest in the 1970s, for the most part selling it has not been a lucrative venture.

The second way Joan managed to raise money was to put together slide shows and, later, video presentations, and travel around the country with them. This was a way for her to share her work with a wider audience, make contacts, and connect with other lesbians around the country. Joan's decision to travel with her images reflects her ingenuity; instead of dwelling on the fact that it was difficult to sell or exhibit her images and giving up, she adopted an innovative way, first used by her colleague Tee Corinne, to raise money and present her images.

As Joan talked about her fundraising efforts, she lamented the tremendous amount of time and energy she spent on fundraising, which took away from the photography and activist work she wanted to be doing:

> The funding is the worst part, especially for a creative person who just wants to make the work. You might have to spend up to three years raising the money for a project, in which time all you're doing is raising money. You're not creating anything except money, and you want to be creating work.

In the early 1990s, Joan decided to take on a new challenge and move from photography to video. With this shift, she began to rely more on grant money, and with the help of a friend she started writing grant proposals and receiving money from foundations. Yet securing grant money proved to be exceedingly difficult, partly because many foundations won't fund films or videos, and partly because many foundations won't fund anything lesbian. Although she was able to get funding from a couple of gay-supportive foundations, like Astraea and the Chicago Resource Center, for the most part Joan had a very hard time getting grants to support her work.

So she decided to abandon grant writing altogether and instead produce, direct, and edit videos for clients, all of whom were nonprofit, progressive, lesbian, LGBT, and/or feminist groups. This shift, although it meant giving up the freedom to develop her own projects, allowed Joan to get away from fundraising and devote more time to her media work.

Although under this new arrangement Joan is not directly responsible for raising the money to fund her projects, the clients Joan works for also operate under serious budget constraints, thereby limiting the possibilities and replicating some of the same obstacles that Joan faced while working on her own.

Joan commented that because she didn't have adequate funds, she often worked with substandard equipment, and that she could have done better work if she had access to state-of-the-art equipment. She also commented on how spending money on her work has resulted in tradeoffs in her lifestyle:

> I could have had a nicer home or car, but instead I had a book. And then another book and then some videos. And I don't regret these choices. I may have less material wealth than some of my friends, but I am very aware that I have a standard of living way above that of most people on this earth.

Joan's social and political convictions were the motivating force behind the difficult financial choices she's made. In her years as a still photographer, Joan often felt that she was completely on her own, without institutional support, without a safety net or cushion to support her.

> You're self-employed, you're running your own business, you have to do all your own bookkeeping and promotion and marketing. I had to self-motivate, I had to self-sustain, I had to self-assign everything I did, and I had to keep going.

Additionally, in the mid-1990s as she passed the 50-year mark, Joan had more difficulty getting work and supporting herself. She commented,

The LGBT community, like any American community, often has a premium on youth and energy over experience. And it was tough–it was emotionally tough, it was financially tough. It's depressing not to be able to make a living when you feel you still have lots to contribute.

One of the ways Joan has managed to sustain her energy is to remain focused on the present, rather than setting goals and projecting into the future. She described this perspective as follows:

> I always think about the thing that I'm doing at the time. If I had said okay, what's my 5-year plan, what's my 10-year plan, like people tell you you're supposed to do when you start a business, I would never have said, "I'm going to be a lesbian photographer and then I'm going to be a lesbian video producer." I've done what I've done because I've managed to train myself not to look ahead about financial security, just take it as it comes and do it step-by-step. If you didn't, you would just say, "there's no way."

In tandem with staying focused on the present, Joan has adopted a very flexible approach to her work. In fact, she seems able to view change as a challenge, rather than a burden. With the passage of time and shifting social and political values, Joan's openness to change and her lack of rigidity have allowed her and her work to survive.

By far, the thing that most sustained Joan's energy for the work was the support she received from individuals, groups, and foundations. In 1997, at a low point in her career, Joan was offered a retrospective exhibition of her photographic work by George Washington University, which was establishing a special LGBT archive. She took the show, *Queerly Visible: 1971-1991,* around the country as part of the National Gay and Lesbian Task Force's 20th anniversary celebration. Before this opportunity, Joan had never exhibited her work before, mostly because preparing it to be exhibited would have been too expensive. As Joan stated, "The show was very helpful to me as a way of putting a ribbon around 20 years of still work."

Clearly, getting the show renewed Joan's enthusiasm. However, it is the effect her work has on lesbians and feminists that lifts Joan's excitement and energy. As Joan talked about the early stages of her career, she described the affirming responses she received from other lesbians:

> The stuff that kept me going was that people loved the work. People wanted the work. People were hungry for lesbian images.

These responses also seem to fuel her excitement for future projects, including the impact she envisioned for her upcoming video, *Women Organize!*, which contains the stories of five women organizers in various social justice movements:

> I'm very excited about the potential it has to go out in the world and inspire young people, young women in particular, to understand that organizing is something they can choose to do and get paid to do. I don't think there's anything quite like it out there.

Joan appreciates the support she received, and she acknowledges that without it she would absolutely have been unable to continue with her work.

> I'm very thankful to all the people who have supported me along the way. All the people who came out and paid their $5 to see the slide shows, and the people who gave me thousands of dollars to publish my books. Without them, the work wouldn't have gone on. The only reason the work went on was because there were lesbians who supported it.

Even more important to Joan than the support from people who view, enjoy, and value her work is the ongoing support that Joan receives from friends, family, and community. Having fun and devoting time to her relationships has become much more important to Joan as she gets older, and likely renews her spirit and allows her to take a break from work.

Joan is clearly an extraordinary woman, a pioneer in the lesbian-feminist movement as well as in the representation of LGBT people. She has accomplished a great deal in her 29 years of media work. Despite the ongoing struggles, she has remained flexible, welcoming growth and change, while staying dedicated to the feminist values that initially led her into the work. Talking with Joan proved to be a fascinating and inspiring experience, for her story offers a portrait of a woman who makes feminism the crux of her everyday life, who faces and combats oppression daily, and who uses her intelligence and creativity in the service of validating the lesbian experience.

Advocacy Meets the Scientific Method

Judith Bradford
J. Alison Hilber

SUMMARY. Dr. Judith Bradford is a social science researcher who has been a key figure in the evolution of lesbian health research. With Caitlin Ryan, Judy was instrumental in creating the National Lesbian Health Care Survey (NLHCS) in the mid-1980s. After assuming the Director-

---

Judith Bradford, PhD, is Director of the Virginia Commonwealth University (VCU) Survey and Evaluation Research Laboratory (SERL) in Richmond, Virginia. She serves on the core faculty for the PhD Program in Public Policy and Administration (VCU Center for Public Policy) and on the clinical faculty in the University Department of Preventive Medicine and Community Health, Medical College of Virginia. She was a member of the Institute of Medicine's scientific panel studying lesbian health priorities, and recently chaired the Methodology Work Group at the DHHS (Department of Health and Human Services) and GLMA (Gay and Lesbian Medical Association) sponsored Scientific Workshop on Lesbian Health, and in July 2000 became the part-time Director of Lesbian Health Research at Fenway Community Health. Dr. Bradford was involved in an interdisciplinary group of Columbia University faculty during the formation of the Center for Lesbian, Gay, Bisexual and Transgender Health. She is passionate about bridging the gap sometimes present between researchers and activists.

J. Alison Hilber, BA, is a 49-year-old lesbian who received her BA in Transpersonal Psychology in 1999 from Burlington College in Burlington, Vermont. Her senior thesis explored the issues of lesbians and body-image. Today she facilitates "Change How You See, Not How You Look" Body Celebration Workshops for women of all sizes, ages and sexual orientations, and is writing a book about the subject. Alison also sings, acts, and gratefully remains employed at her day job in a law office.

Address correspondence to: Judith Bradford, SERL, 921 West Franklin Street, Richmond, VA 23284-3065.

[Haworth co-indexing entry note]: "Advocacy Meets the Scientific Method." Bradford, Judith, and J. Alison Hilber. Co-published simultaneously in *Journal of Lesbian Studies* (Harrington Park Press, an imprint of The Haworth Press, Inc.) Vol. 5, Number 3, 2001, pp. 33-41; and: *Everyday Mutinies: Funding Lesbian Activism* (ed: Nanette K. Gartrell, and Esther D. Rothblum) Harrington Park Press, an imprint of The Haworth Press, Inc., 2001, pp. 33-41. Single or multiple copies of this article are available for a fee from The Haworth Document Delivery Service [1-800-342-9678, 9:00 a.m. - 5:00 p.m. (EST). E-mail address: getinfo@haworthpressinc.com].

33

ship of the Survey and Evaluation Research Lab (SERL) at the Virginia Commonwealth University (VCU), she became involved in the recent Institute of Medicine (IOM) Committee process, which resulted in increased attention to lesbian health at the national level. The IOM Committee recommendations have been instrumental in lobbying efforts by Judy and others for inclusion of LBGT issues in Healthy People 2010, the United States Public Health Service blueprint used by PHS agencies nationwide. Judy's current activities include helping to develop the Lesbian Health Research Institute and serving as the part-time Director of Lesbian Health Research at Fenway Community Health in Boston. *[Article copies available for a fee from The Haworth Document Delivery Service: 1-800-342-9678. E-mail address: <getinfo@haworthpressinc.com> Website: <http://www.HaworthPress.com>*

KEYWORDS. Lesbian, lesbian activism, fundraising

Dr. Judith Bradford and lesbian health care research came out of the closet at about the same time, and the ride has been quite exhilarating for both. In the mid-80s, when she was a Ph.D. student at Virginia Commonwealth University (VCU), Judy was instrumental in conducting the National Lesbian Health Care Survey at a time when lesbian, gay, bisexual and transgendered (LBGT) research of any kind was very much in the closet. Today, a prominent and well-respected scientist, she directs the Survey and Evaluation Research Laboratory (SERL) in Richmond, Virginia, and chairs the Health Policy concentration in the Ph.D. Program in Public Policy and Administration. Both the SERL and the Ph.D. Program are within VCU's Center for Public Policy.

Judy's activism began at the tender age of nine. The eldest of four children, she was born in Rome, Georgia, two weeks before her father shipped out for the Second World War. Shortly thereafter, the family moved back to rural Virginia, where both sides of the family had their roots. In the third grade, Judy confronted the principal of her school on behalf of her friend, Peggy, to complain that children, even those who lived on outlying farms, were not permitted to come to school without shoes. The daughter of an operating room nurse and one of the town's two physician/surgeons, Judy enjoyed many invisible privileges, including immunity from punishment for such "troublesome" behavior. Fortunately, her parents fully supported her penchant to work against the status quo.

Growing up in the South before the civil rights movement, Judy had plenty of opportunity to continue her activism at a time when things were still so

Judith Bradford
Photo by Hollis Newman. Used by permission.

"black and white." When a white child walked down the sidewalk, even elderly African-American people stepped into the street. Judy was expelled from high school because she had shared a room with an African-American girl on an honors trip to Washington, D.C., and then refused to lie about it. The principal of the high school cancelled her scheduled speech at the Monday morning assembly, telling everyone that she was too nervous to give it. This incident also led to the denial of her scholarship at a prominent women's college. She spent a year there anyway, and then left school altogether for a while, to return later on.

Judy's marriage to a man who became a college professor enabled her to finish school, acquiring her bachelor's degree at 24. Living in Lexington, Virginia, she worked, raised her two children, Franny and Max, and gave tennis lessons. She was active in a number of consciousness-raising community efforts unrelated to lesbian and gay issues. When the children were eight and three, respectively, Judy and her husband, Kenneth, decided to separate. Ultimately they divorced, partly because of Judy's emerging recognition of herself as a lesbian. Coming out changed Judy's life completely, and within a year she and her children had moved to Pennsylvania so that she could be with the woman she loved.

J. Alison Hilber
Photo by Cybele Elaine Werts. Used by permission.

By then Judy had her master's degree in Counseling Psychology and was licensed to practice as a mental health counselor. She discovered an emerging organization called the Women's Network that allowed her to apply her passion for community activism. Judy wrote grants and provided mental health and substance abuse counseling in the back room. She put together federal money for displaced homemakers, did life skills training, and set up *pro se* divorce classes in collaboration with legal aid attorneys. During her years at Women's Network, Judy also worked with other community-based organizations and trained students, just as she continues to do today in a very different organizational context.

It was during this time that Judy finally accepted her own coming out by ceasing to have intimate relationships with men and beginning to deal with lesbian issues. The Quaker Meeting she belonged to was very much in the forefront of thought about activist issues. Quakerism's historical processes for doing community development work and supporting community change provided the perfect bridge for Judy between community-based work and lesbian and gay activism.

In 1982, she moved to Richmond. While waiting to obtain Virginia residency so that she could begin her doctoral program at VCU, Judy ran a soup kitchen for a year and helped start a group of organizations that, over time, became an emergency assistance network. Although she had intended to enroll in the Clinical Psychology doctoral program, Judy decided it was not sufficiently oriented towards community change to address her expanding interest in this area. Instead, she entered the Ph.D. program in Social Policy and Social Work, a newly formed joint effort of the Department of Sociology and the School of Social Work. Although Judy was neither a social worker nor a sociologist, the integrative focus of this program and emphasis on applied social research seemed like a natural fit with her developing career interests. It was during the three years of her doctoral program that Judy began her work on the National Lesbian Health Care Survey (NLHCS) in conjunction with Caitlin Ryan, whom Judy considers to be the quintessential lesbian activist.

Judy met Caitlin in 1983 at an early AIDS conference sponsored by the National Lesbian and Gay Health Association in New York. Seeing only men everywhere she looked, Judy was happy to notice an announcement of a women's health meeting. Although she had no idea what it was about, she thought it would be nice to sit in a room with women for a change. Caitlin was running the gathering, which turned out to be an organizing meeting for the NLHCS. When Caitlin and others learned of her specialization in research methodology, Judy became the survey's co-coordinator with Caitlin.

The process of developing and finalizing the Survey was a national cooperative experience. The Survey went through several versions before it was finalized and then pilot-tested in focus groups in different parts of the country. This national exposure was enormously valuable when it came time for distribution. Because there was no list of lesbians from which to draw names randomly, the study used a multi-stage sampling process, or snowball methodology. The first-round distribution centers received 4,000 initial surveys, all numbered and initialed to be traced back to them. Each of those centers was, under certain conditions, allowed to copy and distribute the survey themselves. The result was that surveys were distributed throughout the country, including Native American reservations. One questionnaire that originated in Virginia, first sent to Cuban women in Miami, made its way to Alaska and eventually back to Virginia and into the dataset. Judy used to get calls at 3:00 in the morning from West Coast lesbians who had seen the flyer and wanted a copy of the survey. Ultimately, over the course of six to eight months, nearly 2,000 completed responses were received. It was, in the truest sense, a community survey. To this day, whenever Judy gives a lecture or attends a national meeting, she invariably meets someone who participated in the survey.

Judy gives Caitlin the lioness's share of credit for coordinating and facilitating the distribution process. Her phenomenal activist experience provided a key piece of the project. On the other hand, Judy's job included setting up the sampling methodology, programming and printing the questionnaire, and then coordinating the numbers and analyzing and reporting the results. It was an excellent partnership, and the lesbian community is lucky that they found each other.

It took 18 months to figure out a way to process the NLHCS data. When the director of the Survey and Evaluation Research Lab (SERL) at VCU, a member of Judy's dissertation committee, offered her a position, Judy accepted on condition that the lab provide in-kind support for NLHCS data entry, analysis and reporting. Taking on this project was a real coming out for the organization as well as for Judy. It took several months before the project was referred to as the "Lesbian Health Care Survey," and not just the "Women's Health Survey." Judy even brought in a colleague of hers to do some sensitivity training with the Lab staff on LGBT issues. The Lab now does an enormous amount of HIV-AIDS research and is a very safe place for LBGT people to work, with a higher-than-usual ratio of LBGT employees. Her prominent position at the Lab helped Judy continue the activist work she wanted to do.

In 1986, Judy found herself juggling several critical life and career changes: analyzing NLHCS data, completing her dissertation, graduating, beginning a new job, and blending families with her partner, Holli, who was facing difficult custody issues with her ex-husband. The NLHCS results have been reproduced in various source books and manuals, and, thanks to Esther Rothblum's tenacity, were published as a peer-reviewed article in the *Journal of Consulting and Clinical Psychology* in the early 1990s. All in all, the late 1980s were a very full and dynamic time in Judy's life, and the years since have followed suit.

Within six months of taking the job with the Virginia Commonwealth University SERL, Judy became the director of Health and Social Policy Research; in another year she was co-director of SERL and assumed the directorship in 1991, a position she still holds today. When Judy took over as director, the lab was fiscally precarious; within three or four years, things were very different. It now employs 200 people and has an annual budget of $7,000,000. Once Judy had succeeded in stabilizing the lab's situation, she began to commit more of her time and energy to lesbian health issues. In 1994, she began speaking with colleagues about setting up what has become the Lesbian Health Research Institute (LHRI).

Judy recognized that the political climate in Virginia would make it difficult for LHRI to attract lesbian students and faculty if placed at VCU, so she first initiated a cooperative agreement with the Division of Sociomedical Sciences in Columbia University's Mailman School of Public Health. This Division was developing a Center for LGBT Studies, and the timing for collaborative efforts seemed right. Although there was a lot of mutual and positive interest over the next couple of years, the momentum for LHRI's development was interrupted by a rare and enormously important opportunity for Judy to serve on a committee of the Institute of Medicine (IOM).

The IOM is one of the components of the National Academy of Sciences, where health services research is conducted independent of government control, but still used to inform public policy. With the help of people from LBGT activist organizations, there was a concentrated assault on federal offices to get both attention and money directed towards lesbian health. As a result, the Office of Research on Women's Health in the National Institutes of Health and the Office of Women's Health in the Centers for Disease Control and Prevention (CDC) commissioned a study by the IOM to review the status of lesbian health research and make recommendations about what needed to be done. After a year spent pulling the committee together, nine months of meetings, and an equal amount of time for the IOM peer review process, the report was finally published in January 1999. The IOM recommendations included such things as: increased public and private funding for lesbian health research; the routine inclusion of questions about sexual orientation on data collection forms; consideration of the full range of racial, ethnic and socio-economic diversity among lesbians when designing studies, with special attention to confidentiality and privacy of the study population; and funding of a large-scale probability study to determine the range of sexual orientation and risk/protective factors among women.

In March 2000, the Office of Women's Health Research convened a national meeting of leaders in lesbian research, who spent two days developing an action plan to implement the IOM Committee recommendations. Judy reports that the weekend was a grueling and all-consuming process that had many of the participants' partners threatening mutiny. But having been given this golden opportunity, these women knew they could not back away from their final challenge. The IOM Committee took a huge step towards refocusing national attention on lesbian health research, which had gotten derailed in the early '80s with the onset of the AIDS epidemic.

Having put her other goals and interests in lesbian health during the IOM Committee process, Judy returned to her vision of the Lesbian Health Research Institute (LHRI). LHRI was formed in spring 1999 and became affiliated with the new Center for LGBT Health at Columbia University's Mailman School of Public Health later that year. The School's Division of Sociomedical Sciences graciously provided adjunct faculty appointments to the four LHRI founders and office space for the LHRI coordinator. LHRI founders and coordinator worked together with Center-based faculty to get LGBT health issues included within Healthy People 2010 (HP 2010) and wrote several important documents to implement this process.

"Healthy People" is a major movement within the U.S. Public Health Service (PHS) that began in the 1970s. Every ten years, a document is created that acts as a blueprint for how federal, state and local PHS agencies are to respond to the health needs of the country. Specific health objectives are established and progress tracked through data captured by various national health data sets and surveys. For the first time since the Healthy People movement was initiated, LGBT individuals (persons defined by sexual orientation) are included as priority populations within HP2010. Inclusion of LGBT groups within HP2010 has been constrained by lack of available data and political constraints, but through a concerted effort of LHRI and LGBT Center faculty, in conjunction with national advocacy organizations, inclusion was expanded and a companion document has been written fully dedicated to the health status and needs of our communities. Critical offices within the federal government have implemented internal efforts to ensure that this progress will continue, a result that Judy feels would not have been possible without the significant events of recent years. These include sustained lesbian health advocacy, which resulted in commissioning of the IOM report, the "white paper" and subsequent short paper addressing inclusion of specific objectives written by LGBT Center and LHRI faculty, and the HP2010 advocacy that has taken place over the past 18 months, and a National Lesbian Health Conference in June 2001.

This takes us to a subject that is very near and dear to Judy's heart as a researcher, a scientist, and an activist–the importance of bridging the gap that sometimes separates researchers and activists. Although Judy considers herself an activist by orientation, she has not been overtly political in her efforts since moving back to Virginia and assuming university positions. She has not envisioned herself as the person standing on the stage at a March on Washington, persuading people by force of oratory. As important and necessary as it is, however, to have those front-line, very public activists like Caitlin Ryan forging the path, it is equally important and necessary to have researchers doing the hard science that creates the foundation for the movement. Judy Bradford defines herself as an applied researcher. She believes that the data collected by researchers must have a definable use in the real world. Sometimes, however, academic researchers are perceived as elitists by front-line activists, making productive communication difficult. Often researchers are concerned that their data will be misrepresented, or activists are so worried about misusing data that they hesitate to use the available information. Judy believes that researchers and activists alike must cooperate in moving toward activism that is about changing people's minds and hearts. Her partnership with Caitlin Ryan on the NLHCS is a prime example of the critical work that can be accomplished when researchers and activists work cooperatively and has demonstrated what can happen when these two emphases are successfully united.

Judy is intent on facilitating alliances between research and advocacy, not only for the progression of the movement, but also to create an authentic and effective role for herself and other researchers in the activist journey. She believes that "Healthy People 2010" is a perfect vehicle for uniting researchers and front-line activists. No matter how far apart they might feel, one cannot succeed in this context without the other.

LHRI's founders ended its affiliation with the Columbia Center in June 2001 and began to work on two fronts: strengthening ties between academic and community researchers and developing more coordination among lesbian research groups throughout the country. In response to the growing national agenda for lesbian health, Judy and her colleagues believe that fruitful collaborations among these groups will facilitate the formation of diverse research teams. In turn, this will lead to better studies that more comprehensively reflect the diversity found within lesbian communities.

When asked what advice she would give to young lesbian activists just entering the fray, Judy cautions, "Be careful and pay your dues, but maintain strong focus on what you want and need to do." She also encourages young activists to find mentors in women who have preceded them and who understand the ground rules for making things happen.

Although many parts of Judy's journey have been intimidating, she has no regrets and wouldn't change anything. Judy Bradford is a perfect example of what Audre Lorde meant when she said: "When I dare to be powerful, to use my strength in the service of my vision, it becomes less and less important whether I am afraid."[1]

NOTE

1. Lloyd, Carol, *Creating a Life Worth Living* (HarperPerennial Library, 1997).

How Lesbian Artists Support Their Art

Tee A. Corinne

SUMMARY. This essay examines how lesbian artists from Great Britain, Belgium, Australia, New Zealand, Canada, and the USA have supported their work through a variety of jobs from waitressing to college teaching. Social security, unemployment compensation, family-of-origin assistance, and independent incomes are discussed along with photography as an income-producing skill. Some women felt more comfortable discussing blue-collar jobs than family assistance. The closet remains a necessity for artists who have reached the greatest mainstream success. Although lesbian periodicals have seldom offered money, they have been significant in building audiences for lesbian-themed art and self-esteem in lesbian artists. Finally, the making of art is discussed as a supportive and healing activity. *[Article copies available for a fee from The Haworth Document Delivery Service: 1-800-342-9678. E-mail address: <getinfo@haworthpressinc.com> Website: <http://www. HaworthPress.com> © 2001 by The Haworth Press, Inc. All rights reserved.]*

KEYWORDS. Lesbian, lesbian activism, fundraising

An artist and writer, Tee A. Corinne's work includes *The Cunt Coloring Book, Yantras of Womanlove, Dreams of the Woman Who Loved Sex, Lesbian Muse,* and *Courting Pleasure.* Co-editor of the *Queer Caucus for Art Newsletter,* she writes about art for *Feminist Bookstore News, The Lesbian Review of Books,* and *Lambda Book Report* and co-moderates a Lesbian Art Issues e-mail discussion group. Corinne holds a Master of Fine Arts degree from Pratt Institute (1968). Her art has been included in exhibits at the Armand Hammer Museum and the U.C. Berkeley Art Museum.
Address correspondence to: Tee A. Corinne, POB 278, Wolf Creek, OR 97497.

[Haworth co-indexing entry note]: "How Lesbian Artists Support Their Art." Corinne, Tee A. Co-published simultaneously in *Journal of Lesbian Studies* (Harrington Park Press, an imprint of The Haworth Press, Inc.) Vol. 5, Number 3, 2001, pp. 43-52; and: *Everyday Mutinies: Funding Lesbian Activism* (ed: Nanette K. Gartrell, and Esther D. Rothblum) Harrington Park Press, an imprint of The Haworth Press, Inc., 2001, pp. 43-52. Single or multiple copies of this article are available for a fee from The Haworth Document Delivery Service [1-800-342-9678, 9:00 a.m. - 5:00 p.m. (EST). E-mail address: getinfo@haworthpressinc.com].

Visual art always exists within a political framework, although when art supports the status quo, its politics tend to go unnoticed. Unfortunately, at the beginning of the twenty-first century, most lesbian artists who have succeeded in the mainstream art world are still closeted at the level of press, radio, and television. This is true of art historians as well. Yet, despite the fear, ever-greater numbers of lesbian artists are finding ways to go public.

For many, creating pictures and sculptures with overt lesbian content is a political activity, and it follows that funding for it has seldom come through public channels. The range of strategies that lesbians have used to pay for their art is as varied at the artwork itself. For most lesbian artists, the risks and the gains of producing "out" lesbian imagery have been great. The primary risk is that the mainstream art world will overlook one's production or relegate it to a subcategory of "genre" art. The primary rewards are the joys of doing honest work and the satisfaction of finding an audience for whom one's art has significance.

For this essay I drew upon my own quarter century of experience making art and writing about lesbian art and artists. I also solicited responses from over 100 contemporary lesbian artists about how they have funded their lesbian-themed work.

Although women in loving relationships with other women have been producing art for centuries, lesbian-themed art by lesbian-identified artists in the United States–other than self-portraits and portraits of lovers–did not come into being until the mid-1960s.

Lesbian periodicals have seldom been able to contribute money to the support of lesbian artists, but they have been crucial in building audiences for lesbian-themed work and in giving lesbian artists a sympathetic and much-needed outlet for their work. Seeing her own work in print stabilizes an artist's faith in her art, and this, in turn, helps her to continue working.

Between 1964 and 1966, twenty-one photographs by Kay Tobin Lahusen (b. 1930) were published on the cover of *The Ladder,* a lesbian monthly produced in the United States from 1956 to 1972 by the Daughters of Bilitis (D.O.B.). Kay Tobin Lahusen and her lover, Barbara Gittings (b. 1932), who was editor of *The Ladder,* lived in a one room efficiency apartment and supported themselves with marginal jobs and a small private legacy belonging to Gittings. The magazine was funded by D.O.B. through membership dues and occasional donations.

Barbara Grier, a later editor of *The Ladder,* published covers by Jane Kogan (b. 1939), a painter with degrees from Brandeis and Columbia who had received a Fulbright. Kogan's imagery disappeared from lesbian publications in the early 1970s after *The Ladder* ceased publication. At present, her seasonal job as manager of a bookstore allows her to continue making art.

Self Portrait with a Lover by Tee A. Corinne.
Used by permission.

Unfortunately, *The Ladder* folded in 1972. Several publications which be-gan around that time filled the gap. One of these was *Tres Femme* in San Diego, edited by artist June Parlett Smith (later June Parlett, b. 1947), who was in the process of getting a divorce and had a young daughter. She and the child lived on $251 per month in child support payments while she produced photo-graphs, graphics, and slide shows, and did layout and paste-up for the maga-zine. Since the early 1980s, she has supported her art through full-time work as a nurse.

By the early 1970s, a new wave of lesbian activism was spreading through the U.S. and most of the English-speaking world. In the U.S., publications like *The Furies* and *off our backs* (Washington, D.C.), *Plexus* (San Francisco), *Lavender Woman* (Chicago), and *Big Mama Rag* (Denver) were giving lesbian artists a place to publish their photographs and graphics. Some of the women involved, such as D.C. photographer JEB (Joan E. Biren, b. 1944), created a niche for themselves by doing both mainstream and movement work. In the 1970s, JEB and her lover distributed feminist films through Moonforce Media. They had been saving to buy a house, but broke up shortly before its purchase. In 1979, JEB used her half of the down payment and money contributed by two of her lesbian friends to publish her first book, *Eye to Eye: Portraits of Lesbians*.

Many lesbian artists have favored blue-collar jobs because these jobs free the mind and often pay better wages than other traditional women's jobs, such as clerical work. Canadian painter and sculptor Persimmon Blackbridge (b. 1951) found housecleaning a good way to support her art. "I did that for twenty-five years, and am thinking of taking it up again now that my back injury is better. It pays better than writing, can double as time to mull over art ideas, and it's not the kind of job where you worry in the middle of the night or put in unpaid overtime."

San Francisco Bay Area photographer Cathy Cade echoes Persimmon Blackbridge's comments when she writes, "The good thing about housecleaning was that, once I got started on a particular job, there was something about the physicality of the job that set my mind and creative juices flying."

Photographer and collage artist Honey Lee Cottrell (b. 1945) got her merchant seaman's papers in order to waitress on the Pacific Far East (Cruise) Lines, where she received top dollar, good benefits, and long periods on shore to practice her art. Using money she received from her father's life insurance benefits, she returned to college in her mid-30s and completed a bachelor's degree in film. In her 40s and 50s, she has waitressed at banquets, which often means weekend work, but leaves her weekdays free. With this freedom, she has produced images for exhibition and for publications such as *On Our Backs*, and has consulted for Fatale Films.

Other examples of blue-collar jobs chosen by lesbian artists include running a gardening/landscaping business (photographer Ann P. Meredith, b. 1948) and cooking for an AIDS residence (photographer Katie Niles, b. 1951).

Poet, singer/songwriter, and photographer Ruth Mountaingrove (b. 1923), now in her late 70s, writes, ". . . while I have sold 'Drawing with Light,' my cameraless photography work, as well as my so-called 'straight' photography, and my paintings, I could not have lived on that small income, any more than I could live on seldom-paid book reviews, columns, stories or articles. The foundation of my financial life is Social Security, which I paid into during my years as a research technician and later as a self-employed magazine publisher." Mountaingrove lives in a HUD complex. "The government pays a portion of my rent to the complex and I pay the rest. At one time I paid one-third, and now I pay more than half of the rent. I am still, of course, under the poverty line and have not paid any income tax since I began receiving Social Security when I was 62. You might say SS and HUD are my Trust Fund."

Photography is perhaps the most marketable art-related skill. U.S. photographers Roberta Almerez (b. 1953) and Angela Dawn (b. 1971) have worked in photo processing labs. U.K. photographers Val Williams (b. 1941) and Brenda Prince (b. 1950) started "Format," the first feminist photo agency in Britain. Jill Posener (b. 1953), who was born in Britain and is now a U.S. resident, produces color and black-and-white celebrity portraits for *Curve* and other publications, while continuing to self-publish postcards of her photos of lesbian and feminist-themed graffiti. Marcelina Martin (b. 1950) has developed a market for her sensual photographs through the Internet.

C. Moore Hardy (b. 1955), a freelance photographer based in Sydney, Australia, considers herself a commercial photographer, but has continued to exhibit in gay, lesbian and queer exhibitions as well as mainstream galleries. She writes, "I am in the luxury position of having turned my passion for photography into a lifestyle/income-supporting business. Small as it is, it affords me the money to do almost (there are still a million things I want to do) everything I want to do. I am selective about where I work and who I work for, but larger corporate companies pay the money that allows me to do freebies for community groups/charities. When I retrained in my mid 30's and went to art school, I was never expecting to do what I now do."

Yet, earning one's primary source of income from one's art can be a complex issue. Photographer Lynda Koolish (b. 1946) writes, "I am 'supporting my art' spiritually as well as economically, by not having my work as a visual artist be my day job."

Unemployment or disability incomes have supported or assisted many lesbian artists, sometimes for long periods. Miriam Saphira (b. 1941) in New Zealand writes: "Currently I am living on the Community Wage (unemployment benefit) and supervision of counselors, etc. a few hours a week, so the benefit supplements what I earn, and I have a boarder to help with the electricity etc. I have some bronze designs at the foundry but cannot afford to pay for them, so I lurch from one show to the next, and grow my own vegetables and fruit. Sometimes I do a free lecture, but this morning got offered one for $100 (US $48)."

Figurative painter Lorraine Inzalaco (b. 1946), who spent 20 years living in New York City, has also supported her art in many ways, from waitressing while an art student to designing displays for store windows, showrooms and trade shows. She writes of "attempting to grow and sell grass back in the 70's, but my profit was $7.00 after a month, so I got out of that biz real fast." She "got into the crazy world of decorative wall painting for designers which . . . paid high but I had very little energy for my art. I eventually bought my loft in SoHo and tried to work, paint, go to galleries, and keep up all the stuff you have to do in a co-op. Sleep was not a habit." She became ill with chemical poisoning from turpentine and paints. After collapsing, she was diagnosed with Chronic Fatigue Syndrome. Finally, she moved from NYC to Tucson. The rent from her loft in SoHo provides enough money for living expenses. She "stopped using . . . alcohol, any drugs, oil paints, turps, drama and any other excuse . . . I'm slowly beginning to do my art again."

Success has come in different ways. Sudie Rakusin (b. 1948), one of the best known and most popular lesbian-themed painters and illustrators in the United States, has been widely published in lesbian literary magazines and small-press books, and has published two collections of her drawings. To support her art, she has sold shoes and jewelry, worked for a group of Sikhs, taught continuing education, and modeled nude for art classes. She has tried many kinds of creative merchandising, but what has been most successful is self-publishing. "I've got paintings in my basement holding up my house, but tell other artists to make note cards out of those paintings . . . note cards sell very well."

A few artists, such as cartoonist Alison Bechdel (b. 1960), have been spectacularly successful. Bechdel's comic strip, *Dykes to Watch Out For*, syndicated and gathered into several books, has supported her art. The books are bestselling titles for Firebrand, a major feminist and lesbian feminist publishing house. Without these books, it is doubtful that Firebrand could have continued its activist publishing agenda.

Yet, many artists still struggle to balance their creative lives with successful careers outside the field of art. Lieve Snellings (b. 1954 in Belgium) gives voice to the longing of many artists when she writes, "I work for 80% of my time in the emergency room of a big clinic in Leuven, and I love this job . . . But I would love–no adore–it if I had the chance to work 50% time in the emergency room and 50% in photography."

Since the mid-1980s, university teaching has supported a number of openly lesbian artists. Photographer Gaye Chan (b. 1957) teaches at the University of Hawai'i at Mänoa. Joyce Culver (b. 1947), whose lyrical portraits of lesbian lovers are featured in *Butch/Femme*, teaches at the School of Visual Arts in New York City. Photographer Catherine Opie (b. 1961) teaches at the University of California at Irvine. Her images of transsexuals and gender-bending women and her self-portraits incorporating s/m implications have been widely published and exhibited at the Whitney and the Berkeley Art Museums, proving that occasionally a lesbian artist can carve a mainstream niche for herself while creating fringe-identified sub-cultural imagery.

Several artists teach and write and edit. They always amaze me with their productivity. Painter Elizabeth Ashburn, author of *Lesbian Art: An Encounter with Power*, teaches at and heads the School of Art, University of New South Wales, Australia. Painter and sculptor Harmony Hammond (b. 1944), author of *Lesbian Art in America*, teaches at the University of Arizona, while photographer Deborah Bright (b. 1950), who edited *The Passionate Camera*, teaches at the Rhode Island School of Design.

One hopes that honesty will continue to shine through these academic artists' images, and that, ultimately, they will not be forced to protect their jobs by shrouding their images in irony and ambiguity–traditional refuges of the radical artist.

Important sources of income for British photographer Rosy Martin (b. 1946) are freelance lecturing, teaching, and writing. She notes, "What is needed is a different rate of payment for those who are not working in the academy, and a recognition that without institutional support a whole range of artists/photographers/theorists is being silenced." For instance, with conferences, "In the worst case I have had to pay for registration, travel and accommodation when I have been invited to give a paper. To a certain extent, people only want you as a guest lecturer because you have a profile–but keeping an active profile costs money."

Several women mentioned receiving small grants and gifts of money from friends. Gay men have often supported favorite artists in this way. It is laudable that the photographic work of Jean Weisinger (b. 1954) has received support from Audre Lorde and Alice Walker. One hopes that collecting art by lesbian artists will become a passion among more women.

Born in the U.S. in 1917 and now making her home in Montreal, painter Mary Meigs used her inherited wealth to support the political activism of Barbara Deming and later to make a home with French-Canadian writer Marie-Claire Blais. Meigs wrote about her life and art in *Lily Briscoe: A Self-Portrait,* a book that delighted me with its honesty, although her description of a life of wealth and privilege does not appeal to all tastes.

In fact, Meigs's description of her life of privilege was exactly what I found supportive. Upon my mother's death in 1967, as I was finishing graduate school, I inherited a modest income from investments. When I came out in 1975, I decided to use the freedom this money gave me to create work for which it would be difficult to find public support, including *The Cunt Coloring Book* and the solarized sexual images for which I am best known. Without this support, there is no reasonable way that I could have funded the time-consuming labor that has gone into making these images. In 1981, my mother's money allowed me to purchase and repair a house in rural Oregon. Since that time I have earned my living primarily through writing, teaching, and royalties.

At the end of the film *High Art*, a character accuses the protagonist, a lesbian photographer from a wealthy family, of never having earned what she's received. Soon afterwards, the photographer takes an overdose of drugs. Perhaps it is the fear of this kind of accusation that causes some lesbian artists to hold back information about inherited wealth or about assistance from their families of origin. Another facet of this, however, is that some work would not be produced at all without a combination of money and the willingness to keep and use it. In the 1970s, a filmmaker/photographer told me, "I am a rich bitch and I don't share my money with anyone." I notice that her career has flourished.

If there seems to be a disproportionate amount of struggle in the stories above, perhaps it is because many artists were embarrassed to acknowledge openly the help they had received from family or class privilege. One woman's mother sent her $200 a month to help out, while another woman receives an independent income of $50,000 a year on top of a professional salary. Yet another woman's lover is also her publisher. One artist's father bought her a home in Brooklyn, while another's sent her a portion of his monthly pension check. Vital support also comes in forms that are not always monetary. A photographer's grandmother allowed her to use the grandmother's mailing address and phone number for permanent contact information, so that people and organizations could find her even though her living situation changed frequently. It is an intellectual loss that it still seems easier to stress the hard work and deprivation rather than to note the ways in which our lives have been made easier.

Within this discussion of funding sources, it is also important to honor the ways in which art supports the artist, not financially, but at a deep psychological level. Jean Sirius (b. 1949) supported her lesbian-themed poetry as a typesetter in the 1970s and 1980s. In the late 1980s, she returned to school for a degree in computer science, and also began making collages and working in clay. After she got her degree, she concentrated on making art for three years, supported in part by her lover, Cara Vaughn. When her lover could no longer work because of cancer, Jean cared for Cara at home until her death. During the last year of Cara's life, Jean made a series of large (18" × 18"), paired collages, working on a table at the foot of the bed. She's sure that the meditative state she experienced while doing collage helped her care for her lover better and longer than would otherwise have been possible. Jean has written no poetry in over 15 years, and did one last pair of collages after Cara's death in 1997: a black one and a white one.

For many lesbian artists, lack of access to funding means putting an end to their creative output, at least until their retirement years. Although this is a problem faced by all artists, finding support for minority art is always more difficult than for art that reinforces mainstream imagery.

If any conclusion can be drawn from this informal survey, it is that creativity and diversity mark the funding strategies as well as the work of many openly lesbian artists making identifiably lesbian imagery today. Although some artists are fortunate enough to find a means to live and still continue to create, others struggle for every cent and go into debt to keep faith with their art. In a recent telephone conversation, the now retired Kay Tobin Lahusen, aged 70, spoke of an exhibit of her photographs at the William Way GLBT Community Center in Philadelphia. The images showed demonstrations for homosexual rights held in New York City; Washington, D.C.; and Philadelphia between 1964 and 1969. "I hate to tell you what this exhibit cost me," she said, and then, referring to her earlier self-funded work, she added, "I'm still paying." One hopes that the visibility and social acceptance that lesbians are fighting so hard to achieve will bring with them an increase in appreciation, and funding, for lesbian-identified art.

REFERENCES

Quotes are from e-mail messages or telephone conversations with the author in June and July 2000. Information about artists discussed in this essay can be found through Internet search engines and through the following books.

Ashburn, Elizabeth. *Lesbian Art: An Encounter with Power.* N.S.W., Australia: Craftsman House, 1996. Distributed in the U.S. by Gordon and Breach.
Boffin, Tessa and Jean Fraser, eds. *Stolen Glances: Lesbians Take Photographs.* London: Pandora Press, 1991. Distributed in the U.S. by Harper San Francisco.
Deborah Bright, ed. *The Passionate Camera.* NY: Routledge, 1998.
Bright, Susie and Jill Posener. *Nothing but the Girl: The Blatant Lesbian Image.* London: Cassell, 1996.
Cade, Cathy. *A Lesbian Photo Album: The Lives of Seven Lesbian Feminists.* Oakland CA: Waterwoman Books, 1987.
Corinne, Tee A. *The Cunt Coloring Book.* San Francisco: Pearlchild, 1975; and Last Gasp, 1989.
Corinne, Tee A. *Yantras of Womanlove.* Tallahassee: Naiad Press, 1982.
Hammond, Harmony. *Lesbian Art in America.* NY: Rizzoli, 2000.
JEB (Joan E. Biren). *Eye To Eye, Portraits of Lesbians.* Washington, DC: Glad Hag Books, 1979.
JEB (Joan E. Biren). *Making A Way: Lesbians Out Front.* Washington, DC: Glad Hag Books, 1987.
Kelley, Caffyn, ed. *Forbidden Subjects: Self-Portraits by Lesbian Artists.* North Vancouver, BC: Gallerie, 1992.

Mariechild, Diane and Marcelina Martin. *Lesbian Sacred Sexuality.* Oakland, CA: Wingbow Press, 1995.

Meigs, Mary. *Lily Briscoe: A Self-Portrait.* Vancouver: Talonbooks, 1981.

Saslow, James M. *Pictures and Passions: A History of Homosexuality in the Visual Arts.* Viking, 1999.

Smyth, Cherry. *Damn Fine Art by New Lesbian Artists.* London: Cassell, 1996.

Snellings, Lieve. *Lesbian ConneXion/s Vlaanderen–some day they remember us.* Middelkerke-Leffinge, Belgium: Lover, 1999.

Soares, M.G., ed. *Butch/Femme.* New York: Crown, 1995.

Weisinger, Jean. *Imagery: Women Writers, Portraits by Jean Weisinger.* San Francisco: Aunt Lute Books, 1996.

Changing the World

Elana Dykewomon

SUMMARY. The author explores the contradictions in using/need-
ing/having capital to end the institutions of capitalism. The essay also examines what a cultural worker is, the ways we value our own labor, the
importance of putting our resources into our communities, how we can
sustain activism over time, and how we are inspired and inspire others to
change the world. Michelle Cliff's conceptualization of the application
of thesis + antithesis = synthesis is used as a framework. *[Article copies
available for a fee from The Haworth Document Delivery Service:
1-800-342-9678. E-mail address: <getinfo@haworthpressinc.com> Website:
<http://www.HaworthPress.com> © 2001 by The Haworth Press, Inc. All rights
reserved.]*

KEYWORDS. Lesbian, lesbian activism, fundraising

Elana Dykewomon has been a lesbian cultural worker and radical activist for thirty
years. *Beyond the Pale,* her Jewish lesbian historical novel, was given both the Lambda
Literary and Gay and Lesbian Publishers' awards for lesbian fiction in 1998. Other books
include *Riverfinger Women, They Will Know Me By My Teeth,* and *Nothing Will Be As
Sweet As The Taste.* She was an editor of the international lesbian feminist literary journal *Sinister Wisdom* from 1984-1995. She lives happily in Oakland with her partner,
among friends, trying to make trouble whenever she can.
Address correspondence to: Elana Dykewomon, 8008 Winthrope Street, Oakland,
CA 94605 (E-mail: dykewomon@yahoo.com).

[Haworth co-indexing entry note]: "Changing the World." Dykewomon, Elana. Co-published simultaneously in *Journal of Lesbian Studies* (Harrington Park Press, an imprint of The Haworth Press, Inc.) Vol. 5,
Number 3, 2001, pp. 53-62; and: *Everyday Mutinies: Funding Lesbian Activism* (ed: Nanette K. Gartrell, and
Esther D. Rothblum) Harrington Park Press, an imprint of The Haworth Press, Inc., 2001, pp. 53-62. Single or
multiple copies of this article are available for a fee from The Haworth Document Delivery Service
[1-800-342-9678, 9:00 a.m. - 5:00 p.m. (EST). E-mail address: getinfo@haworthpressinc.com].

53

I [had] a firsthand knowledge of the enormous amounts of capital with which white men are able to convey their view of the world, to the world. As long as we exist under capitalism, what we are able–as Black women, Third World women, lesbians, feminists–to do may well come down to capital, after all. . . . I think about the Marxist dialectic: thesis, antithesis, synthesis. Thesis = feminism/lesbian-feminism/belief in collective empowerment; antithesis = a dependence on capitalist modes to create a financial base which will underwrite revolution; synthesis = the revolution in which resources will be shared equally and our various enterprises will be assured of survival.

–Michelle Cliff, "Notes for a Magazine"
Sinister Wisdom 24, Fall 1983

Years before I also was an editor of *Sinister Wisdom*, I read Michelle Cliff's last reflections on putting out the magazine and felt she had articulated a large part of the problem in the lesbian and women's movement I saw struggling around me. We have always been undercapitalized–we don't have enough money; we don't take money seriously and we hold suspect those who do take money seriously. Very few lesbian activists think in terms of million dollar projects (urban cooperative housing, a lesbian technical institute) while men routinely finance shopping malls and trucking fleets. Nevertheless we believe in our work; we believe it is possible to make a more just world; and many of us feel a strong desire to express our love in the concrete terms of moral action.

So it's easy to be caught in conflict here, with Audre Lorde's voice echoing in our ears, "The master's tools can never dismantle the master's house." We have no tools besides money to fund our work. We need postage, computers, staple guns; we need schools, clinics, radio stations. The *way* we work, the institutions we develop, don't have to–and should not, if you ask me (and you did, didn't you?)–mimic the master's hierarchies. But no way can we do without the master's dollar. So we get trapped in the riddle: how can you develop alternatives to hierarchy when you are dependent on hierarchy to eat?

I remember reading Emma Goldman's autobiography when I was in my 20s–hanging around the Northampton Valley Women's Center, circa 1972–in a study/discussion group centered on the feminist institute we hoped to get funding for.[1] I was shocked by how landlords evicted her, how, at one point, she ran an ice cream parlor: but wasn't it apparent to them that she was *Emma Goldman*? She had work to do: she was doing it. Why did she have to pay rent too?

Is this just naive willfulness? Those women activists of the Progressive Era–they charged a few cents admission to their lectures, and people came. They were hired by political parties or labor unions; they understood that peo-

Elana Dykewomon
Photo by Susan Goldberg. Used by permission.

ple needed to pay dues and take up collections. The desperate urgency of life left them no room for self-doubt.[2] Those women fund-raised, wrote articles, gave speeches on soapboxes to workers leaving factories, went to the homes of rich women and talked about sweatshops and prisons. They worked sixty-hour weeks and went on strike in the freezing cold. (Suddenly I hear myself: activism was harder back then. Us kids, we had it easy. Well, actually we did: if we were white-skinned and our parents had secure work.) They "sacrificed" for the visions they had, although many of them would likely scorn the word sacrifice.

And the activists of my generation also "sacrificed" for our visions, though we also, at least in our twenties and thirties, did not think of it that way. If you come to identify your own well-being as dependent on the well-being of a group, then working for that group's strength and power is a privilege–an exciting, purposeful way to live your life. But even a purposeful life has to be funded.

Naturally I have my own story about reconciling vision with practical reality, but before I get into that, I want to be clear about what money is. (Oh right, in a sentence? Economists write volumes about the symbolic function of currency; Hollywood spends a lot of energy making money seem sexy and fun, the ultimate American experience. What sentence are you going to come up with to change that?)

Money is a weapon of terrorism against those whose access to it is systematically limited. It is much more efficient than brutal force (though it is often backed up by selective force) at defining social position, particularly for all women, and men of color. Recently I watched the film *Out–The Making of a Revolutionary* about the political prisoner Laura Whitehorn–a Jewish lesbian who decided that armed struggle was a necessary and moral way to oppose U.S. racism and patriarchal violence at home and abroad, and spent 15 years in federal prisons for being in a radical group that set off a bomb in the U.S. Senate.[3]

What got to me, again, watching this film, was the background footage of Harlem slums, of the ravaged African American schools of Chicago, where children go to school without breakfast, how Black Panthers were killed for creating a kids' breakfast program. Someone does not want African Americans to have money, plain and simple. There is absolutely no reason why slums need to exist in the United States besides that we, collectively, will them to be there.

The broad racist uses of capital are clear. Against women, monetary violence, as all violence, is more individualized, cloaked as "welfare" or buried under the propaganda of marriage and dependency. Capitalism has created its own conflicts with its patriarchal root: women are cheaper to hire, and women need the freedom to be consumers. The independence of working and making choices has created a mass of women that patriarchy does not quite know what to do with, besides paying us 73 cents on the dollar. But the friction created by independent, if not very well organized, masses of women appears to create three levels of backlash: psychological (aimed at body image and appeals to motherhood), religious (witness The Promise Keepers and various strains of fundamentalism) and violent (consider the recent rapes in Central Park–or just watch the 11 p.m. news for the latest murders of women).

If we stare at this reality, at all the levels of how our culture and government uses capital, and force when necessary, to perpetuate violence, to keep the majority of people always uncertain about how they will be able to fund their lives (let alone their visions), then armed rebellion can certainly seem like the moral choice.

But to attempt to blow up the Federal Reserve or the Pentagon because, as an individual, you cannot bear the violence done to you and in your name for another day, becomes the same kind of capitulation to the myths of individualism our culture feeds us at every turn. No lone hero–or even cadre of ten/coven of thirteen–can take out capitalism if the mass of people could care less. And right now, capitalism is enjoying a fantastic surge of popularity–socialism has been "proven" a failure with the collapse of the Soviet Union, and day trading can make "anyone" rich. Laura Whitehorn talks, in the film, about how she now feels that strategic armed resistance has to be part of a mass movement–it can't exist on its own.

So we come back to the opening problem: how do we fund the revolutionary imagination, the revolutionary institutions, that can change the fundamental social organization of our culture? Michelle Cliff continues what I quoted above by saying "the only way to traverse the antithesis is to keep sight of the synthesis." That is, when we use capitalism, we need to keep our vision in front of us, and not be distracted. A white woman CEO and Tina Turner's success do not make a revolution. Cliff says hold on to the synthesis: keep your vision in front of you, even as you need to work on a pragmatic, often reactive basis–but that's not enough for many, maybe not for most. In a sound-bite, instant gratification country, how can lesbians achieve/promote the resolve that keeping "sight of the synthesis" requires?

That is, what can inspire individual women to put energy and resources into building a better world, and to keep at it for twenty, fifty years? I sit here staring at the screen and talk to myself: well, here's where your own story may be relevant. Here's why so many lesbians are contributing their stories to this volume. Why did we, why did I, decide that the path I wanted to take was towards the liberation of women, economic justice, lesbian creativity? Out of our individual motivations, can we piece together universals, ways of inspiring or giving courage to others?

In the early sixties, I was one of those adolescent lesbians who, living without any possible role models, decided to kill herself.[4] At twelve and thirteen, I tried fairly seriously, and was locked up for the better part of two years. When I was in the first mental hospital, they gave me the Oz books to read, thinking they were harmless entertainments. But in Oz, I found out, all creatures give according to their abilities and take according to their needs. A very nice system, Dorothy says, but I don't think it would work in Kansas. Why not? The 12-year-old me thought: why not? I looked at the world and it was easy to see that a better form of social organization was necessary. In college, I went to protests, rallies, signed petitions (against the Vietnam war, against local racism), but the organizations were overwhelmingly male, permeated by egotistic posturing. Though I didn't have an analysis then, I had revulsion.

Here's the part where I'm supposed to say: the women's movement was a revelation to me. But it's much more complicated than that. What drew me in first was gay liberation–but the gay movement of the early '70s was overwhelming male and, although those men were easier to talk to than the straight guys in SDS, it wasn't fun making coffee for them. The first women's consciousness-raising group I went to was extremely straight, and I felt like the fat dyke from Mars. But eventually, after graduating college, through a series of accidents, I found the Valley Women's Center in Northampton, populated by lesbians and straight women who were not talking about getting men to do the housework, but how to end the war effectively, develop women's skills, question hierarchies and bring about radical systemic change.

So I got swept up and in. It was exciting to feel part of something. How was it funded? In bits and pieces. I lived on welfare and volunteered much of my time to the women's center.[5] I stayed on welfare, as I recall, until I got an advance of $1000 for *Riverfinger Women* (about a third of which I gave away to lesbians and lesbian organizations). Around that time I was about to or already working for The Women's Film Coop, which I, along with four other women, inherited from a group in New Haven that started with a few films, and by which I was eventually paid $50 a week.

Fifty dollars a week was a lot of money in 1974–or so it seemed to me. I paid no taxes on it, and I walked to work from the close-to-slum apartment I shared with my printer friend Carol. We each paid $40 a month for rent and utilities and–what else did I need that $160 a month couldn't cover? Working class friends have had to bring my background privileges to my attention more times than I'd like to admit: I always knew my father would bail me out (pay medical bills, spring for a car), even when we were most estranged. Conceptualizing middle-class privilege as a resource that's part of how you fund revolution is one way to deal with it, but having the private escape route of money means you cannot necessarily be counted on to share the fate of those who don't. What I've found to be the most important lesson is to keep being part of community–to apologize (and mean it), learn from my mistakes, and keep working.

In my 20s, when so many women from different backgrounds were doing this, it seemed easier (or was it because I was 20?). I worked part-time jobs when I could get them–art gallery secretary, short-order cook, lecturer on women's media at the local colleges. Oh–and we scammed. Not often, but sometimes. Has the statute of limitations run out? Plane tickets, insurance money. When we organized conferences, we fronted the money or paid the bills afterwards, doing everything as cheaply as possible. I asked the wealthier women I knew for money to support a lesbian land cooperative idea that didn't work out, and to print my second book, which I wrote by taking a summer off, living on the royalties of the first.

In the Film Coop, as a community organizer and as a writer, I thought of myself as a cultural worker: someone whose "product" is part of the community she lives in. The basic idea is that every lesbian needs appreciation and respect for the work she does, but no one needs to be a "star"; and cultural work should serve the community it comes from.[6]

Deciding to be a cultural worker instead of "aiming" for the *NY Times* bestseller list is definitely a choice. There were many ways I internalized various forms of women-hatred that made me feel "unmarketable"–fat butch dyke ex-mental patients have never been front office hires. When any of us decide to take low-paying movement jobs or support our volunteer hours with dead-end work, it's important to look at issues of self-esteem and self-deprecation. It's one thing to choose not to compete because competition is essential to the hierarchical manipulation of the scarcity mentality, and another because we're afraid we won't succeed, we'll be the last one chosen for the team. To a certain extent, my commitment to the work I did was reinforced by the fact that I could not fit into a business suit, wear make-up or heels. But as a writer, I had a lot more confidence, and so my choice to be a cultural worker was much clearer.

Sometimes I blamed that choice when I felt I couldn't write because too many women were looking over my shoulder–but every writer has to contend with being a part of or apart from her community. Basing my work in the lesbian movement has been frustrating at times, but mostly it is fantastically rewarding–I have wonderful conversations and friendships with lesbian writers and readers internationally; I've seen younger women take up some of my ideas and expand them, making them their own. Nothing beats knowing you've touched other women's lives, and that the ideas you were part of will survive long after you've been forgotten–except maybe seeing that you have the power to create more freedom for yourself and others.

This was why I, and I think many other lesbians, willingly sacrificed "career goals" for endless meetings and the creation of lesbian and women's art and institutions. And we did make things: books, music, conferences, actions, baseball teams. In Northampton we had a women's center which became a socialist feminist center (the Valley Women's Union), staffed entirely, and consistently, on volunteer labor: it ran a speakers' bureau and consciousness raising groups, sponsored anti-Vietnam War activities, organized rape speak-outs, did crisis intervention, participated in local and national conferences and many more things that I've forgotten. Out of that, lesbians met and organized: a women's press, the Women's Film Coop, a lesbian garage, a women's restaurant, a lesbian space and businesses, newsletters, classes, study groups, dyke patrol (a community volunteer self-defense action group).

Many of us were discouraged because the revolution we thought was imminent never came; or because we developed the same kind of schisms that other radical movements had; or because we engaged in painful personal dynamics that mirrored our families of origin/society as a whole. We did change the world, but not in the vast, sweeping ways we imagined. Was our imagination wrong?

If anything, I think we didn't imagine wildly and widely enough. More than anything, we were underfunded. We bickered over tiny resources. We didn't know how to use the tools of capitalism. We were rightfully wary about being bought off (more than one fantastic women's project bit the dust in fighting over whether or not to take money from the Playboy Foundation). And still, many of us kept working, trying to bring radical lesbian analyses to bear on whatever situations we found ourselves in.

All those years I was frugal–working for whatever I needed to support the lesbian work I wanted to do, using my class privileges for some necessities and any luxuries. I learned to print in a government training program (CETA), and then started a lesbian distribution company with Dolphin Waletzky, printing two of the books we distributed. The longest I held a full time, "regular" job I ran the sign shop of a department store chain. I quit when I was offered the editorship of *Sinister Wisdom* in 1987–and supported the magazine as a night-shift typesetter. In my late thirties and early forties, I worked harder than I'd ever worked before–three to four nights a week typesetting, 20-50 hours a week on *Sinister Wisdom*. Certainly I didn't put out *Sinister Wisdom* alone–I had lots of help, and other women, particularly Caryatis Cardea (co-editor from 1991-94), made substantial sacrifices of time and resources to make it happen (and gave me time off to write). In 1993 or so I decided to go back to school to get an MFA so I could teach (which I have for the last five years, until this fall), since carpal tunnel was making typesetting for a living miserable.

Then my father died, leaving me a half million dollars I had no idea he had (still somewhat estranged, I expected him to live another twenty years and leave somewhere between 20-50 thousand). Imagine my surprise to suddenly be rich. Being the beneficiary of the class lottery is, of course, the trouble any woman would like to have. The short story is that now I can fund my work myself–and other work I believe in. I go back to the idea of synthesis: keeping the vision in front of me. But money turned it around: where before I had to believe that although I gave up "fame and fortune" for the greater good, now I have to believe that I can work for the greater good while having fortune (and a little notoriety, if not exactly fame).

Money seduces: I'm fat, fifty and disabled and want to write books. I'm taking the time now to try and do that, not having to scrounge for time as I did when I was younger. But I no longer live so frugally–I buy new cars, I go out to eat where and when I want. Capitalism is weird. I've been both smart with the money and extremely lucky to have had it at the beginning of this bizarre stock market surge: I've given about $200,000 away and spent another hundred thousand (a lot of that on taxes–paying taxes is, I think, the most immoral thing I do), and still have more than I started out with.[7]

So I joined the S.F. Bay Area group 100 Lesbians and Our Friends, which encourages us to give money to lesbian projects and individuals, to stretch the idea of what we think we can give. In a time when, because of historical luck and the work we did in the Second Wave, more lesbians than ever before have disposable income, it's crucial to put that money into our communities–to fund the revolutionary visions we have in ways that let lesbians do the work, not just scrape by. It's crucial to keep each other talking about economic justice–and putting our money where our talk takes us.

Recently I was on a book tour which reminded me of why I love living as an out dyke–everywhere we went, we met dedicated, thoughtful activists, young and old, from many backgrounds. One night my traveling companion, Tryna Hope, and I were having dinner in a noodle house in Leeds, England, with the writers Barbara Burford and Joy Howard. We agreed that maintaining a utopian imagination was crucial to our own senses of well-being and to having hope for lesbian activism. So we made a solemn vow, stacking our fists in a tower: to eat noodles and change the world.

For possibility, for inspiration, renew this vow in some way every day: laughing at how it's impossible, the impossibility of a bumble bee's flight or finding money for your most-hoped for project: change the world.

NOTES

1. We didn't, although many high-powered, relatively well-connected white feminists tried everything they could imagine at the time. Foundations rarely gave (give) money to women's projects (I remember reading statistics of 3-8%)–that's why women created our own. But I suspect all the women's and lesbian funds combined have fewer resources than the Ford Foundation.

2. No, that's a romanticization. I read the letters Pauline Newman wrote in 1910 to Rose Schneiderman, while Newman was on the road, organizing women workers. Her letters were full of loneliness, of ambivalence and anger towards the various movement power structures she had to deal with.

3. I urge you, whether you think you agree or disagree with this position, to see the film. The political prisoners in the United States–and we have many of them–are highly principled, moral, thoughtful, engaging folks, worth hearing out.

4. My first motive: to make a world where fat eleven-year-old lesbians don't feel they have to die.

5. General Assistance welfare was much easier to get in 1971 than it is now, and after I told the social worker I was a lesbian, I was rarely pushed to move or find work. At the time, I thought it was a good thing to take money from the state to fund revolutionary and creative work (and hey, I still apply for NEA grants, although they never give them to me). The ability to think of it that way was a function of my own middle-class arrogance, of ignorance about what welfare has meant to working class and poor people.

6. This doesn't mean it has to be "social realism" or simplistic (women are good/men are bad, for instance). It means it has to be thoughtful, accessible and honest. Experimental art can definitely be all three.

7. Many of us get the message that we must keep this kind of information private, for a hundred reasons. I think privacy about money is part of the problem. What greater risk is it to admit you have money than to say you have none? Women with money separate themselves from women who need money by maintaining silence. And it helps in not dealing with the money–not figuring out what you need, what you can give away, what your priorities are.

Lesbian Giving–and Getting:
Tending Radical Roots
in an Era of Venture Philanthropy

Marcia M. Gallo

SUMMARY. Lesbian philanthropy is rooted in a tradition of radical giving. Without the inspiration and vision of the small, community-based "alternative" foundations of the late 1960s and 1970s, with their commitment to "change, not charity" and to funding grassroots groups dedicated to social justice, today's profusion of queer organizations would not have been possible. Lesbians and bisexual women–both as donors and as activists–have been central to both movements. Today, contributions from individuals are responsible for the vast majority of the 1999 increase in overall giving–an increase of $15.80 billion over 1998, to a record $190.16 billion. (Since 1997, giving has increased by more than $15 billion annually.) But the questions that inspired a

Marcia M. Gallo is a lesbian activist who worked as a civil rights and civil liberties organizer for the ACLU of Northern California in San Francisco from 1978 until moving to New York in 1995. In New York, she joined the staff of the Funding Exchange and has spent the last five years working with donors to fund progressive groups throughout the United States and internationally. She is also completing her PhD in U.S. History at the City University of New York Graduate Center, focusing on social change, gender and sexuality issues. Her dissertation will be on the Daughters of Bilitis, the first lesbian organization in the U.S.

Address correspondence to: Marcia M. Gallo, Director of Donor Programs and Development, Funding Exchange, 666 Broadway, #500, New York, NY 10012 (E-mail: marcia.gallo@fex.org).

[Haworth co-indexing entry note]: "Lesbian Giving–and Getting: Tending Radical Roots in an Era of Venture Philanthropy." Gallo, Marcia M. Co-published simultaneously in *Journal of Lesbian Studies* (Harrington Park Press, an imprint of The Haworth Press, Inc.) Vol. 5, Number 3, 2001, pp. 63-70; and: *Everyday Mutinies: Funding Lesbian Activism* (ed: Nanette K. Gartrell, and Esther D. Rothblum) Harrington Park Press, an imprint of The Haworth Press, Inc., 2001, pp. 63-70. Single or multiple copies of this article are available for a fee from The Haworth Document Delivery Service [1-800-342-9678, 9:00 a.m. - 5:00 p.m. (EST). E-mail address: getinfo@haworthpressinc.com].

63

groundbreaking re-evaluation of traditional philanthropy thirty years ago still remain: who is giving, and to which groups? Now more than ever, it is vitally important for lesbians to recognize that the intersection between the radical philanthropic movement–which seeks to disrupt the power relations of traditional charitable giving–and the lesbian/gay/bi-sexual/transgender movements–which seek at least to dispel homophobia and at best to disrupt heteronormativity–is where both can become more inclusive, representative, and revolutionary. *[Article copies available for a fee from The Haworth Document Delivery Service: 1-800-342-9678. E-mail address: <getinfo@haworthpressinc.com> Website: <http://www. HaworthPress.com> © 2001 by The Haworth Press, Inc. All rights reserved.]*

KEYWORDS. Lesbian, lesbian activism, fundraising

Shortly after she was hired five years ago as the Funding Exchange's first openly lesbian executive director, Ellen Gurzinsky was asked by a long-time donor whether there was "a gay agenda" at the national office. Gurzinsky replied, "Yes, there is–and it's about economic justice, affordable health care, an end to domestic and state-sponsored violence . . . your basic list of social justice concerns." Gurzinsky's retort was right on point. It is exactly the vision of an intertwined, *progressive* queer political agenda and a philanthropic one that makes lesbian giving, and getting, challenging, especially at a time when capitalist values and institutions are being reified with a vengeance.

As a national network of activist-controlled, community-based foundations, the Funding Exchange and its 15 member funds are among the elders of the 1970s alternative philanthropy movement. Funding small, grassroots groups selected by community activists has been part of the Funding Exchange commitment to support radical social change and alter the traditional power relations within foundations. Through network grants such as the North Star Fund's early support of New York City's Gay and Lesbian Pride March, the Funding Exchange became one of the nation's first sources of foundation support for lesbian and gay organizing.

And that support has only increased over the years. In 1990, the OUT Fund for Lesbian and Gay Liberation was established. Started with a large donation from a progressive gay man, who gave away not only part of his inheritance but the power to determine which groups would benefit from it, the OUT Fund has been a vital source of funding for queer organizations working for social justice. And it has been vital both because of the relatively low level of funding

Marcia M. Gallo

generally available to progressive queer groups and because of the activ-ist-centered process through which the grants are made.

Since 1991, OUT has given away over $800,000 to more than 100 groups, some of them for multiple years. Of these, about 17 percent were for les-bian-specific projects. Sandra Laureano, director of the Grants Program for the Funding Exchange national office, says that they are seeing an increase in re-quests from lesbian-specific projects. "We're also seeing an increase in the number of lesbian donors, as well as a rise in the number of straight allies will-ing to fund lesbian and LGBT groups." These are hopeful developments. As

Gurzinsky's comment makes clear, the progressive potential of a link between radical philanthropy and the identity politics of the lesbian/gay/bisexual/transgender movements has not always been obvious to donors or to organizers.

As lesbian activist and scholar Alexandra Chasin notes, "(T)wo simultaneous strategies can enable diverse people to gain true cultural and economic equality. One, liberal identity-based social movements who fight the good and necessary fight for rights need to strengthen their coalitional activity, working more closely with other identity-based movements. Two, premiums on equal access to all social institutions and benefits and on equal opportunity must inform the progressive platform across lines of identity."[1]

This holds true for radical philanthropy. In the last five years, I've had the privilege of collaborating with generous people who are committed progressive activists. Many of them are lesbians or bisexual women, but not all. In fact, finding straight allies to support radical LGBT projects is an important part of our fundraising strategy. It requires identifying donors who recognize that such projects are a crucial part of transforming traditional philanthropy. On the other hand, finding LGBT projects that incorporate a broad social justice vision in their work can be just as difficult.

REMEMBERING THE RADICAL ROOTS
OF LESBIAN PHILANTHROPY

The first alternative community foundations were established more than 25 years ago by a handful of wealthy inheritors shaped by 1960s activism. These women and men radically altered traditional philanthropy forever, building on the vision of groups such as the Brotherhood Crusade in Los Angeles, the African American communities' alternative to the local United Way, and RESIST in Boston, a foundation established in 1967 to give small grants throughout the country for progressive organizing.

The growth of lesbian philanthropy has been intimately connected to this radical tradition. As Katherine Acey, Executive Director of the Astraea National Lesbian Action Foundation in New York, notes, the 1977 founding of Astraea "was a radical act. As one of the first women's foundations in the country–preceded only by the Ms. Foundation, the Barbara Deming Fund, and Women's Way–we were in the vanguard of a newly-emerging women's funding movement."

Lesbians are a diverse assortment of generous folks. We give individually, as institutions, as groups of friends, across race and ethnicity, class lines, and geography, to a variety of issues, and we give strategically. We support lesbian health organizing and legal advocacy, coming-out groups, community centers, lesbian-specific art and culture. We fund groups working on queer family issues, LGBT think-tanks and community archives. We are helping to institutionalize queer studies in a variety of academic settings.

At the same time, lesbian philanthropists at all giving levels recognize that our struggles for liberation are part of a broader social change agenda. This is the strategic part. So we also give to coalitions that challenge racism, sexism and homophobia, poverty and the growing economic divide, in the U.S. and around the world. We help fund the protests at WTO meetings. We support educational reform and the organizing of day-care workers. We raise our voices, and give our dollars, to challenge a culture of greed and violence.

And it's a good thing we do. Money for progressive social change–including LGBT groups in general and lesbian-specific projects in particular–is still hard to come by. Within the Funding Exchange network of progressive funds, for example, over $64 million has been given in the last twenty years to locally-based organizations working for social justice. Compare this to the $190 *billion* Americans gave to charity in 1999. And only about 13 percent of the philanthropic pie goes to direct public benefit and human services programs.[2]

Nancy Cunningham directs the Working Group on Funding Lesbian and Gay Issues in New York. The Working Group was established in the early 1980s to press for more LGBT monies from mainstream foundations. Cunningham notes that while the pool of potential funders has grown, particularly in the last four or five years, it is still the case that only .5 percent of foundation dollars go to LGBT groups. "We estimate that lesbian-specific projects probably receive less than half of that amount," she says. Cunningham points to the success of the Working Group's Partnership Initiative, which teams traditional community foundations and local LGBT groups. They've awarded over $2.2 million in matching grants, which requires the expansion of fundraising for underserved communities within the queer movements, including people of color, lesbians, youth, and elders.

As our communities expand, and our institutions survive, the issue of structural reorganization–known in philanthropic parlance as "capacity building"–becomes more and more critical. Christie Balka directs the Bread and Roses Fund in Philadelphia, one of the oldest alternative foundations in the country. She tells the story of a recent discussion with lesbians and gay men about philanthropy, and notes that "it became clear that we were speaking two different languages–lesbians saw money as a gift, whereas the men mostly talked about it as an investment." The AIDS crisis politicized many gay men and the government's inaction meant that alternative institutions had to be created, usually with monies contributed by both gay men and lesbians. But the crisis had the unintended side effect of strengthening the organizational capacity of those groups run mainly by gay men. "The levels of sophistication are very different today among LGBT groups and lesbian organizations," she noted. "In Philadelphia there are about 100 LGBT organizations. Of these, only two of the lesbian organizations are staffed. There is no lesbian organization with a single full-time staff person." Balka notes that the lesbian groups that do exist are supported by a relatively large donor base with many small donations.

Recognizing the need for capacity building among lesbians, Shad Reinstein and Jody Laine are two Seattle activists who have funded a special technical assistance project for lesbian organizers in Washington state. The new Washington Lesbian Organizing Project (WALOP) brings together 25 diverse lesbian/bi/trans women from a variety of racial, economic and geographic backgrounds for two intensive weekends of training. Sessions will tackle "the isms" as well as project development, fundraising, media, and board development. Reinstein explains that the impetus came from the awareness that "lesbian projects would get to a specific level of development, and then seem to stagnate. This project tries to push lesbian organizing to the next level, as well as create a lesbian political network throughout Washington state."

This commitment is echoed by Léonie Walker, a lesbian philanthropic advisor and activist. She and her partner, Dr. Kate O'Hanlon, a lesbian health activist, feel it is critical to make commitments to insuring that our organizations survive and grow. "We need to think more deeply about stabilizing the institutions that have proven themselves. We need to be giving multi-year grants, for general support–'no strings' grants. For the first time, in 2000, both Astraea and the National Center for Lesbian Rights finally have $1 million budgets, and our organizations are celebrating 10th and 20th year anniversaries. This in spite of the fact that sources for lesbian funding are still very low." She shares a concern that there is somewhat of a divide among lesbians, especially those capable of being major donors: "among my peers, activism is not even a hobby. They don't spend the majority of their time going to meetings, events, writing fundraising letters, and sending 8 million emails." Walker says she can count "on one hand" the number of out wealthy lesbians who have given significant gifts (over $100,000) and she acknowledges that while anonymity is still a big issue, so, too, is information and education. "The 'mainstream' issues, the ones we learn about in the media, are the ones that catch most people's attention, including lesbians," she says. "But there is so much potential out there for lesbians to give money–especially if they are understanding the growing economic divide in this country."

Katherine Pease is the former Executive Director of the Gill Foundation, which was established by Quark software creator Tim Gill to promote LGBT philanthropy. "We gave away $8 million in 1999, with 45 percent going to national LGBT organizations," she reports. Gill also prioritizes groups in non-urban communities. With regard to funding for women's projects, Pease said that the overall numbers have certainly increased over the last five years, but the percentage of proposals that Gill receives from lesbian/bi projects is still only about 5 percent of the total.

SOCIAL JUSTICE VERSUS SOCIAL ENTREPRENEURSHIP?

Katherine Pease maintains that there's "nothing monolithic" about lesbian donors–"they reflect the breadth of society, and they are progressive as well as conservative." She also cautions that she sees a "new economy of philanthropy" in which funders are bringing business values to their giving. "And that is women and men alike, including LGBT ones."

The "new donor" Pease notices wants business plans, more accountability, and a level of professionalism from the groups she or he funds. Certainly the era of "venture philanthropy"–and entrepreneurial values–is what is being heralded by the mainstream media. The July 24, 2000 issue of *Time* magazine, with its focus on "the new philanthropists," profiled only white, presumably heterosexual, mostly male dotcom millionaires who have started megafoundations. Most of their philanthropic largesse seems to be devoted to increasing computer use and insuring that tomorrow's workers (and customers) will be able to do their jobs. With the exception of Tim Gill and a few others, many technophilanthropists shy away from funding projects that challenge the status quo, ignoring groups which question the conditions that enable a few to prosper fabulously while most people are plunging deeper into debt.

This is an issue of concern for many progressive philanthropists, regardless of sexual orientation. Will future funders be less tied to visions of social justice? Can we incorporate the demands of new donors who are more and more attuned to–and may be increasingly uncritical of–global capitalism?

As activist philanthropists, we need to approach this challenge as we would any complicated organizing situation. We will need to show our true colors and not shrink from our commitment to progressive politics. At the same time, we may need to reframe how we describe what we believe in and what it is we want to support. It is not a contradiction to request progress reports from grantees while pushing donors to give unrestricted gifts and to recognize that, more often than not, social change is both difficult to quantify and a long-term process.

It may well be that the connection between LGBT identity politics and radical philanthropy can help both movements survive and grow. For example, we should appeal to lesbian activists of all ages and at all giving levels to support those institutions that have survived–and, in turn, have helped us survive–the last thirty years, from the Esperanza Center in Texas to the Highlander Center in Tennessee. We can talk about "capacity building" and organizational development in terms that successful businesswomen and men can warm to without selling out our constituencies. We can hold out for a vision of economic justice that doesn't drop out sexuality, race, and gender. We can keep working for–and funding–a movement that is inclusive, representative, and revolutionary. In fact, we can do no less.

REFERENCES

1. Alexandra Chasin, *Selling Out: The Gay & Lesbian Movement Goes to Market* (New York: St. Martin's Press, 2000), 243.

2. "Charitable Giving Shows Big Jump in 1999," *Grassroots Fundraising Journal,* Vol. 19, Number 4, August 2000.

Shoestring Science

Nanette K. Gartrell

SUMMARY. Nanette K. Gartrell, MD, is a psychiatrist, teacher and re-searcher who has served on the faculties of Harvard Medical School and the University of California, San Francisco. For the past thirty years, without relying on major grants, she has been gathering data to depathologize lesbianism. Her earliest investigations contributed to the effort to remove "homosexuality" from the list of mental disorders. More recently, Dr. Gartrell has been conducting a national, longitudinal study of lesbian families. In this overview of her research career, Dr. Gartrell discusses the strategies that she has used successfully for pursuing scientific investigations on a shoestring budget. *[Article copies available for a fee from The Haworth Document Delivery Service: 1-800-342-9678. E-mail address: <getinfo@haworthpressinc.com> Website: <http://www.HaworthPress.com> © 2001 by The Haworth Press, Inc. All rights reserved.]*

KEYWORDS. Lesbian, lesbian activism, fundraising

Nanette K. Gartrell, MD, is Associate Clinical Professor of Psychiatry at the University of California, San Francisco. She is the author of more than 50 publications, and is the editor of *Bringing Ethics Alive* (Haworth, 1994). Dr. Gartrell has discussed other aspects of her activist career in "Lesbian Feminist Fights Organized Psychiatry" (in Chesler P, Rothblum ED, Cole E, eds. *Feminist Foremothers in Women's Studies, Psychology, and Mental Health.* Haworth, 1995) and "Out in Academic Psychiatry" (in Mintz B, Rothblum ED, eds. *Lesbians in Academia.* Routledge, 1997). She has a private psychotherapy practice in San Francisco, and also volunteers her psychiatric services to chronically mentally ill homeless people.

Address correspondence to: Dr. Nanette K. Gartrell, 3570 Clay Street, San Francisco, CA 94118 (E-mail: Ngartrell@aol.com).

[Haworth co-indexing entry note]: "Shoestring Science." Gartrell, Nanette K. Co-published simultaneously in *Journal of Lesbian Studies* (Harrington Park Press, an imprint of The Haworth Press, Inc.) Vol. 5, Number 3, 2001, pp. 71-78; and: *Everyday Mutinies: Funding Lesbian Activism* (ed: Nanette K. Gartrell, and Esther D. Rothblum) Harrington Park Press, an imprint of The Haworth Press, Inc., 2001, pp. 71-78. Single or multiple copies of this article are available for a fee from The Haworth Document Delivery Service [1-800-342-9678, 9:00 a.m. - 5:00 p.m. (EST). E-mail address: getinfo@haworthpressinc.com].

Students are always surprised to learn that I have funded my own research. They assume that I have been supported by grants from the National Institutes of Health (NIH) during my thirty-year career as an academic. Aspiring researchers expect to be trained to write grant proposals, and to receive federal funding before a project is undertaken. Only the activist students grasp the politics of governmental support; the others are amazed to learn that the NIH has funded only one major study on lesbian healthcare to date (7/2000).

While Esther and I were developing the list of topics for this volume, she suggested that I share my perspective as an activist lesbian researcher. I hope this account will provide some useful research strategies to those who are long on determination, but short on resources.

STUDENT ACTIVISM, 1967-76

I came out during my freshwoman year at Stanford (1968) when lesbianism was still considered a mental illness according to the *Diagnostic and Statistical Manual of Mental Disorders (DSM)* (American Psychiatric Association, 1968). One positive outgrowth of attending college during the Vietnam War was that I learned strategies for grassroots activism in the antiwar movement. Those were the days when copy machines were "liberated" by employees working "overtime," so that demonstration leaflets and flyers could be reproduced. I did my share of liberating, leafleting, marching, and protesting, along with many other student activists. When I shifted my focus to eliminating homosexuality from the *DSM,* some of those antiwar tactics came in handy.

Through literature reviews, I knew how dangerous the lesbianism-as-illness concept could be. Untold numbers of lesbians had been imprisoned or institutionalized because of their lesbianism. Many had been forced to undergo treatments–including electroconvulsive therapy–in futile attempts to change their sexual orientation (Katz, 1976). It was clear to me that nonhomophobic studies on lesbians were sorely needed.

The *DSM* is formulated by mental health professionals to reflect the current state of knowledge about human psychology. If a diagnosis no longer reflects the prevailing sentiment of most mental health professionals, then it can be modified or eliminated. Did most psychiatrists in 1971 really still believe that homosexuality was a disease? I decided to find out. I approached my senior research advisor about studying psychiatrists' attitudes toward lesbians. He agreed to sponsor my project and to pay for paper and outbound postage. As a scholarship student with limited economic resources, I would have been unable to proceed without such support. I negotiated with a biostatistician to do

Nanette K. Gartrell (with ER)
Photo by Cathy Cade. Used by permission.

data analysis in exchange for co-authorship on publications generated by the project.

I "liberated" the copy machine at Stanford's Dean of Students office, where I had a work-study job, to duplicate the questionnaire I had developed and pilot-tested. I surveyed members of the American Psychiatric Association (APA) and found that most considered lesbianism a normal variation of sexual expression. To my surprise, respondents were more hostile about my "failure" to provide return postage than they were negative about lesbianism. The survey results motivated my advisor, who was the APA's Program Committee chair and later became its President, to include nonhomophobic presentations on lesbigay issues at APA annual meetings. These educational fora helped pave the way for the removal of homosexuality from the *DSM* in 1973 (a process that, in the end, came down to a vote by the membership).

During the time that I was gathering responses to my survey, a report was published claiming that gay men had lower testosterone levels than heterosexual men (Kolodny et al., 1971). It was accompanied by considerable public speculation that homosexuality was biologically mediated. Although we now live in an era where the unraveling of the human genome may confirm the genetic determinants of many behaviors, in the 1970s, most lesbian and gay people feared the consequences of such scientific endeavors. With homosexuality still defined as a mental illness, straight researchers typically searched for a "cure," generating data to reinforce their preexisting homophobic attitudes. One glaring problem was that most of the research on lesbigay mental health prior to the 1970s utilized psychiatric inpatients or prison inmates as subjects–hardly a representative sample of the overall lesbigay population. I was interested in replicating the Kolodny study without homophobic bias.

My advisor had access to a lab where, at no cost to us, hormone levels could be measured through a radioimmunoassay technique. I assembled a group of healthy, gay male student volunteers and drew their blood for testosterone measurements. In exchange for assistance with the assays, the lab technician accepted co-authorship. Using the same research design and analysis as the Kolodny report, we found that gay men had significantly higher testosterone levels than their heterosexual counterparts (Brodie, Gartrell, Rhue, & Doering, 1974).

Several years later as a medical student at NIH, I conducted the same study on lesbians. I happened to be doing a neurology externship at the time. The chief of my section told me when I arrived that I could study anything that interested me (assuming that I would select a topic related to neurological disease). When I appeared in his office with a cost-free proposal to measure testosterone levels in lesbians (using a radioimmunoassay lab at NIH, exchanging co-authorship for lab assistance, recruiting and phlebotomizing the participants myself), he was impressed with my ingenuity and allowed me to proceed with data collection.

I solicited lesbian volunteers at various community events in Washington, D.C., explaining that I was testing the hypothesis that lesbianism was caused by elevated testosterone levels. Even though I had no money to reimburse them for their time or blood, a sufficient number of lesbians agreed to participate. I provided a shuttle service (my '69 VW Bug) out to NIH for the venipuncture, in order to increase compliance. I drew blood on the first three days of menses from each participant. The heterosexual volunteers were Mormon women without children who were fulfilling their mission by donating their blood to science.

All participants in my NIH study had normal testosterone levels (Gartrell, Chase, & Loriaux, 1977). This finding helped to dispel the homophobic notion that lesbianism could be "cured" by a reduction in testosterone levels.

WOMEN'S MENTAL HEALTH ADVOCACY, 1976-86

During my psychiatric residency and early years on the Harvard Medical School faculty, my research interests grew naturally out of the various political agendas I advocated. For example, I collaborated on a study that documented the psychological impact of sexism in medical training (Lloyd & Gartrell, 1981). I also looked at gender differences in the ages at which children learn correct anatomical names for genitalia (Gartrell & Mosbacher, 1984). All these studies involved administering paper-and-pencil questionnaires, with data analysis by volunteer biostatisticians.

In 1982, I was appointed National Chair of the American Psychiatric Association's (APA) Women's Committee. I called for an APA-sponsored investigation into the problem of sexual abuse by psychiatrists. I developed and pilot-tested a questionnaire to be completed anonymously by all U.S. psychiatrists. Two years later, it became clear that the APA intended to stall the investigation indefinitely out of a concern that documenting the prevalence of sexual misconduct by psychiatrists might discredit the profession. Unwilling to sit by passively while this issue was swept under the rug, several Harvard colleagues and I decided to gather the data independently.

APA officials assumed that the investigation could not proceed if they denied me the membership mailing list, but I thought of another way to obtain the addresses I needed. I contacted the Harvard Continuing Medical Education (CME) office to inquire about access to physician mailing lists for CME courses. I obtained information about purchasing a mailing list of U.S. psychiatrists (pre-printed labels, sorted by zip code) from a national clearinghouse.

Using my Harvard affiliation, I devised a "dummy" CME course on medical ethics, referring loosely to presenting data on physician misconduct. I withdrew $500 from my checking account in the form of a cashier's check that I submitted along with the course description. Two weeks later I received the mailing labels I needed.

The postage for such a large survey was quite costly. An insider at NIH had told me that there was no likelihood of government funding for the project, because it was far too "controversial" (translation: any project that might discredit physicians would never be funded). Since the mailing labels would have become obsolete if I had taken too much time for fundraising, I used my savings to pay for postage ($2000). To obtain the best possible response rate, I included return postage. I applied for a postal permit in order to use self-addressed envelopes with a bar code that debited my postal account only if the questionnaires were sent back. Two biostatisticians at the Harvard School of Public Health analyzed the data, again in exchange for co-authorship. The study was exempt from review by the Human Subjects Committee since neither Harvard patients nor federal grants were involved.

Data from this and subsequent studies have been used to promote criminal statutes prohibiting sexual abuse by health professionals, to support malpractice claims by victims, to educate consumers about nonabusive care, and to develop preventative educational programs in medical and mental health training (Gartrell, Herman, Olarte, Feldstein, & Localio, 1986; Gartrell, Herman, Olarte, Feldstein, & Localio, 1987, 1988; Gartrell, Herman, Olarte, Localio, & Feldstein, 1988; Herman, Gartrell, Olarte, Feldstein, & Localio, 1987). In addition, despite considerable opposition, the American Medical Association (AMA) and the APA amended their ethics codes to specify that sexual contact with patients is unacceptable. If I had not funded these studies myself, there would have been no data documenting the severity of the problem, and the APA and the AMA could have successfully buried the issue for at least another decade.

LESBIAN FAMILY STUDY, 1986-PRESENT

In the early 1980s, increased access to donor insemination (DI) led to a baby boom among lesbians. In 1986, I began the National Longitudinal Lesbian Family Study, a 30-year study designed to provide descriptive data on a population of lesbian families in which the children were conceived by DI. For the past fourteen years, this study has documented the everyday realities of child rearing in a homophobic world (Gartrell, Hamilton, Banks, Mosbacher, Reed,

Sparks, & Bishop, 1996; Gartrell, Banks, Hamilton, Reed, Bishop, & Rodas, 1999; Gartrell, Banks, Reed, Hamilton, Rodas, & Deck, 2000).

By the time I started this study, I had given up any hope of outside funding for my research. I assumed that a study on lesbian families would be too controversial for the NIH. If I had waited until I had been able to collect enough donations to support the project, I would have lost the opportunity to document the first wave of this important sociological phenomenon. My only alternative was to budget my research as part of my personal expenses and work longer hours to increase my income. Fortunately, in recent years the study has received a number of small grants from various foundations, including An Uncommon LEGACY, Horizons, Joyce Mertz-Gilmore, Gill, Arcus, and the Lesbian Health Fund, which have helped to defray a small portion of the $70,000 annual expenses.

A colleague once told me that it was more cost-effective to support my research through private practice than to spend hundreds of hours each year preparing NIH grant proposals. Since I have never experienced the "joy" of receiving government funding or the frustration of waiting for it, I have been able to seize the moment, investigating problems of political import in a timely manner. I have also been able to pursue issues that interested me, and therefore to remain passionately involved in my research. The lack of federal funding for my investigations has affected neither my ability to publish my findings in scholarly journals nor the amount of attention my work has received.

Additionally, as an independent researcher, I have had the luxury of consulting with colleagues whose expertise I value, rather than having to quell the anxieties of homophobic review committees. If NIH ever becomes progressive enough to fund projects like mine, perhaps I will consider applying for support. Or perhaps, by that time, I might be too set in my ways to allow any government "interference" in my work.

REFERENCES

American Psychiatric Association. (1968). *Diagnostic and statistical manual of mental disorders (2nd ed.)*. Washington, DC: Author.

Brodie, H.K.H., Gartrell, N., Rhue, T., & Doering, C. (1974). Plasma testosterone levels in heterosexual and homosexual men. *American Journal of Psychiatry, 131*(1), 82-83.

Gartrell, N., Banks, A., Hamilton, J., Reed, N., Bishop, H., & Rodas, C. (1999). The national lesbian family study: 2. Interviews with mothers of toddlers. *American Journal of Orthopsychiatry, 69*(3), 362-369.

Gartrell, N., Banks, A., Hamilton, J., Reed, N., Bishop, Rodas, C., & Deck, A. (2000). The national lesbian family study: 3. Interviews with mothers of five-year-olds. *American Journal of Orthopsychiatry,* in press.

Gartrell, N., Chase, T., & Loriaux, L. (1977). Plasma levels in heterosexual and homosexual women. *American Journal of Psychiatry, 134*(10), 1117-1119.

Gartrell, N., Hamilton, J., Banks, A., Mosbacher, D., Reed, N., Sparks, C., & Bishop, H. (1996). The national lesbian family study: 1. Interviews with prospective mothers. *American Journal of Orthopsychiatry, 66*(2), 272-281.

Gartrell, N., Herman, J., Olarte, S., Feldstein, M., & Localio, R. (1986). Psychiatrist-patient sexual contact: Results of a national survey. I. Prevalence. *American Journal of Psychiatry, 143*(9), 1126-1131.

Gartrell, N., Herman, J., Olarte, S. Feldstein, M., & Localio, R. (1987). Reporting practices of psychiatrists who knew of sexual misconduct by colleagues. *American Journal of Orthopsychiatry, 57*(2), 287-295.

Gartrell, N., Herman, J., Olarte, S., Feldstein, M., & Localio, R. (1988). Management and rehabilitation of sexually exploitive therapists. *Hospital and Community Psychiatry, 39*(10), 1070-1074.

Gartrell, N., Herman, J., Olarte, S., Localio, R., & Feldstein, M. (1988). Sexual contact between psychiatric residents and educators: Results of a national survey. *American Journal of Psychiatry, 145*(6), 690-694.

Gartrell, N., & Mosbacher, D. (1984). Sex differences in the naming of children's genitalia. *Sex Roles, 10*(11/12), 869-876.

Herman, J., Gartrell, N., Olarte, S., Feldstein M., & Localio, R. (1987). Psychiatrist-patient sexual contact: Results of a national survey. II. Attitudes. *American Journal of Psychiatry, 144*(2), 164-169.

Katz, J. (1976). *Gay American history: Lesbians and gay men in the U.S.A.* New York: Thomas Y. Crowell Company.

Kolodny, R., Masters, W., Hendryx, J., & Toro, G. (1971). Plasma testosterone and semen analysis in male homosexuals. *New England Journal of Medicine, 285*(21), 1170-1174.

Lloyd, C., & Gartrell, N. (1981). Sex differences in medical student mental health. *American Journal of Psychiatry, 138*(10), 1346-1351.

The Jewelle Gomez Stories
as Told to Amanda Kovattana

Jewelle Gomez

Amanda Kovattana

SUMMARY. Fiction and the performing arts are powerful tools for cultural activism. As Jewelle Gomez tells the story of how her black lesbian vampire novel, *The Gilda Stories*, was brought to the stage, it becomes clear that many people who would not otherwise seek out such stories are exposed to the stories of minorities via plays. Part of this retelling illus-

Jewelle Gomez is a cultural activist, poet, author and playwright. Her work has appeared in numerous periodicals including *The San Francisco Chronicle*, *The New York Times*, *The Village Voice*, *The Advocate*, *Ms. Magazine*, *Essence Magazine* and *Black Scholar*. Her novel *The Gilda Stories* is a double Lambda Award winner. She has taught creative writing and popular culture on the east and west coasts at Hunter College, Rutgers University, New College of California, and San Francisco State University. She is the former executive director of the Poetry Center and American Poetry Archives.

Amanda Kovattana divides her time between her writing life and the hardware store. As a professional organizer she is privy to an intimate view into the untidy lives of others. She rescues her clients from their stuff and their house by installing storage systems, fixing stuck doors and leaky faucets, and doing other minor repairs. She writes non-fiction essays based on insights gleaned from seeing how people really live. She attempts to bring together her California perspective, her mother's British sensibilities, and her father's Thai family life into a wry global perspective. Her poems and essays have been published in the anthologies *Dyke Life*, *Encountering Cultures*, *On My Honor*, and *The Lesbian Polyamory Reader*.

Address correspondence to: Jewelle Gomez, 206 Fairmount St., San Francisco, CA 94131.

[Haworth co-indexing entry note]: "The Jewelle Gomez Stories as Told to Amanda Kovattana." Gomez, Jewelle, and Amanda Kovattana. Co-published simultaneously in *Journal of Lesbian Studies* (Harrington Park Press, an imprint of The Haworth Press, Inc.) Vol. 5, Number 3, 2001, pp. 79-86; and: *Everyday Mutinies: Funding Lesbian Activism* (ed: Nanette K. Gartrell, and Esther D. Rothblum) Harrington Park Press, an imprint of The Haworth Press, Inc., 2001, pp. 79-86. Single or multiple copies of this article are available for a fee from The Haworth Document Delivery Service [1-800-342-9678, 9:00 a.m. - 5:00 p.m. (EST). E-mail address: getinfo@haworthpressinc.com].

trates how arts funding is controlled by politics. Jewelle Gomez also demonstrates her activism by teaching lesbians how their money can be used in powerful ways to encourage the changes they would like to see in the world. *[Article copies available for a fee from The Haworth Document Delivery Service: 1-800-342-9678. E-mail address: <getinfo@haworthpressinc.com> Website: <http://www.HaworthPress.com> © 2001 by The Haworth Press, Inc. All rights reserved.]*

KEYWORDS. Lesbian, lesbian activism, fundraising

"Well, there's the name on the invitation job," Jewelle Gomez offered as we pondered what funding lesbian activism means and the different ways she participates in that activity. I was visiting Jewelle one May morning in the beautiful Craftsman style home she shares with her partner Diane.

From her dining room table, sipping tea and breaking into large muffins, I took in the stunning view of downtown San Francisco. Jewelle Gomez was indeed a name in our fair city–she sits on the advisory board of the James Hormel Center at the Public Library and used to run the Poetry Center at San Francisco State University. She refers to herself as a "cultural worker," a term that embodies the art and politics of her life.

I had last seen her speak after the dance performance, by Urban Bush Women, in the adaptation of her novel *The Gilda Stories*. A powerful woman in any context, she was unlike any lesbian I had ever seen. Her hair in long, long dreadlocks framed a pretty round face of color, of somewhat indeterminate heritage. I liked the possibilities. She had presence, commanding the stage in a soft spoken but experienced manner, a big woman wearing a dress, a Goddess, a creator who had just wowed the audience with a rich tale of black lesbian vampires that spanned the century from the days of American slavery to the present.

Sitting in the audience at that performance, in a packed house at the Yerba Buena Center for the Arts with the usual uptown dance theatre subscribers in their fine clothes, I was struck by a large contingent of elegantly dressed, handsome, black women assembled in one row and searched the audience for other signs of diversity. There was a flamboyant black gay man, several artsy straight feminist sorts, some dance students and a few lesbian couples. As a dance theatre enthusiast, I was used to a largely white audience of a certain non-political, well-heeled class coming to watch half-naked, muscled young bodies performing unthinkable movement. To have a dance piece bring to-

Jewelle Gomez

gether not only a story line with words, but also women of color within a cross-dressing, lesbian context, was a rare treat indeed.

Jewelle spoke that night of the importance of bringing black stories to a national audience. Talking to her in her home, she was an earnest teacher of the importance of lesbian money being raised to fund lesbian projects. It was not until I asked how she herself came out that I began to piece together the integrated life of a writer who is also a black lesbian feminist activist. Her ten years working at the New York State Council on the Arts and as a panelist for various other art funding agencies was in itself political, while supporting her artistic life as a writer. In those positions her lesbian feminist perspective might mean the difference in funding often-marginalized artists as well as artists of color.

Born in Boston and raised by her great grandmother, her early work life was spent at the studio of WGBH-TV as a writer/script editor and production assistant, then later in New York she also worked for public television and in Off Broadway theatre. Her first political experiences came during the tumultuous period of the Civil Rights movement in the 1960s. But her feminist political perspective came together when she came out in the mid-70s. At the time, the gay community was very underground, often existing largely in bars. Jewelle

Amanda Kovattana
Photo by Warren Hukill. Used by permission.

had gone in search of a meeting of Salsa Soul Sisters, a lesbian of color group in New York City. All she knew was that they met in a church on Thursday nights somewhere in the Village and she was determined to find them. When she couldn't, she was alarmed. Even the lesbian/gay hotline had no idea where they held their meetings. She was so angry at how lesbians could still be invisible, the incident stayed in her mind and became a turning point in her involvement in lesbian politics.

Politics and activism were not, however, where she would find the community of lesbians of color. Where she did find them was in the theatre community. At that time she worked as a stage manager on a show written by a black lesbian, Alexis De Veaux, a cultural icon of Harlem and Brooklyn. She was editor of *Essence* magazine as well as a teacher. She and her partner Gwendolyn Hardwick held monthly Salons, called Flamboyant Ladies, at their Brooklyn apartment. The Salon was so popular that it became a hotspot of cultural exchange for all. Even members of the elusive Salsa Soul Sisters showed up there eventually. It was at these gatherings that Jewelle developed herself as a writer and was opened up politically.

Only women were invited to perform at Flamboyant Ladies, although men were often in attendance. Nor was the audience limited to the black community; all were invited, and they all came. The diversity of the attendees characterized the Salon, and the full-on lesbian energy was a first for Jewelle. It was a politically consciousness-raising scene without being completely focused on politics.

Artists of color in the '60s and '70s were intrinsically political just by presenting their perspective in a white world, and to have a lesbian perspective at all was heady stuff. Money for the Flamboyant Ladies Salon was raised at the door by donations to pay for the food and drink. People hung out for hours. Dancers and musicians entertained as well as poets and writers. Jewelle first heard June Jordan read there, and Edwina Lee Tyler drummed. Jewelle read her poetry and later read her first vampire stories at the Salon. The audience was mesmerized by them, wanting more, and with their encouragement, Jewelle wrote *The Gilda Stories*. The Salon experience is captured in one of the chapters of the book as a salute to those women who helped make its writing possible.

"Literature is an important political tool," Jewelle explains. "It gets people thinking. They see vampires, but they are thinking about feminism." Indeed, the reader is seduced into the compelling story of the black, lesbian vampires as they carry on their underground life. The main character lives a long time, carrying the reader through history, giving perspective to the changes that take place. In this fashion, history, political thought and feminism are entwined in the narrative. It was while writing the book that Jewelle supported herself working as an administrator with the New York State Council on the Arts. She calls that turn of events ironic. "I make a career of giving out money after growing up on welfare."

In rhythm with her characters, she wrote at night from 10 p.m. until 2 a.m. Not a schedule conducive to having a relationship, she notes. In 1991 the book was published by Firebrand Books and has gone on to 5 more printings.

A few years later the black dance company Urban Bush Women received a commission by a funder in New Orleans to do a piece about death, time travel and history. They were unable to find a script that captured all those themes until someone gave the Company director a copy of *The Gilda Stories*. Although known as a feminist dance company, it was not a lesbian-oriented company, but they liked the story and commissioned Jewelle to collaborate on the script. She agreed to work on the project providing the main character remained a lesbian. The stipulation caused no particular concern. Thus began a three-and-a-half-year process to bring together the script, choreography by Jawole Willa Jo Zollar, and music written by Toshi Reagon, daughter of Berniece Johnson Reagon, the founder of the internationally known a capella group Sweet Honey in the Rock.

The dance community is funded by all manner of cultural institutions, including the National Endowment for the Arts which provided grants to the Gilda project during its creation. The company was also supported with residencies at places such as Jacob's Pillow, Colorado Dance Festival and Hanscher Auditorium at the University of Iowa. The NEA funding for the project came in three tiers–one grant at the start, another after a workshop presentation of some of the material and then (it was assumed) a final grant for the process leading to the full production.

Bones and Ash: A Gilda Story had a partial script, music, and choreography, and received the first two of the NEA grants. By the time it came to applying for the third and final grant from the NEA, the lesbian content of the script had become clear. What happened next would not surprise those familiar with gay and lesbian culture, but it completely upset the dance company. The NEA Board overturned the peer panel recommendation for funding, and refused to award the final grant. Despite the work samples submitted for the proposal, which included tapes of the music, the script, and all the elements leading to the final phase of production, the Board claimed that the project was not ready.

For Jewelle, who herself had served on NEA panels, it was clear that the Endowment Board, a group of political appointees who have the final vote, was creating a smokescreen to conceal the real reasons for their lack of continued support. After reading a transcript of the Board meeting, Jewelle knew that the word "lesbian" was carefully never mentioned. Members of the Board who were willing to go to bat for the project, including one who knew Jewelle's work with the State Arts Council of New York, were ignored. "This is what it means to be a lesbian," Jewelle told the company. "These are the limitations of straight, public funding. Being out as a lesbian can cut you off from funding arbitrarily." The company understood and persevered, getting other money to finish the project. The play opened in 1996 and toured for a year from Maine to Boston to Seattle to San Francisco, hitting the big performance cultural centers, exposing broader and broader audiences to not only black stories, but also lesbian content. Trusting subscribers at venues such as the Bates Dance Festival in Maine, who had season tickets and sat down to whatever was offered, found themselves watching black lesbian characters. The black audience, drawn by Urban Bush Women as a black company, saw lesbians in action. Dance festivals brought the play to dance lovers. Vampire enthusiasts in their black capes and white make-up filled the front row of many a performance. And of course lesbians came, particularly in Maine where they filled up rows and rows of the packed house.

That a play can so effectively bring together such diverse strata of society is a testament to the political power of the performing arts. It becomes clear in this context why we must nurture diversity in these expressive languages of the arts. "Funders have a difficult time giving money to artists who are not mainstream, middle of the road. No one wants to be embarrassed by having their name on a controversial piece of art. I find their timidity embarrassing. If you look at any of the awards given to artists, especially writers, in this country almost without exception, you won't find a writer whose work wouldn't get approval from the *Reader's Digest* crowd. That's why we have to fund each other."

Jewelle now devotes a good portion of her activism to talking with lesbians about how their money can be a powerful political tool and is sorely needed by the lesbian community, especially in the arts. From her days working with arts funding agencies on the east and west coasts, she saw how women, particularly women of color, often held themselves back when looking for project funding. Young male artists "with as much experience as would fit in a teaspoon" would, on the other hand, apply for grants aggressively, left, right and center.

"When it comes to funding, lesbian projects are the last to be considered even by the lesbian community," Jewelle explained. Why so many lesbians give more money to AIDS causes and generic Gay causes than to lesbian causes puzzles Jewelle. She recalled working in the 1980s with the lesbian literary magazine *Conditions*, and the difficulty the editors had getting lesbians to make the leap to subscribe annually, even though readers were aware that subscriptions were the primary way to sustain the publication. "Lesbians just don't seem to believe their dollars are worth as much as anybody else's. Truth is our dollars are worth more because they can do more in places where no one else is giving."

In her work with a group called 100 Lesbians and Our Friends, she gets to discuss just that issue: how lesbians decide to give money. The group, which has actively avoided creating a formal organization, holds meetings to discuss the emotional and psychological elements that go into the decisions that lesbians make about giving money. The idea is to have lesbians see themselves as philanthropists and to stretch themselves to give more than they ordinarily would. "People throw $25 into solicitation envelopes without thinking about a plan for giving. Why not make the dollars have a bigger effect?" Jewelle asks.

At the meetings checks are made out by members who pick the recipients. They range from large organizations such as the National Center for Lesbian Rights to the local lesbian performance space, Luna Sea. Each meeting brings new members and the names of new lesbian organizations. Sent in batches under the name 100 Lesbians, the checks give the members a sense of being part of a large gift and lesbian organizations receive increased funding with no effort.

One Hundred Lesbians and Our Friends has raised $92,000 this year thus far and expects to meet its $100,000 goal before the year is out. "Lesbians need to be visible as donors; the word lesbian needs to be visible," Jewelle says. "Because lesbians are connected to feminism we are capable of bringing about progressive political change. Our money may be one of the ways we help do that."

Jewelle Gomez lives her own advice that a writer need not retreat from the world. Now 51, she shows no sign of quitting this life of art blended with political activism. She is on the board of the Open Meadows Foundation (openmeadows.com) which gives seed grants to projects supporting women and lesbians. She is currently collaborating with Harry Waters Jr., a gay man she knew from New York theatre days. They are working on a play about James Baldwin and Lorraine Hansberry, some sections of which she read at this year's Queer Cultural Festival in San Francisco. Jewelle, who was paid a fee for this reading, called that check the first actual funding of the project so far. When it is more developed the collaborators will begin to seek financial support from theatres and grant makers, perhaps even the NEA.

Not content with just being the "name on the invitation," Jewelle left me with the impression she was looking forward to another half century of life as a cultural worker.

A Burning Love for Lesbian Literature

Barbara Grier

Rhonda J. Factor

SUMMARY. Barbara Grier's enjoyment of and commitment to lesbian literature have been guiding forces in her life. While working non-professional jobs for little pay, she managed to find money to buy the books she loved. Her enthusiasm led her to devote considerable time and energy to *The Ladder* while simultaneously working a full-time job. When *The Ladder* was no longer financially viable, she founded Naiad Press, and, for the first nine years of its existence, continued to hold a full-time job. In 1982, she became the first paid employee of Naiad, which enabled her to focus exclusively on her passions: writing, editing, and publishing lesbian literature. *[Article copies available for a fee from The Haworth Document Delivery Service: 1-800-342-9678. E-mail address: <getinfo@ haworthpressinc.com> Website: <http://www.HaworthPress.com> © 2001 by The Haworth Press, Inc. All rights reserved.]*

KEYWORDS. Lesbian, lesbian activism, fundraising

Barbara Grier is the founder and publisher of Naiad Press and has been a lesbian activist for over fifty years. She has written numerous books, including *The Lesbian in Literature* and *Lesbian Lives,* contributed to various anthologies, and coedited several books. She lives with Donna McBride, her partner of thirty years, in Tallahassee, FL.

Rhonda J. Factor is a graduate student in clinical psychology at the University of Vermont. She is also a massage therapist and facilitates anti-heterosexism workshops for schools and non-profit organizations.

Address correspondence to: Barbara Grier, Naiad Press, P.O. Box 10543, Tallahassee, FL 32302.

[Haworth co-indexing entry note]: "A Burning Love for Lesbian Literature." Grier, Barbara, and Rhonda J. Factor. Co-published simultaneously in *Journal of Lesbian Studies* (Harrington Park Press, an imprint of The Haworth Press, Inc.) Vol. 5, Number 3, 2001, pp. 87-94; and: *Everyday Mutinies: Funding Lesbian Activism* (ed: Nanette K. Gartrell, and Esther D. Rothblum) Harrington Park Press, an imprint of The Haworth Press, Inc., 2001, pp. 87-94. Single or multiple copies of this article are available for a fee from The Haworth Document Delivery Service [1-800-342-9678, 9:00 a.m. - 5:00 p.m. (EST). E-mail address: getinfo@haworthpressinc.com].

When Barbara Grier came out to her mother at the age of twelve in 1945, she encountered the same encouragement, appreciation, and humor she had always known from her mother. It had never occurred to Grier that she might not have her mother's whole-hearted support and approval. Knowing her mother's attitude was a rarity, particularly at that period in time, Grier described herself as "blessedly lucky" to have had the family she did. In contrast to many other parents who stigmatize and denigrate their children, Grier's mother helped her daughter to cultivate a sense of her own unique capabilities. So, when Grier discovered the curious word that described her, she knew that being a lesbian must be part of what distinguished her as intelligent and insightful. Grier's sense of herself as a worthy, bright, and articulate person who had the support of those most important to her enabled her to proudly embrace her desires.

Grier grew up in the Midwest, the oldest of three girls. Everyone in the family read a great deal. "We all read, all the time," she recalled. She remembered hearing about one of the books her mother read in the summer of 1933 while pregnant with her. Radclyffe Hall's *The Well of Loneliness* had met with an outcry when published a few years earlier. Perhaps her mother's reading had "marked" her, Grier joked.

Grier became interested in lesbian literature when she was about sixteen and began collecting all kinds of lesbian titles. "I'm a collector by nature," she said, "and every time I would read anything that had lesbian content, I would collect it." Finding money to buy books, however, was no small task.

After high school, Grier went right to work. Not having a college diploma, she worked in non-professional positions for little pay. Her jobs simply provided money to support her and her passion for collecting lesbian literature. Over the years, she held various jobs in retail stores, banks, libraries, and collections (consumer credit counseling).

Her expectations of work were quite different from those of young people today. "When I was growing up," she recalled, "it was taken for granted that your purpose in life was to work. You wanted the job and you wanted as many hours as they would give you." Those who grew up during the depression experienced a constant and pervasive sense of scarcity. The concept of people having disposable income did not exist. Nonetheless, Grier managed to parcel out money for collecting books. Every cent not designated for a pressing expense, and sometimes even lunch money, went towards buying books.

The collection became a central focus in Grier's life. She learned a great deal about locating hard-to-find books from Jeannette Howard Foster, the author of *Sex Variant Women in Literature*. Foster, 39 years her senior, shared her "burning love for lesbian literature" and became a mentor as well as a good friend.

Barbara Grier

Rhonda J. Factor
Photo by Tage Lilja. Used by permission.

While Grier was exploring lesbian culture through collecting books in Denver, Colorado, and the Kansas City area, women in California were forming the first national lesbian organization in America, Daughters of Bilitis (DOB). Beginning as a social alternative to the bar scene, it subsequently became political through challenging negative images of lesbians and demanding lesbian rights (Faderman, 1991). Thus, when Grier came across *The Ladder,* the official magazine of Daughters of Bilitis, she was immediately drawn to it. She began subscribing in 1957 with its fifth issue. "I remember looking at that little magazine," she recalled, "and thinking, 'this is what I'm going to spend the rest of my life doing.'"

Given her passion for lesbian books, Grier was perfectly suited to write book reviews for *The Ladder*'s "Lesbiana" column. She then went on to become, first, the *Ladder*'s fiction and poetry editor, then the magazine's editor, and finally its publisher. In her work with *The Ladder*, she corresponded with Marion Zimmer Bradley, with whom she assembled several early bibliographies of gay and lesbian literature–what they called "checklists."

Running a magazine solely on volunteer labor was quite a challenge. All the time and energy that went into the magazine was done on top of a full-time workweek. Not doing the work she most enjoyed was out of the question for Grier, and making a living at it was equally out of the question. There was no funding from any outside source. The women who worked on the magazine had no choice but to rely on their own resources. "You wanted to get something done, you figured out a way to get it done." Occasionally, a note in *The Ladder* would ask for donations: stamps or pens or typewriter ribbon. "Once a young woman sent us a box of pens," Grier recalled. "We were just astonished. It was like somebody had sent us gold bars!"

The efforts and resources of the volunteers and the money from subscriptions were able to sustain *The Ladder* through the early '70s. In 1972, *The Ladder* had 3,800 paid subscriptions but no advertising. At that time, no companies were willing to risk an association with a lesbian publication. Neither liquor companies nor tobacco companies even considered it. As the magazine grew, subscription costs no longer covered the cost of publication, and, without another way to increase income, the magazine could no longer survive.

The creativity and resourcefulness of Grier and the other women in the print media movement, however, meant that lesbian publishing would continue, albeit in a different form. The last issue of *The Ladder* came out in October of 1972. Soon afterwards, a woman approached Grier wanting to get her lesbian book published and distributed. Fortunately, this woman had a few thousand dollars to make that happen, and Naiad Press was started. Fliers were sent to *The Ladder*'s mailing list advertising the upcoming publication. Naiad was founded on January 1, 1973 and, one year later, Naiad's first book was published. Initially, distribution was difficult, given the lack of an organized network of lesbian or women's bookstores; however, by publishing one book a year in the early years, costs were kept in check until distribution became easier.

As she had with her work on *The Ladder*, Grier met the demands of running a publishing company while working a full-time job. She and her lover, Donna McBride, lived together first in the greater Kansas City area, then in Tallahassee, Florida, and ran the Press from their home. They would get up at 5 o'clock in the morning. McBride would go to the small shed outside the house and pack books while Grier did book work inside. At 7 o'clock, they'd shower, eat, and leave for work. After a full day's work, they'd come home, do more book work and packing and go to bed at 11. The next morning, they'd wake up at 5 and the routine began again. On Saturdays, they "only" worked eight or nine hours, while their three or four hours of work on Sundays felt like "hog heaven."

By January of 1982, Naiad Press had grown enough to support Grier as its first paid employee. The salary, however, was a significant decrease from what she had been earning at the already low-paying non-professional jobs she worked at. Her lover, McBride, joined her as a paid employee in June of that year, also taking a significant pay cut to do the work she wanted to do.

After leaving their day jobs, they were able to devote all their energy and time to Naiad. Still, they continued to work considerably more than the standard 40-hour workweek. Grier stated that, since turning 66, her goal this year has been to reduce her hours to a 40-45 hour workweek, which would be the least she's worked since the age of 13.

The growth of Naiad Press over the years has been a result of Grier's hard work and talent as a publisher, as well as changes in the cultural landscape and transformations in the book-selling and distributing industries. In 1974, Naiad distributed to about three bookstores found through *The Ladder*'s mailing list. In the late '80s, Naiad contracted with two or three specialty distributors who mostly worked with small, alternative bookstores. Outlets at that time consisted mainly of women's bookstores and gay and lesbian bookstores. Grier observed that, since the mid-90s, three-quarters of women's bookstores and gay and lesbian bookstores have closed down. "You can't run Joe's diner when the world eats at McDonald's," she said. In five to ten years, she predicts that all but the largest independent bookstores will have gone out of business. However, with mainstream bookstores now eagerly catering to the lesbian and gay readership, Naiad has found a comfortable niche there.

Naiad currently distributes through Ingram, the world's largest book distributor, and a dozen smaller distributors. Naiad titles can readily be found in large, mainstream bookstores, including Borders and Barnes & Noble. Wider distribution and the development of an increasingly visible national lesbian market have helped Naiad grow from publishing one book a year in 1973 to thirty-two books in 1999. Overall, Naiad Press has published about 450 books, and several hundred of these titles have been translated into half a dozen other languages. About 300 of those books were published since the late '80s when distribution began to include mainstream bookstores.

While Grier is pleased with the increased access wider distribution allows, she also believes it's important for lesbians to know about the history that preceded the current climate of relative tolerance and increased visibility. She believes that young lesbians, like the population at large, are at risk of losing a sense of history. "Literature is part of our written history and people are reading less now than in the past." While she noted that using computers requires some reading and writing skills, she believes that sustained absorption in books has diminished. Though an increasing number of books are being published, people are actually reading less.

Not surprisingly, Grier's advice to young lesbian activists today is to "read about your history. Find out about yourself. Have some concept of where you began and where the people before you began." Gaining knowledge about the past can be empowering for young lesbians. "Learn that wonderful fact," she urged, "that you can hardly find a famous American woman poet who was not a lesbian." Or, for example, learn that lesbian literature in America did not begin with *Patience and Sarah* or *Rubyfruit Jungle* but with the first novel ever published in the United States. The lesbian-themed *Ormond, or The Secret Witness* by Charles Brockden Brown was privately printed in 1799. Knowledge of longstanding history provides a sense of connection with the past and excitement about discovering what came before. "I think it's wonderful that we weren't invented yesterday."

One of Grier's greatest joys is her contribution to enhancing access to this history. In 1993, she donated her massive gay and lesbian book collection to the James C. Hormel Gay and Lesbian Center of the New Main Library in San Francisco. About 75% of the collection was uncatalogued, which means that publications in that collection had not existed in any other public archive or library. Grier treated the collection as if it were "a living child," leaving forty- and fifty-year-old books in almost mint condition. Her donation has helped to make the Hormel Center the largest lesbian and gay archive in the United States. Currently, the Center receives considerable funding, which will enable the archive to be stored and accessed on-line. Grier shared her fantasy that, fifty years after she's gone, someone in Zanzibar will be able to access the entire collection at home.

When asked what, if anything, she would have done differently, Grier had difficulty coming up with an answer. "I've been lucky in my life," she stated, "in that I've always loved what I was doing. I've done a progression of things that logically fit together. Collect books. Write about books. Publish books. Give books away in mass quantities. And sell books. I wouldn't change my life. I'd do the same things." Reflecting on her role in facilitating social change, Grier described her work as "an unusual kind of activism, one that didn't involve holding hands with people. I'm good with books," she added, "and that's what I chose to do."

Grier does sometimes wish she had been a bit more practical from a business perspective. In her desire to create a more humane and kinder work environment for her employees, she feels she may have gone a bit too far. Decisions based on her idealism seem to have limited Naiad's growth in the long run.

Grier also wishes she "might have been a shade less believing in the things that weren't going to happen. I thought that by the time I was 66, all the civil rights would have been won and Vermont would not be the only state honoring same-sex unions." But perhaps Grier brought so much energy and enthusiasm to her work precisely because she had those expectations. Although her high expectations for greater social change may have led Grier to some disappointments, there is no doubt that others have benefited enormously from her idealistic vision.

Grier's engagement in the sociocultural climate continues. She observed, "We are the last group that it is okay to hate. It's perfectly acceptable in most social settings to revile gay men and lesbians." Given the difficulties this creates for young lesbians and gay men first coming out, including an extremely high suicide rate, she emphasized the importance of reaching parents. "We have to make it possible for mothers and fathers to be supportive and helpful, or we're going to have disastrous trouble." Knowing how significant her own family's support was, she advocates continued struggle to help parents accept their children's choices and allow them to embrace their desires, as she has.

REFERENCES

Brown, Charles Brockden. (1799) *Ormond, or The Secret Witness,* New York: G. Forman for H. Caritat.

Brown, Rita Mae. (1973) *Rubyfruit Jungle,* Plainfield, VT: Daughters, Inc.

Faderman, Lillian. (1991) *Odd Girls and Twilight Lovers: A History of Lesbian Life in Twentieth-Century America,* New York: Penguin Books. p.149.

Foster, Jeanette H. (1956) *Sex Variant Women In Literature; A Historical and Quantitative Survey,* New York: Vantage Press.

Hall, Radclyffe. (1929) *The Well of Loneliness,* New York: Covici Friede.

Miller, Isabel. (1972) *Patience and Sarah,* New York: McGraw-Hill.

Funding the National Center
for Lesbian Rights

Kate Kendell
Ruth Herring

SUMMARY. The Executive Director and Development Director of the National Center for Lesbian Rights (NCLR) describe NCLR's growth over the past 23 years in the context of lesbian feminist activism and increasing philanthropy among lesbians. NCLR's activist lawyering on family, youth, immigration and elder law issues is radical work that is transforming the lives of ordinary lesbians, and which depends on the fi-

Kate Kendell became NCLR's Executive Director in 1996. She is also Adjunct Professor of law at Hastings College of Law, UC Berkeley Boalt Hall School of Law, and New College School of Law. She recently served as a volunteer director and major donor fundraiser for the campaign to oppose Proposition 22 in California. Kate is a nationally recognized litigator and spokesperson on lesbian civil rights and appears regularly in major mainstream and lesbian and gay media. Under her leadership, NCLR's budget has grown from $500,000 to $1 million since 1996. Kate and her partner, Sandy Holmes, have a five-year-old son, Julian. Kate also has a 20-year-old daughter, Emily.

Ruth Herring joined the staff of NCLR in 1997 as Director of Resource Development, where she oversees all fundraising for the organization. She has 15 years of fundraising, management, organizational development and Board experience with organizations including Lambda Legal Defense and Education Fund, the New York City Gay and Lesbian Anti-Violence Project, Lincoln Center for the Performing Arts, and the California Abortion and Reproductive Rights Action League.

Address correspondence to: Ruth Herring, NCLR, 870 Market St., #570, San Francisco, CA 94102 (E-mail: herring@nclrights.org).

[Haworth co-indexing entry note]: "Funding the National Center for Lesbian Rights." Kendell, Kate, and Ruth Herring. Co-published simultaneously in *Journal of Lesbian Studies* (Harrington Park Press, an imprint of The Haworth Press, Inc.) Vol. 5, Number 3, 2001, pp. 95-103; and: *Everyday Mutinies: Funding Lesbian Activism* (ed: Nanette K. Gartrell, and Esther D. Rothblum) Harrington Park Press, an imprint of The Haworth Press, Inc., 2001, pp. 94-103. Single or multiple copies of this article are available for a fee from The Haworth Document Delivery Service [1-800-342-9678, 9:00 a.m. - 5:00 p.m. (EST). E-mail address: getinfo@haworthpressinc.com].

nancial support of lesbians. The organization's earliest financial supporters were lawyers, who remain a core group of donors today. NCLR has grown as increasing numbers of lesbians grasp the personal connection between the organization's legal victories and the effect of discrimination in their own lives. NCLR has also built a professional fundraising infrastructure and major gifts program, which are key to its long-term institutional growth. In recent years the feminist philanthropy movement and NCLR's own donor activists have helped lesbians express their activism by giving back to their community through charitable contributions to lesbian organizations, including NCLR. NCLR will continue to advance lesbian civil rights by maintaining strong relationships with current donors and finding creative ways to meet its greatest fundraising challenge: how to reach the vast majority of lesbians who are quietly living their lives and are not part of any organization. *[Article copies available for a fee from The Haworth Document Delivery Service: 1-800-342-9678. E-mail address: <getinfo@haworthpressinc.com> Website: <http://www. HaworthPress.com> © 2001 by The HaworthPress, Inc. All rights reserved.]*

KEYWORDS. Lesbian, lesbian activism, fundraising

Donna J. Hitchens founded the Lesbian Rights Project in 1977 as a small program of Equal Rights Advocates, a feminist law firm in San Francisco. Seed funding was a $10,000 grant from the Berkeley Women's Law Foundation. Today the National Center for Lesbian Rights (NCLR) is a freestanding organization with a million-dollar budget, most of which is raised from individual lesbian donors. The growth experienced over the course of 23 years by NCLR in many respects is a history of the funding of lesbian activism in this country. This article will focus primarily on the development of NCLR given that we know the organization and best understand its growth. However, we believe that the changes in funding and activism experienced by NCLR are shared by many non-profit, social change institutions.

Much has changed in 23 years, not the least of which is our understanding of "activism" and how it happens. But what exactly what do we mean by "lesbian activism" and why do we need to fund it? Ask twenty lesbians that question and you may well get twenty different answers. For those of us at NCLR lesbian activism means, in part, changing institutions that discriminate or deny justice and equality based on gender or sexual orientation. These changes can be brought about by grassroots organizing, political lobbying, legal advocacy,

Kate Kendell
Photo by Rick Gerharter. Used by permission.

Ruth Herring
Photo by Rick Gerharter. Used by permission.

dialogue and discourse, agitation and civil disobedience, or in some ways simply by living a life unbounded by traditional notions of gender conformity.

The phrase "funding lesbian activism" may at first blush appear an oxymoron. When we cut our teeth as baby lesbian feminists in the '70s and early '80s, activism was supported by our passion, commitment, drive and great expectations for changing the world. We all know of women, and have heard the stories of others, who made great sacrifices in order to be activists for lesbian rights. Just twenty years ago the idea that a radical lesbian feminist could be paid for doing activist work was a ludicrous and suspicious idea. Ludicrous because few would contribute resources to someone to do such work, and suspicious because if someone wanted to do such good and important work she shouldn't expect to be paid for it and maintain her integrity.

NCLR's work is activist lawyering, not a concept everyone grasps easily. The idea that social change could occur through mainstream institutions, which had been mechanisms of discrimination, was a relatively novel idea at the time of NCLR's founding. In 1977 courts around the country routinely ruled against lesbian or gay litigants in employment, sexual privacy, family law, housing, the military and virtually every other issue. Prior to the early 1970s there were few national organizations focused on the rights of lesbians or gay men that focused on mainstream institutions as vehicles for social change. Given the well-founded suspicions most lesbians and gay men had about the justice system, it is not surprising that NCLR's early funding came from donors who were lawyers. It was not difficult to convince other lawyers that working to change the legal system is a valid expression of lesbian feminist activism, that it is, in fact, radical. Nor was it difficult to explain that in order to have a chance of succeeding in our court challenges we needed paid, experienced lawyer-activists. Lesbian lawyers were our earliest supporters and it was in those early years that NCLR learned what any successful non-profit activist organization knows–donors give when they feel a connection to the work. Lesbian lawyers who worked in the court system and themselves were agents of change knew change was possible, and supported NCLR's efforts to target that change on behalf of lesbians. Many of these same lawyers, and legions of others, today remain a core group of our donors.

But in order to build an organization, NCLR needed to widen the circle of supporters beyond lawyers. Explaining to non-lawyers why they should care about and support a lesbian legal organization was essential to our growth. The success of any activist effort dependent on funding is based on ensuring that potential supporters connect with the work. While there may at times be other motivations for giving (i.e., guilt, obligation, and pressure), the sustained support required to build an effective lesbian activist organization must be based on making a clear connection between the work and its relevance to the life of the donor. While many of us give money to organizations based on a connection with the issues–e.g., the environment, reproductive choice, or death penalty–doing work on behalf of lesbians provides the chance to demonstrate that "the personal is political" and that support for lesbian identified social change can transform us at the most personally relevant level. Our job as fundraisers has been to help donors discover their own personal stake in NCLR, and how our victories and our challenges directly affect their own lives.

When Donna Hitchens began doing this work 23 years ago, a significant focus was on family issues, an area of the law that had been virtually ignored by other queer identified organizations in part because it was believed that such issues only affected lesbians, and in any case were rare. What Donna discovered, and what we continue to find, is that issues affecting family–custody, adoption, access to reproductive technology, partnership protection, marriage–largely do involve lesbians and now raise some of the most challenging and groundbreaking opportunities for lasting change. Family law work also provides an opportunity for the telling of real-life stories that chillingly demonstrate the importance of NCLR's work in this area. In 1983, the story involved Sharon Kowalski, who was severely disabled in an auto accident, and her partner, Karen Thompson, who was shut out of Sharon's life by Sharon's parents, who totally denied their lesbian relationship. Karen fought an excruciating eight-year legal battle with Sharon's parents, which she ultimately won. This fight was a wake-up call to the lesbian community. The Thompson/Kowalski story was a personal tragedy that scared us profoundly because it could have happened to any one of us. Karen became a lesbian hero, an activist fighting for her life with her partner, using the law to challenge those who denied her family. Lesbians around the country raised money and gave money and organized in their communities to help Karen with her legal expenses. Karen spoke tirelessly about the need for lesbian couples to complete basic legal documents to secure their relationships, which helped bring this issue to national attention. The Lesbian Rights Project participated in this case and became known to a wider national community of lesbian activists.

The Thompson/Kowalski story is but one example of why there have been such profound changes in giving by lesbians to lesbian identified organizations. This story creates a clear connection between the work of, in this case, NCLR and the lives of lesbians who want to assure that the story is not repeated. Stories of tragedy and triumph have peppered the lives of lesbians across the country and have helped to create an understanding of the urgency of eradicating discrimination against lesbians. As we at NCLR have heard these stories we've responded and modified or added to our work, first with the addition of a Youth Project, then with an emphasis on immigration, and most recently with the launch of our Elder Law Project.

On every one of these issues, our work is establishing new legal precedents that have a direct, personal effect on lesbians. For example, in 1987, NCLR created the legal mechanism of second-parent adoption, which is now used in 23 states to ensure that non-biological lesbian mothers are recognized as full legal parents. We participated in the case in Vermont that just resulted in the creation of the nation's first "civil unions" for lesbian and gay couples. This historic legislation provides same-sex couples with more than 300 legal rights previously guaranteed only to heterosexual married couples. Our lawsuits and advocacy are creating the first legal protections for young dykes who are standing up to fight discrimination at school based on their sex, sexual orientation and gender expression. We have helped teenage lesbians gain release from abusive psychiatric institutions; we recently won a case that enabled a gay student club to meet on school grounds in conservative Salt Lake City; and we are assisting high schools across the country to enact non-discrimination policies that protect LGBT students. We have won political asylum for lesbians who had been terribly abused and persecuted in their home countries. In our newest work on behalf of LGBT elders, we are providing free legal advice on practical issues such as access to nursing and other health care, and estate planning. And, every year, NCLR attorneys and law clerks provide free legal advice to more than 3,000 lesbians who would otherwise have no access to the legal system.

NCLR's work is life changing work, and our growth reflects the fact that more and more lesbians are discovering NCLR's relevance in their own lives. But there is also another force at work: lesbians are developing their identity as donors. The feminist philanthropy movement of the past twenty years has helped create a community ethic among straight and lesbian feminists that giving money and time to organizations are activist deeds and are essential to changing the world. "Donor-activists," many of them out lesbians, are organizing across the country to galvanize women to think about their philanthropy and the profound role of money in our lives. Lesbians at every level of the economic spectrum are giving more because they are being asked to give, because some of them can afford to give more, because there are now strong feminist organizations they want to support, and because they see the world changing for the better. It comes back to the personal: giving is another expression of lesbians' personal power. Many organizations that rely on women generally, and lesbians specifically, as supporters and donors have experienced recent growth in both the number of donors and the size of gifts. This growth is directly attributable to a shift in the perspective women have about money and giving. This shift for NCLR is due to our own donor-activists who have been visible and vocal about the importance of giving as a "tithe," giving back to the community and being an agent for further change.

Raising money effectively in order to build an institution requires far more than compelling programs and personal connection with your donors. It requires a staff and volunteer infrastructure, professional expertise and knowledge of how to apply the proven rules of non-profit fundraising. Fundraising infrastructure takes a long time to create, and NCLR has worked hard to develop ours. We have always taken the basic rules of fundraising to heart. Begin by asking people you know, then widen the circle of people you know, ask often and in many different ways, ask for well-defined needs, say thank you often, be accountable to the community you serve, spend donors' money wisely to further your mission.

In the past five years, during which NCLR's budget has doubled, the major growth in our income has been from lesbian donors giving $1,200 or more each year. Only in the last three years have we asked for–and received–gifts of $10,000 or more. Lesbian major donors are now realizing that their investment in NCLR is an excellent investment. Our 23-year track record of legal accomplishments, our growing national profile in the LGBT movement, and our professionalism inspire their confidence. We are realizing that it is time to ask for–and expect to receive–gifts of this size. These donors are very excited to be leaders in supporting an explicitly lesbian, feminist legal organization and inspiring their peers to give.

As we have nurtured our major donors, we have also continued to seek ways to expand our national membership of lesbians who give $35 a year. In this area of fundraising, the tried and true methods are not proving adequate. These days, a typical non-profit organization can expect to gain 750 new members if it mails a new member request to 100,000 people who are already donors to similar organizations. Our major obstacle is that there are only a handful of mailing lists of primarily lesbian donors in the country. The vast majority of lesbians are not on any list at all, so our dilemma is how do we reach them cost effectively in order to invite them to support our work? We are being creative, as all fundraisers must be. We are finding ways to make NCLR more visible on the Internet, especially on the largest lesbian and gay sites; we are developing our own Website to attract more visitors; we are getting more coverage in the mainstream and LGBT media. Perhaps the greatest challenge for NCLR, and for every other lesbian identified organization, is visibility among those most likely to be supporters or clients. There still exists a healthy skepticism from lesbians when it comes to politics and law. Many lesbians continue to be closeted and thus are even more difficult to identify or reach. But reach them we must, not only in the interest of the growth and strength of NCLR, but, more importantly, to assure that lesbians who suffer discrimination understand that there may be recourse. Our mission requires that we always work to increase our visibility.

NCLR's growth provides ample evidence that lesbians' commitment to funding lesbian activism is robust while also capable of far greater breadth. We are proud to be an institution that makes real change in the lives of lesbians, and with their continued support we intend to realize our vision of a world in which every lesbian lives free from discrimination.

Lesbian Activism in Silicon Valley

Kathy Levinson
Karen L. Erlichman

SUMMARY. Kathy Levinson is a Jewish lesbian mother who advocates for social justice. Her activism arose out of experiences in childhood and her years as a college athlete at Stanford. As a senior executive at Charles Schwab & Co., Inc. and most recently the President and Chief Operating Officer of E*TRADE Group, Inc., she forged a successful career in busi-

Kathy Levinson is the former President and Chief Operating Officer of E*TRADE Group, Inc. As its "Master of Logistics," she kept E*TRADE running like a race-tuned Ferrari between 1996 and 2000. She is currently concentrating on her wide range of philanthropic and community service interests. Kathy was named "Community Role Model" at the LA Gay & Lesbian Center's Women's Night 2000 and was awarded the Davidson/Valentini Award by the Gay & Lesbian Alliance Against Defamation (GLAAD) for her support of equal rights. In 1999, she was named one of the "25 Top Unsung Heroes on the Net" by *Inter@active Week Online*, as well as the top executive in the "gfn.com Power 25" by *Gay Financial Network*. *OUT Magazine* included her as one of the "OUT 100," the most influential gay men and lesbians of 1999. In addition, *San Francisco Business Times* named her one of the "100 Most Influential Business Women in the Bay Area" in 1999 and one of the "50 Most Influential Bay Area Women" in 2000. Kathy established the Lesbian Equity Foundation of Silicon Valley to support new initiatives that explore the intersections between sexual orientation, gender and Judaism as a way to bring about social justice. She holds a BA in economics from Stanford University.

Karen L. Erlichman is a clinical social worker in private practice in San Francisco, as well as a lesbian writer and activist. She teaches at the University of California-San Francisco, and at San Francisco State University.

Address correspondence to: Kathy Levinson, 555 Bryant St., #1500, Palo Alto, CA 94301.

[Haworth co-indexing entry note]: "Lesbian Activism in Silicon Valley." Levinson, Kathy, and Karen L. Erlichman. Co-published simultaneously in *Journal of Lesbian Studies* (Harrington Park Press, an imprint of The Haworth Press, Inc.) Vol. 5, Number 3, 2001, pp. 105-112; and: *Everyday Mutinies: Funding Lesbian Activism* (ed: Nanette K. Gartrell, and Esther D. Rothblum) Harrington Park Press, an imprint of The Haworth Press, Inc., 2001, pp. 105-112. Single or multiple copies of this article are available for a fee from The Haworth Document Delivery Service [1-800-342-9678, 9:00 a.m. - 5:00 p.m. (EST). E-mail address: getinfo@haworthpressinc.com].

ness and technology. A well-known and visible figure in gay, lesbian, bisexual and transgender, women's and Jewish philanthropy and activism
nationwide, Kathy's greatest aspiration is to change the world one person
at a time, one conversation at a time, one dollar at a time. *[Article copies
available for a fee from The Haworth Document Delivery Service: 1-800-
342-9678. E-mail address: <getinfo@haworthpressinc.com> Website: <http://
www.HaworthPress.com> © 2001 by The Haworth Press, Inc. All rights reserved.]*

KEYWORDS. Lesbian, lesbian activism, fundraising

Lesbian activism takes many forms, from the flamboyant to the serious,
from the personal to the historical. Lesbian Avengers eat fire, and Ruth Ellis
celebrates 100 years of pride as an African-American lesbian. Ellen DeGeneres
comes out on national television–the conspicuous act of a high-profile star–and
a determined woman, through her everyday actions, persistently challenges the
status quo. For Kathy Levinson–a 46-year-old Jewish mother, philanthropist,
community activist, and former President and Chief Operating Officer of
E*TRADE–activism means leading a exemplary lesbian life to create change
in the San Francisco Bay Area, the Silicon Valley, and beyond.

One of four children, Kathy grew up in an upper-middle-class, professional,
Jewish family in Topeka, Kansas. Her father was a clinical psychologist; her
mother became a social worker after the children had grown up and left home.
Kathy characterizes her younger self as "different–Jewish, a tomboy, smart,
and not deferential to boys." Kathy describes her family's Jewish identity as
primarily social rather than religious. She remembers attending *"Blintze
Brunches"* at the local Reform temple, and knowing that her father had donated *"tzedakah"* (charity) to Jewish causes.

Very early in her life, Kathy was exposed to prejudice and racism. When
she was 12, her family moved to Massachusetts. They were advised by a real
estate agent that Jews were not welcome in certain neighborhoods. Kathy also
recalls a local program that existed when she was an adolescent called "A
Better Chance," in which "disadvantaged" young men of color were invited to
live in a group home to receive a good education and better opportunities. "A
Better Chance" seemed to make the white people of the town feel good about
themselves, but it did virtually nothing to welcome or weave these young
Black men into the fabric of the community. Moreover, when Kathy started
dating one of these young men, she became the object of scorn and criticism.
Nevertheless, she stood her ground in a way that stimulated others to become
conscious of their prejudices, and perhaps to discard them.

Kathy Levinson
Photo by Clark Ivey. Used by permission.

Kathy identifies her experience as a female college athlete as the true begin-ning of her activist days. As a student at Stanford University before Title IX, she protested the poor treatment and inadequate funding and support endured by women athletes. As a result, she helped to create the Organization of Stan-ford Women Athletes (OSWA), a campus organization whose mission was to fight for the rights and privileges of women athletes at Stanford.

Karen L. Erlichman

Kathy and her former partner came out together and were a couple for 19 years. "[At first] we were together but not actively engaged in the lesbian community." In the early 1980s, her partner worked for Kathy at Charles Schwab & Co., Inc. At one point, they were called into a meeting with the Human Resources Director, who informed them that because of the company's policy against spouses working in a reporting relationship, or even in the same department, they could not continue working together. After examining a copy of the policy, Kathy pointed out that the policy referred only to married spouses. He responded that they were, for all intents and purposes, equivalent to a married couple, which then led to Kathy's request that they receive spousal benefits. The opportunity to raise awareness came up, and she responded to it at the moment. Kathy says that this conversation was the catalyst for the company to develop a policy on domestic partners health insurance.

Finding her own voice and following her heart have taken Kathy down a long road of opportunities and challenges. "Being a lesbian you are different, [like] being a woman in a male-dominated career. This is the foundation of my activism. You can either compromise and assimilate, or be who you are, be successful and be true to yourself." She describes herself as a "contextual activist" who responds to opportunities for activism and visibility on a daily, if not momentary, basis.

Kathy has always felt an obligation to give back, possibly part of her Jewish heritage. In Judaism, the concept of mitzvah is very core and basic to what it means to be Jewish. Strictly translated, it means commandment and it refers to being "commanded to provide for those less fortunate." Kathy's philanthropy has taken on many forms–giving money, time, mentoring, or merely a supportive ear as she worked toward making a difference in her community.

A variety of organizations, from the National Center for Lesbian Rights to a gay and lesbian organization in Haifa, Israel, have been recipients of Kathy's generosity. She has also contributed to the Mid-Peninsula Jewish Day School, which both her daughters attend. As major donors, she and her partner were given the opportunity to name two of the classrooms. "I'm not interested in having my name appear on the classroom door," Kathy says; instead, they named the two rooms the Martin Luther King Jr. Room and the Lyon-Martin Room (after Del Martin and Phyllis Lyon). Kathy is involved in school-wide efforts to teach children about philanthropy and to encourage them to participate in community activism and *tzedakah*.

Kathy has been learning about strategic philanthropy. She is more focused in her giving, and setting priorities about where her money will be used most effectively. She is proud to have co-founded the Lesbian Equity Foundation of Silicon Valley, a donor-advised fund that is housed at and administered by the Community Foundation of Silicon Valley (CFSV). "CFSV is mostly rich straight white men, but it's where I live and who I want to change." Kathy explained that in the CFSV annual report, which goes to all the Silicon Valley community leaders, the Lesbian Equity Foundation and all its funding recipients are listed. Kathy is less interested in public recognition than in being "out" as a tool for social change.

Committed to maintaining her visibility as a lesbian in the corporate world, Kathy spoke at a 1999 conference on philanthropy in Silicon Valley. She was one of about 20 presenters, most of whom were men. When it was her turn to present, she talked about E*TRADE, and then began to talk about herself. Although she hadn't planned it in advance, she ended up coming out and discussing the importance of women's philanthropy and lesbian visibility. Afterward, many people came up to her, some with tears in their eyes, and thanked her for "using the L word on stage."

Once Kathy made the decision to have children, she became politically visible as a lesbian parent. There were many incidents during Kathy's pregnancies when people asked questions about her conception, her marital status, and her plans for motherhood, which offered the opportunity for her to come out as a pregnant lesbian. "I am committed to educating people in every interaction in life, to make a better world for my kids." Kathy's daughters are an integral part of her activism. "My kids know that they're part of a lesbian family." Becoming a mother has influenced Kathy to "answer every question as if my kids were in the room." She says her kids would know and object if she was to censor herself or pretend to be other than who she is. "I can't compartmentalize who I am; I'm all of me."

She teaches her daughters about her political causes; the children are involved in community service and donated some of their own money to the No-on-Knight campaign to defeat Proposition 22, the California amendment that defined legal marriage as the relationship between a man and a woman. "My kids are really aware of the world. They can tell you who's running for president, what propositions were on the ballot. Activism and philanthropy are a family affair."

Kathy describes the demands of her life as "exhausting." In the corporate world, she doesn't "get support every day for being who I am."

> For twenty years in my work life, I have spent every day around people who are *not* like myself. There are not enough of us. Why is it that there are so few lesbians and gays who are willing to be visible and take a stand, to stand up and change the world?

Kathy recently read an article by Stanford Business School professor Deb Myerson that describes "how I think of myself to a tee. [Myerson refers to] what I call 'contextual activism' as 'tempered radicalism.' She talks about tempered radicals making incremental change, working from the inside, ensuring that you get invited back. I have struggled with walking the fine line between assimilation and compromising myself and my integrity every day of my working life."

Kathy donated a great deal of time and money to the No-on-Knight campaign. Kathy also contributed to the Stanford Women's field hockey team. That donation exemplifies her theory of "mindful" philanthropy: the funds go to the women's field hockey team, and, if Stanford eliminates the team, the money reverts to the Gay, Lesbian & Bisexual student center. It can never be diverted into the general Athletic Department fund.

Kathy has faced many challenges associated with being so visible as a lesbian philanthropist and activist. At times people have been intrusive and unwilling to respect Kathy's privacy or her right to make choices about where she donates her money. She has been inundated with requests for funding such things as lesbian bars that don't fit her mission. Some people assume "that, just because I'm a lesbian, I will give money to [any arbitrary] lesbian cause." Kathy also finds the media exposure difficult to deal with. She has been interviewed in the *Wall Street Journal* and the *San Francisco Examiner,* and has been identified as a lesbian in these articles. "It's a challenge to be visible as an activist and protect my children."

Being with her family helps Kathy renew her commitment to activism. Motherhood injects passion into her work for social justice. She also finds it rejuvenating and affirming to be "in a nurturing environment among other lesbian and gay activists," citing the 1993 March on Washington and the annual NCLR dinner as two examples. Being around "smart, active lesbians" inspires her.

Kathy also feels renewed by knowing straight people "who have come to see me as a 'normal' person and really support the challenges in my life." She values the opportunity to "change somebody's mind," and gives the example of inviting neighbors over to her home. "They go home changed people. They see my kids are really aware of the world. They see we have *Shabbat* dinners." When Kathy attended this year's NCLR gala event, she and her partner purchased two tables, and the invited guests included two straight men and four straight women, all of whom she describes as strong allies. At the No-on-Knight fundraiser she co-hosted in 1999, at least half the people in attendance were heterosexual. "We can reach those straight people who are supportive but somewhat clueless about homophobia."

She takes her responsibility as a business leader who is female, lesbian and Jewish very seriously. "Everything we do is a chance to make a difference, like *tikkun olam*" [a Hebrew expression meaning 'repair the world']. Everything is either better or worse, nothing is really neutral." She is committed to changing the world one person at a time, one conversation at a time, one dollar at a time. "It is all about how you live your life and [remain] true to who you are without compromising what you believe in."

Kathy first "retired" six years ago, with the intent of focusing on philanthropy and community service. However, she became enraptured with the Internet, and within a short time her brief consulting assignment at E*TRADE turned into a multi-year career. Regarding her more recent retirement from E*TRADE, Kathy says, "I had the best job in the corporate world and it was both exciting and rewarding to define and create a different kind of corporate culture. Now the time has come for me to give back. You know, it's often said we spend our first 20 years learning, the next 20 earning, and the following 20 returning. I just felt that I needed to get to that 'returning' stage sooner. I have been very fortunate in my life and career and I am thrilled to have the resources, experience, and relationships to be able to make the world a more welcoming place for my children and others that follow."

Daughters of Bilitis
and the Ladder that Teetered

Del Martin
Phyllis Lyon

SUMMARY. This article traces the economic history of the Daughters of Bilitis, the first national Lesbian organization, and its periodical *The Ladder*. Besides membership, subscriptions and fundraisers were monetary donations and in-kind "gifts" from businesses. Staff labor was volunteer. Compensation for authors was DOB's guarantee of full rights to their own work. Funding was precarious until an anonymous donor came to the rescue. Funds were funneled through a member/friend who singularly decided what project to back. Officers of the organization were not privy to an overall plan, nor any accounting of how the funds were spent. In the end, secrecy was the undoing of DOB as a national organization and the demise of *The*

Del Martin and Phyllis Lyon were co-founders of the Daughters of Bilitis in San Francisco in 1955. Martin was its first president and Lyon the first editor of its periodical *The Ladder*. They were active in the Homophile Movement of the 1950s and '60s and joined the Feminist Movement when the National Organization for Women formed a Northern California Chapter in 1967. Their book *Lesbian/Woman* was first published in 1972. Although they continued to work together on many other fronts, they also took on separate issues: Martin's book *Battered Wives* became the catalyst for the Domestic Violence Shelter Movement. Lyon co-founded the National Sex Forum and later The Institute for Advanced Study of Human Sexuality. Their present concerns are ageism and aging issues, Lesbian history and visibility.

Address correspondence to the authors at 651 Duncan Street, San Francisco, CA 94131 (E-mail: lymar@mindspring.com).

[Haworth co-indexing entry note]: "Daughters of Bilitis and the Ladder that Teetered." Martin, Del, and Phyllis Lyon. Co-published simultaneously in *Journal of Lesbian Studies* (Harrington Park Press, an imprint of The Haworth Press, Inc.) Vol. 5, Number 3, 2001, pp. 113-118; and: *Everyday Mutinies: Funding Lesbian Activism* (ed: Nanette K. Gartrell, and Esther D. Rothblum) Harrington Park Press, an imprint of The Haworth Press, Inc., 2001, pp. 113-118. Single or multiple copies of this article are available for a fee from The Haworth Document Delivery Service [1-800-342-9678, 9:00 a.m. - 5:00 p.m. (EST). E-mail address: getinfo@haworthpressinc.com].

113

Ladder as well. *[Article copies available for a fee from The Haworth Document Delivery Service: 1-800-342-9678. E-mail address: <getinfo@haworthpressinc. com> Website: <http://www.HaworthPress.com> © 2001 by The Haworth Press, Inc. All rights reserved.]*

KEYWORDS. Lesbian, lesbian activism, fundraising

Daughters of Bilitis began in 1955 with eight women: four Lesbian couples, four blue-collar workers, four white-collar workers, two Lesbian birth mothers, and one Filipina and one Chicana. What was later called "politically correct" happened by chance, not design.

By the end of its first year DOB had fifteen members, only three of the original eight founders remaining. We decided to make an all-out push. We would publish a newsletter and hold monthly public discussion meetings in a downtown hall. We sublet a tiny office from the Mattachine Society. One member donated a desk. We bought a used typewriter and filing cabinet. Several San Francisco businesses "donated" small items like pens, pencils, paper clips, staples and typing paper.

The newsletter soon became a magazine. Readers contributed manuscripts, letters, postage stamps, and small donations besides membership dues, subscriptions and occasional ads. One sent eight packages containing about 6000 duplistickers for use in mailing *The Ladder*. "They were lying around unused at my office and were about to be discarded."

The first three issues were run off on the Mattachine mimeograph. When it gave out, Macy's sign shop came to the rescue. Several Lesbians worked there on the offset press. *The Ladder* staff typed the magazine on paper plates and they printed them before or after regular working hours. One day when *The Ladder* was on the press the boss came into the shop. One worker rushed toward him with a very loud enthusiastic "Good morning," detaining him at the door. Another stepped in front of the stack of pages that had already been run off, blocking them from his view. The forewoman, who had been feeding the press, frantically looked for a replacement. She didn't dare ask either of her helpers to move, so she shouted above the whirr of the press, "I'll be through with this job in just a few minutes." He waved, "That's all right, you're busy. I'll come back later."

This call was too close for comfort. By that time we had become more solvent. We had received some recognition in the alternative press and a lot by

Del Martin and Phyllis Lyon

word of mouth. We had difficulty keeping up with the mail that was pouring in. Pan Graphic Press, a Mattachine-connected private business, offered to print *The Ladder* for a nominal fee. But the volunteers still had to type the stencils and had the same tedious job of collating, folding and stapling by hand, and mailing to do when the pages dried.

The downtown public meetings were drawing considerable interest. A series of lectures by attorneys, psychologists, psychiatrists, employment and marriage counselors was held to dispel some of the "public's" fears and anxieties. A few attendees braved it to become DOB members or subscribe to *The Ladder.*

In 1956 to be an active member of DOB there was an initiation fee of $5.00 and dues of $1.00 per month. Associate members paid $2.50 plus 50 cents a month. Subscriptions to *The Ladder* were $1.00 a year. In response to an anonymous letter praising *The Ladder*, the editor added, "At the risk of sounding mercenary, those of you who don't want to reveal your names could throw a few anonymous dollar bills in an envelope to help the cause."

One anonymous donor sent a $50 bill, a huge sum for those days. Unfortunately we received the envelope and an accompanying note, but not the money. Thereafter we recommended postal money orders, which do not require the signature of the sender.

In June 1957 subscriptions were raised to $2.50. One reader sent $8.50 to encourage us to establish a New York Chapter. An attorney sent $10 for subscriptions "to people who ought to read *The Ladder.*" To encourage readers to get friends to subscribe, DOB offered to send three sample copies. By December we had 55 members and 400 subscribers. Because of the demand by new subscribers, DOB promised to reprint three, then the first five, issues of *The Ladder*. Advance payments were requested. Despite good intentions, it never happened. There just wasn't enough income to cover the cost. During the first three years membership would swell, then drop. Publication costs went up, while DOB's bank account dwindled.

San Francisco members also handled volumes of mail and sponsored fundraising activities–parties, brunches, picnics, spaghetti feeds, and holiday cocktail receptions. Some events were open to Gay men when we realized that on average they earned considerably more money than did women.

In 1958 internal problems surfaced within the Mattachine organization. But Los Angeles and New York were forming DOB chapters, and there was interest in Chicago and Rhode Island. So we dared to move out on our own. We rented a suite of offices on O'Farrell Street downtown and found a new printer.

For those who doubted its legality or permanency, the Daughters of Bilitis became a full-fledged, non-profit, California corporation in 1959. The Secretary of State accepted the articles of incorporation filed by Kenneth Zwerin, our pro bono attorney. Later he also obtained non-profit tax-exempt status for DOB with the Internal Revenue Service. We happily told our readers that their donations to DOB could be deducted from their federal income tax. Much later we found that DOB had an organizational tax exemption which was not extended to donors. Our error probably didn't make any difference. We doubt that anyone dared to declare DOB contributions on their tax returns.

The response to the September 1959 report in *The Ladder* on the survey of its readership and the November 1959 issue on "Organized Homosexual Issues in San Francisco Election" drew new readers. Subscriptions to *The Ladder* were boosted to $4.00. Immediate renewals up to two years were allowed at the old rate of $2.50.

By 1960 DOB chartered three new chapters to join San Francisco: Los Angeles, New York, and Chicago. And a new business venture, the DOB Book and Record Service, came into being. The Los Angeles Chapter produced a 45 record featuring Lisa Ben singing two Gay folk songs, "Cruising Down the Boulevard" and "Frankie and Johnnie," on the DOB label. It sold for $1.98.

Available books were mainly self-published through a vanity press. Also in 1960 DOB sponsored the first National Lesbian Convention. It was held in the penthouse of the Whitcomb Hotel on San Francisco's Market Street. Registration for the one-day forum, including lunch and banquet, was $15. Morning and afternoon sessions (without meals) were $2.00 each. More than 200 attended, topping those held by ONE and Mattachine. The Homosexual Detail of the San Francisco Police Department dropped by to find out more about the Daughters. Their primary interest was, "Do you advocate wearing clothes of the opposite sex?"

The following day DOB members met in their biennial Business Meeting. That evening Charlotte Coleman, owner of The Front, a Gay bar, closed early and treated DOB members to a private party and celebration. As her contribution to DOB she often donated or obtained food and drinks at wholesale rates for our fundraisers.

After the Tavern Guild was organized in 1962, bar owners closed their establishments on Monday nights and held auctions to raise money for existing community organizations and projects. People donated things they wanted to clean out of their closets, many of which were white elephants that no one wanted. So bids were made for someone else as a joke, and the same junk items would show up at the next auction. Each auction brought in $1,000 or more. Profits also included fun, camaraderie and good will between Gay men and Lesbians.

In the mid-60s, with Shirley Willer of the New York Chapter as conduit, an anonymous donor began to subsidize *The Ladder* by sending $3,000 cashier's checks to individual officers of DOB who in turn signed them over to the organization. This boon made it possible to publish *The Ladder* on slick stock and make it the polished magazine we had all hoped for. With a more attractive format came manuscripts from some established authors.

Some of the funds were invested in a Sacramento Lesbian mother custody case in which her sexual history was thoroughly probed and found wanting as a credential for good parenting. No one questioned the father's parenting skills. The presumption of his heterosexuality was enough. DOB helped finance an appeal which resulted in the California Appeals Court decision that custody could not be based solely upon the sexual orientation of the parent, but rather on "the best interests of the child."

Since members had participated as guinea pigs in various research studies on Lesbians, Florence Conrad, DOB's research director, in 1967 decided it was time to see what effect the studies had had. Because this would be a reversal of the usual procedure (this time Lesbians wanted to study the professionals who usually study them), Conrad felt subjects probably wouldn't cooperate with a known Lesbian organization. She took her idea to Dr. Joel Fort, director of the Center for Special Problems, an agency of the San Francisco Public Health Department. With the help of Drs. Fort and Claude Steiner, a questionnaire was developed and sent, under the auspices of the Center, to a sample of 163 scientifically selected Bay Area psychiatrists, psychologists, and social workers. Cost of printing and mailing came from DOB's anonymous donor. Of the 147 who responded, the results were so contrary to the party line of their associations that it took three years to get a journal to publish "Attitudes of Mental Health Professionals Towards Homosexuality and Treatment" (Psychological Reports, 1971).

The anonymous fund (more than $100,000), for all its positive support, ultimately led to the demise of *The Ladder* and the Daughters of Bilitis as a national organization. Shirley Willer, elected in 1966, was the first national president who did not reside in San Francisco. Chores at the national office were left to the vice president, who was not functioning well. Willer was out of contact, traveling most of the time organizing chapters–reviving some and creating new ones, about fifteen in all. Each of them received checks to set up offices and publish local newsletters.

The 1968 DOB convention was held in Denver, put together by Willer at the last minute, omitting the usual public forum and holding only the obligatory DOB Biennial Business Meeting. Thus, it was poorly attended. Rita Laporte became the new national president with Gene Damon (Barbara Grier) to continue as editor of *The Ladder*. As time approached for the 1970 DOB Convention in New York, Laporte and Damon apparently feared they would lose control of *The Ladder*. So Laporte "lifted" the mailing list and other DOB properties and moved the operation to Reno, Nevada. Although the June/July 1970 issue of *The Ladder* appeared to be under the aegis of DOB, it was in reality already an independent non-profit publication.

Attorneys advised DOB that the move across the border to Reno made a lawsuit a federal case that could take years to settle. At the New York Convention members decided not to file suit, dissolved the national board, whose chief function was to publish *The Ladder*, and freed chapters to put their money, time and energy into local endeavors. It was hoped that the chapters would still maintain a loose coalition of mutual concerns. It never happened. Willer, who had no position in DOB after 1968, continued to fund publication of *The Ladder* after 1970. By 1972, *The Ladder* died. Willer stopped funding it. In the end, despite its 3,800 subscribers, it could not survive without the support of the organization that spawned it.

Changing Hearts, Changing Minds:
An Interview with Dee Mosbacher, MD, PhD

Dee Mosbacher
Kimberly F. Balsam

SUMMARY. This article is comprised of excerpts from an interview with Dee Mosbacher, MD, PhD, a psychiatric consultant and lesbian ac-

Dee Mosbacher is a psychiatrist, activist, filmmaker, and the founder and president of Woman Vision, a non-profit educational media production company. She directed and co-produced the Academy Award-nominated film *Straight from the Heart*. Her documentaries, *Closets Are Health Hazards: Gay and Lesbian Physicians Come Out* and *Lesbian Physicians on Practice, Patients, and Power*, have been used in medical school sexuality courses and conferences throughout the United States, Canada, and Europe. Dr. Mosbacher's documentary credits also include *Out for a Change: Addressing Homophobia in Women's Sports*, which was awarded a National Educational Media Award. She has served on the boards of various organizations, including the American Medical Students Association, Lyon-Martin Women's Health Services, the National Gay and Lesbian Task Force (NGLTF), Pitzer College, the American Association of Physicians for Human Rights (now GLMA), and California Pacific Medical Center. Dr. Mosbacher has received many awards for her service to the LGBT community.

Kimberly F. Balsam is a doctoral student in the Clinical Psychology Program at the University of Vermont. Her research, teaching and clinical interests focus on the psychology of women and lesbian/gay/bisexual psychology. She has been active in the violence against women movement since 1990. Her current research projects include studies of lesbian mothers, incarcerated women, and trauma and victimization in lesbian, gay, and bisexual populations.

Address correspondence to: Dr. Dee Mosbacher, 3570 Clay Street, San Francisco, CA 94118 (E-mail: Dmosbacher@woman-vision.org).

[Haworth co-indexing entry note]: "Changing Hearts, Changing Minds: An Interview with Dee Mosbacher, MD, PhD." Mosbacher, Dee, and Kimberly F. Balsam. Co-published simultaneously in *Journal of Lesbian Studies* (Harrington Park Press, an imprint of The Haworth Press, Inc.) Vol. 5, Number 3, 2001, pp. 119-128; and: *Everyday Mutinies: Funding Lesbian Activism* (ed: Nanette K. Gartrell, and Esther D. Rothblum) Harrington Park Press, an imprint of The Haworth Press, Inc., 2001, pp. 119-128. Single or multiple copies of this article are available for a fee from The Haworth Document Delivery Service [1-800-342-9678, 9:00 a.m. - 5:00 p.m. (EST). E-mail address: getinfo@haworthpressinc.com].

tivist who has expressed her visions of social change through documentary films. Dee describes the beginnings of her political activism in the social change and women's health movements of the 1960s and 1970s and her evolution as an activist filmmaker over the past two decades. She explores the process of fundraising, the importance of working collaboratively, her experience balancing activism with her work as a psychiatrist, and the rewards of making films that have an impact on people's lives. She also discusses her visions for the future and provides recommendations for young lesbian activists. *[Article copies available for a fee from The Haworth Document Delivery Service: 1-800-342-9678. E-mail address: <getinfo@Haworthpressinc.com> Website: <http://www.HaworthPress. com> © 2001 by The Haworth Press, Inc. All rights reserved.]*

KEYWORDS. Lesbian, lesbian activism, fundraising

Dee Mosbacher is a woman with visions of change. As a psychiatrist working with severely mentally ill patients and the agencies that serve them, she has been intimately involved with the process of change on both the personal and institutional levels. As a lesbian activist, she has expressed her vision of social change through the medium of film. Her efforts have not gone unnoticed; her 1994 film, *Straight from the Heart,* was nominated for an Academy Award. Currently, Dee is working on three diverse projects: a film about Phyllis Lyon and Del Martin; *Radical Harmonies,* a film about the history of women's music, and *Fundraising from the Heart,* which documents the creative fundraising strategies of a woman who raised $100 million for world hunger.

In the midst of her demanding schedule, I caught up with Dee and spoke with her about her life, her activism, and her visions for the future. I was impressed with her enormous dedication and her ability to articulate the many insights she has gained through her work. Following are excerpts from that interview.

How did you get involved with lesbian activism?

I guess it really began in college. I was doing some anti-war work in the late 1960s and early 1970s. Then I moved to Washington, D.C., and became active in various causes. First it was the anti-war movement, then the abortion rights movement, and then I joined the socialist worker's party.

So the beginnings of your activism weren't with lesbian activism per se, but with other political and social justice issues. How did that change?

Well, I came out! It happened in the course of being an abortion rights activist, and then I got political in more woman-centered issues such as the

Dee Mosbacher
Photo by Nanette K. Gartrell. Used by permission.

women's health movement. I guess being an activist as a lesbian came to fruition when I was in medical school in Houston. In 1979, when I started, I had originally planned to give up activism and focus on being a medical student. I thought it would be a rough road academically and I wouldn't have time to do politics. But politics was in my blood, although my relatives have a very different political agenda from mine. My father raised millions for the Republican Party. He served as Secretary of Commerce under George Bush. My Republican brother ran for senator and lieutenant governor in Texas, and then for mayor of Houston.

This is an aside. I came across a reference to you and your father in a 1992 Philadelphia Inquirer *article that I found very interesting. Can you tell me the story?*

I was asked by Pitzer College to give the first commencement speech by a graduate. Coincidentally, my father, who was then the Commerce Secretary

Kimberly F. Balsam
Photo by Kerri Ashling. Used by permission.

under President Bush, was the commencement speaker at nearby Claremont Men's College that same day. I began my speech with the following anecdote: "Dad and I had breakfast this morning. We had a look at each other's speeches. He would have used mine, but he's not a lesbian. I would have used his, but I'm not a Republican" (Philadelphia Inquirer, 20 September 1992, p. L1). The audience seemed to find it quite amusing.

To return to your story . . . what happened in medical school that brought you back to activism?

Well, it was not a friendly environment. Once on our bulletin board there was a big sign that said, "Kill the queers." I would say that the homophobic climate motivated me, but I was also inspired by meeting other students who had the courage to stand up and be counted. Having them as role models helped me, so I tried to be a role model for people who were coming in behind me. I became active in the American Medical Student Association and was elected to be one of the trustees at large. I got a lot of requests to speak as an out lesbian medical student to a variety of medical schools across the country. Being a medical student with limited time, I couldn't really do this. The idea came to me to do a slide and audiotape presentation about homophobia in medicine. I wanted to make something that could be used as a presentation around the country so that people who were afraid to come out in their medical schools didn't have to. They could use this presentation and not focus all of the attention on themselves.

So you came up with a creative way to get your message out there . . .

Yes. Joan Biren, who has been an activist, photographer, and videographer for many years, worked on this with me. It has gone all over the country to medical schools and sexuality courses. It's been really helpful in breaking the ice and starting discussions about human sexuality and sexual orientation.

Was this your first involvement with any kind of filmmaking, so to speak?

Yes, it was, and I soon realized that it was a really great tool. When I got a little further down the road, Joan and I made a video called *Lesbian Physicians on Practice, Patients and Power*. It was filmed at the Women in Medicine conference in Provincetown.

In the beginning, these projects were funded out of my own pocket. I was lucky enough to come from a wealthy background and had some money to put into filmmaking. That video was also not terribly expensive to make because the production was more like home video than broadcast quality.

Then I kind of went off on a different track. I was always a jock as a kid and stopped doing that when I went to college. I wasn't really conscious of this at the time, but as it turned out, one of the main reasons was internalized homophobia. I think I'd been programmed to think that if I were a jock as a grown woman, I would be thought of as a lesbian. I think that's the message that a lot of girls and young women get. So I wanted to make a video about homophobia in sports. I started doing that, and, in the midst of production, the radical right was starting to produce videos such as *Gay Rights, Special Rights*. Things were getting pretty nasty, and I was inspired, so to speak, by one of those reactionary videos to do sort of a "Homophobia 101" video aimed at white, Christian, church-going audiences. So I started working on *Straight from the Heart* and that's when I started trying to raise money.

You were starting to put more time and energy into filmmaking?

I thought in the beginning that I would be able to finance the videos myself, but it became apparent that in order to make a broadcast quality video, the budget was out of my range. So I started going to individuals to raise money and I recruited someone to work with me who started writing some grants. It was a real uphill battle. Many foundations have concerns about financing video. People wonder how you are going to distribute it. And then of course the subject matter is not of interest to some. When you consider that less than .03% of all philanthropic dollars are awarded to lesbian and gay issues annually, it's pretty scary.

Were you aware of that statistic when you started fundraising?

No, nor was I aware of how much of my time would be taken up raising money. I really went into that pretty naively. I was just thinking I would sort of muddle through and bring in some income with the finished product to defray some of the costs, and that it wouldn't cost that much. The lesbian physician video cost something like 12 to 15 thousand dollars, but *Straight from the Heart* cost 90 thousand. *All God's Children*, which was a "Homophobia 101" film geared towards African-American church-going audiences, was about 150 thousand. They've all been in that range or higher since then. More and more of my time has been taken up raising money to get the videos done. I started a non-profit called Woman Vision in the early 1990s in order to get tax-deductible contributions. I decided to go that way instead of making this a for-profit venture that people would invest money in and then get their investments back.

So was it disappointing to find that you were spending so much time on fundraising, when you initially went into this to make films?

Yes, it's just something that's necessary to be able to make the videos. I don't think of myself as a particularly social person, and the amount of socializing that needs to happen to do the fundraising is not really comfortable for me, not something I would choose to do if I didn't have to. I end up having to attend a lot of social and political events for networking purposes.

How have you kept your morale and stamina up?

I've kept my day job, which is psychiatry. I work with the most mentally ill folks, and I really like the work a lot. I enjoy working with other caregivers in a

collaborative way. That really keeps me sane. It feels good, and it's something that I know I'm good at. I think that my work is valued. With the fundraising, everything has to come from me, and that gets a little tiring.
You said that you had hired someone to help you with the fundraising. Do you still have help?

Yes, I still do have someone doing some of the nuts and bolts of it. It became clear after a while that I really needed someone to be in a supporting role. I'm sort of a control freak, so it's been a little bit difficult to relinquish some of the control. But along with that comes relinquishing some of the responsibility, which is the good side of it. For instance, with both the Lyon-Martin film and the history of women's music film, I've taken Margie Adam as an associate producer. Joan Biren is directing the Del and Phyllis film. Boden Sandstrom is the co-producer for the history of women's music project and Judith Casselberry is the associate producer, along with Margie Adam. My willingness to work collaboratively has really paid off. It has been extremely helpful after all for me to share the responsibilities and the artistic control. That was the thing I was most worried about losing.
What was your worst fear?

That the films would be something I didn't want them to be–that they would say something that I didn't believe in or want to say. But I have worked very well collaboratively, and the folks I am working with are excellent collaborators as well, so it's been fine. It's really my issue–just not wanting to let go of the control. I still feel like the buck really does stop with me, but I realize that I'm beholden to other folks who are my comrades, and with whom I might occasionally disagree on an aesthetic or political issue.
Do you think those kinds of conflicts have been useful in any way?

Yes, I think they've been very helpful. I realize that I'm not very good asking for help. That's my personal work-in-progress. I have a Board of Directors that I am learning to rely more on. That's been hard for me, too. They're all really busy folks, and I have a hard time asking them to do things.
But the flip side is that getting all of these other people involved has allowed your vision to grow even bigger than you might have imagined.

Yes, I think so.
Being both a filmmaker and a psychiatrist is an interesting combination of roles. When you started medical school, what was your vision for your career, and how has your activism made an impact on it?

When I started medical school, I actually had just gotten a PhD in social psychology and had focused on schizophrenia, so I knew that I wanted to be a psychiatrist. After medical school, I was Medical Director for mental health down in San Mateo County, which was a pretty big job, and at some point when I got more into the filmmaking, I decided to stop doing that. I loved it, but it was hard to do with my filmmaking schedule. So now I'm an independent consultant with San Francisco Community Mental Health and the Progress Foundation. Both have been really great about being flexible when I need to go away to be on location for shoots. So it's really a perfect situation.

The filmmaking, and the many wonderful people I've met in the course of this work, have broadened me intellectually and emotionally. I think my skill as a psychiatrist and as an administrator has really enhanced my filmmaking ability. I've done a lot of the interviews in the films and really enjoy doing that. It's been quite synergistic.

There are certainly challenges to raising funds for lesbian-related projects. What are some of the strategies that you have found to work well?

In terms of the format, house parties and benefits have been quite successful. A lot of people have held house parties for many of the different projects we have been involved with. Most people come to these events expecting that they will be asked for money. We usually show a clip of the video, talk about the costs involved, and make a pitch for people to give money. That works pretty well. We've had some benefits that have been successful, too. We had one recently for Woman Vision that raised over $10,000, which we were very happy with. Sometimes we go to individuals and ask for donations. We've gotten some grants from the Legacy fund and from Astraea. The lesbian/gay-centered organizations tend to give money to Woman Vision.

Have you ever gotten money from more mainstream foundations?

Yes, we have. Another big part of our work is increasing our exposure with the videos that we've already made. We've been looking for ways to work with institutions such as churches, schools, and legislatures to use our videos in different settings. So we have raised money from a number of "straight" organizations or foundations to promote and distribute the videos.

So they've been supportive of those activities, but not as much of the film production?

Right, particularly the more recent films, which some of them view as more cultural and political.

Are there any fundraising tactics that you tried that didn't work or were particularly discouraging?

Well, when you approach individuals to ask for donations, there are always some who will not be interested in your projects. We had a few forays into making T-shirts with the titles of films on them that didn't make as much money as we thought they would. We also tried a couple of distribution tactics that didn't work as well as we expected, like sending mailers to colleges and universities to see if they would purchase the video.

You've been involved with this for a long time. How has being a lesbian activist changed for you over the past two decades?

You have to take the long view. I don't know that I'm going to see marriage or domestic partnership legalized in my lifetime. It's a matter of putting one foot in front of the other and keeping the spirits up. Sometimes it is discouraging. Sometimes I feel like we're not as generous to our own causes as we should be. We have to support each other in our work, and we really need to call the straight world on not supporting lesbian issues. My impression, and the statistics back this up, is that straight people don't give to LGBT causes. We need to approach them and remind them that we've been active in many other causes and now we need their help. We have not effectively been able to break into that huge market of straight people who are progressive enough to think about giving money to LGBT causes. We really need to be more assertive about that. I say "we" and I mean myself as well. I haven't really gone to my straight friends. I think that is, on some level, about internalized homophobia as well. When we don't go to straight folks and say "Look, this is important, this is a social justice issue, and I want your support," we're internalizing that lack of esteem.

On a personal level, what are the greatest rewards of your activism?

It's incredibly gratifying. I've heard story after story of how the films have affected people. For instance, someone wrote and told me that her sister-in-law had kicked her son out because she found out he was gay. This person got *Straight from the Heart* and showed it to her sister-in-law. She was so moved that she called her son and reunited with him. There's story after story like that; it's really amazing.

When you look back on how you've done things, are there any stellar moments that stand out to you about being a lesbian activist?

On a lot of different levels, having my work appreciated. *Straight from the Heart* was nominated for an Academy Award, and I have to say, that was a blast! I never in my wildest dreams thought something like that would happen. But also, I feel just blown away when I hear the stories of how the films have touched people's lives. I also think that having a message and a vision that I want to see translated is what keeps me going.

On the flip side, what are your biggest regrets as a lesbian activist?

I suppose I wish I had been better able to avail myself of people's willingness to help and that I'd been more adept at using the help that people offered. I'd say that was one of my biggest shortcomings and it's made my job more difficult. It was kind of lonely at times. Lately I've moved toward working more collaboratively, but I wish that it had happened sooner.

What are your goals for the future, beyond everything you've already accomplished?

My fantasy is for me to go to somebody and say, "I want to make this film" and for them to say, "Okay, here's a couple hundred thousand dollars to do it."

I'd love it if the videos themselves generated enough income so that I could rely more on that and less on fundraising. I guess all of my hopes and aspirations revolve around having the money to do the work that we want to do. I'm equally as committed to getting the videos out and doing organizing and trying to change people's hearts and minds in terms of homophobia. I know how useful the videos can be, and my goal is to get them into as many hands as possible.

So it's not about the art of filmmaking, but about using films as a tool for change . . .

I really consider myself a lesbian activist who makes films, rather than a filmmaker.

What are your greatest concerns for the future of our movement as prominent lesbian activists approach their senior years?

Actually, I'm much more concerned for the welfare of the aging activists themselves. I am concerned because activism often does not pay well. These women may not have adequate health insurance. They may not have adequate money to live on or adequate resources to retire. Over the last 30 years, I have helped to support a number of lesbian activists at times when they have had limited financial resources, and I expect to do even more of that as we all grow older. Most of us who are doing this never speak publicly about this issue, but I'm doing so for the first time because I think it is very important for younger generations of lesbians to recognize the need to support each other in our struggles, whether they are political, financial, or personal.

What words of advice would you offer to a young lesbian activist today?

Think creatively! The Internet has opened up a whole new world that folks my age–that is, over 50–are becoming involved in. One of my big regrets is that I took so long to develop a Website. The existence of broadband, which will allow us to share high-resolution video and films through our computers, is greatly increasing opportunities to get information to people. There are many opportunities out there for young activists; the key is to be as creative as possible. There are also a lot of challenges, and I think a big part of those challenges has to do with our willingness to work and to solicit in the straight world. That's the next big step. I really admire the activists who are confronting that on an institutional level. A lot of the work that we are doing is with the straight world, trying to increase tolerance. That is my vision for our future.

Time Is More Valuable than Money

Marcia Munson

SUMMARY. Marcia Munson, a feminist, gay rights, and environmental activist for the last thirty years, has chosen to reserve a significant portion of her life for doing volunteer work by living simply and working part time at the IRS (Internal Revenue Service). While choosing to retain the simple lifestyle of the '70s in order to pursue her activist dreams, the author recognizes that the '70s model of self-funded activism no longer works today. During the 1970s, volunteers were often able to support their projects with funds from their own pockets, or could scrape by on small salaries provided by CETA grants and work-study money. In the 1980s, fundraising events to raise money gained popularity. By the 1990s, many non-profit organizations operated primarily with paid staff, and the main volunteer activity had become raising money. Looking back at '70s activism, Munson points out that the services of a skilled, experienced volunteer can be as valuable as money to an organization. *[Article copies available for a fee from The Haworth Document Delivery Service: 1-800-342-9678. E-mail address: <getinfo@haworthpressinc.com> Website: <http://www.HaworthPress.com> © 2001 by The Haworth Press, Inc. All rights reserved.]*

KEYWORDS. Lesbian, lesbian activism, fundraising

Marcia Munson has been a feminist, gay rights, and environmental activist for the last 30 years. She sees lesbian community involvement work as her vocation, and her paid work at the IRS (Internal Revenue Service) as a way to support her dreams. Address correspondence to: Marcia Munson, P. O. Box 40370, San Francisco, CA 94140.

[Haworth co-indexing entry note]: "Time Is More Valuable than Money." Munson, Marcia. Co-published simultaneously in *Journal of Lesbian Studies* (Harrington Park Press, an imprint of The Haworth Press, Inc.) Vol. 5, Number 3, 2001, pp. 129-135; and: *Everyday Mutinies: Funding Lesbian Activism* (ed: Nanette K. Gartrell, and Esther D. Rothblum) Harrington Park Press, an imprint of The Haworth Press, Inc., 2001, pp. 129-135. Single or multiple copies of this article are available for a fee from The Haworth Document Delivery Service [1-800-342-9678, 9:00 a.m. - 5:00 p.m. (EST). E-mail address: getinfo@haworthpressinc.com].

129

Once upon a time, as recently as the early 1970s, most lesbian activism I knew of was accomplished by dedicated volunteers who worked part-time at low-paying jobs. During our off hours, we worked nearly full-time organizing demonstrations, starting child care centers, opening bookstores, and inventing women's resource centers and battered women's shelters. We always talked of finding a "rich woman" to fund our projects, but that was just a dream. Those of us doing volunteer work usually paid for the supplies we needed ourselves.

In the 1970s, a woman like myself without children to support could work at a minimum wage job, pay for rent and food, and still have money left over to spend on activism. By the late 1970s many of us had figured out how to turn our projects into tax-exempt organizations so that we could qualify for work-study money or CETA (Comprehensive Employment and Training Act) federal grants. When another woman and I started the Clatsop County Problem Pregnancy Hotline in Seaside, Oregon, in 1975, we had no outside funding. Working out of our own homes, we contributed about $30 each for placing ads in local newspapers and printing flyers. With this small investment, we served hundreds of women.

Inspired by our success, we gathered a dozen women interested in starting a Women's Resource Center in nearby Astoria, Oregon. After forming a non-profit corporation and applying for 501c(3) tax-exempt status, we became qualified to hire students on work-study grants from nearby Clatsop Community College. Most of our group then signed up for a couple of classes at the college. (The favorite was a Women's Studies class that one of our members taught.) We each applied for financial aid, got work-study grants, and hired ourselves to work at the Women's Resource Center we had started. Most of us contributed a few dollars a week to pay for the office rent and utilities. The Women's Resource Center existed like that for a few years until the health and legal information referral services we offered were absorbed by a county government agency.

In 1977 my girlfriend and I decided to share our Girl-Scout-learned survival skills with other women by starting the Women's Wilderness Institute Northwest (WWIN). We each loaned the organization $900, which enabled us to buy 10 backpacks and sleeping bags at wholesale prices, print and mail the first year's brochure, and rent a Post Office box. If all went well, the trip fees we collected would allow us to repay ourselves and to fund the next year's program. We planned to continue working at our previous part-time jobs–she was a ski patroller, I was a cross-country ski instructor–to pay our living expenses. At this point, one of the women we had recruited for the Board of Directors suggested we apply for CETA funding to pay a Program Director's salary. We applied for and got the grant. Three years of CETA funding allowed me to de-

Marcia Munson

vote full time to developing a year-round program of backpacking, bicycle touring, and cross-country skiing courses.

By the time CETA funds were no longer available, trip fees were generating enough money to pay the director's salary plus organizational expenses. WWIN continued as a self-supporting non-profit organization in Portland, Oregon, for the next 5 years, always offering reduced trip fees to any participants who expressed a need. Unfortunately, in 1984, after a series of poor financial decisions by the third Program Director, an exhausted Board of Directors was forced to dissolve the organization.

By 1980, when I left WWIN and moved to Colorado Springs, I had figured out that I was never going to be a big moneymaker. I had no interest in medicine or law, and I'm not competitive enough to make it in the business world. Making a career out of my volunteer work only fed my workaholic tendencies–the 60- or 70-hour workweek I had put in at WWIN taught me that I needed to separate the feminist, activist, environmentalist community work that I loved from my livelihood. In the 1980s I chose part-time blue-collar work, first as a forest fire fighter and then as a mail carrier. This allowed me to live comfortably while working less than full time, leaving plenty of time for projects that won my heart. As a blue-collar worker in the 1980s, I could still afford to pay for the out-of-pocket expenses of my volunteer projects, but I saw that most other women could not. Lesbians not working as professionals were mostly stuck in female-dominated jobs that paid poorly. Holding fundraising events to raise the money for postage, printing, and rent was essential to every volunteer project I participated in throughout the 1980s.

In Colorado Springs, I became involved with a group of lesbians who dreamed of starting a Women's Cultural Center in town. I could see that paying for such a project out of our own pockets was no longer possible. The times had changed economically. Rents had soared, but salaries had not increased comparably. Those of us with time to dream and volunteer had no extra cash to contribute to this project. Many of the lesbians in town had turned their volunteer work into paid careers by starting the Women's Health Service Center, but for them this work was a more-than-full-time, all-consuming commitment. A few of the lesbians in town followed demanding professions that took all their time but provided them with extra cash. A lawyer and an electrician were big donors to the Women's Cultural Center, but most of the funds came from events like the $5-a-plate spaghetti dinner/talent show, which almost every dyke in town could afford to attend–and most did!

The Colorado Springs chapter of the National Organization for Women took most of my time in the early 1980s. After that, I spent a year planning social events for the Dykes of Estes (in Estes Park, Colorado, population: 5000). Then I joined the steering committee of The Lesbian Connection (TLC), a

300-member social organization in Boulder, Colorado. It was through TLC that I recruited the 150 volunteers who gathered signatures and distributed leaflets to pass Boulder's gay rights ordinance in 1987. It was also through TLC that I planned the New Year's Eve dance that raised the funds to pay a chunk of the gay rights ordinance's campaign costs. While I was technically a full-time Post Office employee in the late 1980s, I was actually able to take frequent weeks of unpaid leave from my mail-carrier position when my volunteer work became too demanding, as long as I could think up some plausible excuse!

When I moved to San Francisco in 1989, I could see that the economic reality of being an activist was far different from what I had experienced in Oregon in the 1970s or in Colorado in the 1980s. It was obvious that I would have to work full-time at almost any job I could land just to pay rent on an apartment, dress appropriately for city life, and have a normal urban social life. Instead of continuing as a mail carrier, I got a desk job as a federal bureaucrat at the Internal Revenue Service (IRS)–a job that was far less exhausting. Knowing I had no interest in devoting myself to a new career that would demand 60 hours a week, as many of my new acquaintances were doing, it seemed that I had two choices. I could plod along in a 40-hour-a-week IRS job, moving up the career ladder, and maintain a middle-class existence, or I could cut my expenses, work part-time, and have plenty of time to volunteer and play. I chose to cut expenses and play.

Now I'm still a seasonal worker after 10 years with the IRS, usually taking three or four months of time off without pay each year. I say "no thanks" to the frequent promotion offers that would mean more money, but less free time. The months off allow me time to write, hike, camp, travel, visit friends, and generally get recharged for the eight or nine months each year when I work at my low-stress job and devote most of my free time to a major volunteer project. My activities have ranged from serving on the Board of the San Francisco Chapter of the National Organization for Women, to playing clarinet in the Lesbian and Gay Freedom Band. I have worked on the Governing Committee of the Gay and Lesbian Activity Group of the Sierra Club. I started a short-lived newcomers' group called "Lesbians Welcoming Women." I recruited and supervised 100 volunteers for a National Center for Lesbian Rights fundraising dinner, taught "safer sex" workshops at the Billy deFrank Community Center, and worked for Tom Ammiano's mayoral campaign. I have also pursued dozens of minor activities, such as ushering for the Women's Philharmonic Orchestra.

Certainly, many lesbians who work full-time in high-powered jobs occasionally have time for volunteer work, but I have far more time and enthusiasm than the average lesbian my age. It's my life work, building community and

making the world a better place in which to live. I choose to follow that vocation in my free time, and work part-time to support my habit of volunteering.
These days, meaningful volunteer work is getting more difficult to find.
When I volunteer at lesbian cultural events, I feel that taking tickets at the door
or selling refreshments during intermission is not the best use of the volunteer
skills I've developed over the years. I always seem to be on the lookout for the
right volunteer opportunity. Most lesbian and gay organizations in San Francisco seem geared towards raising enough money to pay staff to do the work.
"Volunteering" usually consists of performing some menial task at an event or
working to raise funds. "Membership," rather than being a call to activism,
consists of little more than paying annual dues.

This organizational structure might have made more sense in the 1990s,
when there were fewer highly skilled and dedicated volunteers like me. But I
predict that there will many more such volunteers in the years to come. Organizations need to realize that a dedicated, highly qualified, 10-hour-per-week
volunteer doing work they might otherwise pay an employee ten to a hundred
dollars an hour to perform is indeed a "major donor." Development directors
need to cultivate such volunteers and find ways to use us to build organizations. Community organizations need to learn to recruit and utilize experienced volunteers, instead of expecting every new volunteer to start at the
bottom stuffing envelopes. I think this will be the organizational development
challenge of the decade, as more of us dykes with '70s values, a lifetime of
skills, and lots of mid-life zest retire.

Last year I read a survey showing that most Americans would choose more
free time over a pay raise, and I chuckled and thought, "So why don't you actually make that choice?" But I know why most people make different choices
than I do. Most people in this country have become accustomed to a level of
material comfort that keeps them trapped in demanding jobs. Many are influenced by social pressure to acquire more and more possessions, since material
wealth has come to signify success in our culture. For me, planning to have
time to travel, write, volunteer, and relax for several months each year requires
a lifestyle few of my peers could tolerate. I live in a tiny 11´ x 13´ apartment; I
drive a car way past its prime. On vacations I camp out or stay at inexpensive
youth hostels.

Sometimes events force me to re-examine the unusual balance of career,
lifestyle, free time, and volunteer activism I have chosen for myself. Once, a
woman I was dating warned me, "You'll never find a girlfriend unless you
move to a bigger apartment!" And my lover's son, just out of college, landed a
job that paid the same as mine. When something like that happens, I have to
stop and remind myself of how lucky I really am. I know I have traveled more
in the last 10 years than almost anyone I know. My list of accomplishments in

the last decade is something to be proud of. I picture the envy of my home-owner friends when I tell them that I can vacuum my floor in only five minutes. When I think of the millions of people in third-world countries living in cramped conditions with no running water, I realize that my lifestyle is actually quite luxurious. I know that American-style overconsumption is one of the greatest threats to environmental preservation. My simple lifestyle serves as a model that encourages others to question their choices. But best of all, it allows me the luxuries I most value: time to travel, time to relax, and time to do meaningful volunteer work.

Rainbow Philanthropy

Martina Navratilova

Nanette K. Gartrell

SUMMARY. Martina Navratilova was the first professional athlete to proclaim her lesbianism. After retiring from a stunning tennis career, Martina Navratilova has emerged as a prominent author, television commentator, and public speaker. She is an influential advocate of lesbigay causes, and a major contributor to the lesbigay community. This article describes Martina's *"passion [and] #1 cause"*–the Rainbow Endowment. *[Article copies available for a fee from The Haworth Document Delivery Service: 1-800-342-9678. E-mail address: <getinfo@haworthpressinc.com> Website: <http://www.HaworthPress.com> © 2001 by The Haworth Press, Inc. All rights reserved.]*

Martina Navratilova has won more overall titles than any other woman or man in tennis history. By August of the year 2000, Martina had won 1438 singles matches, and her career earnings exceeded twenty million dollars. She was named "Athlete of the Year" numerous times, as well as "Athlete of the Decade." Martina has served as president of the Women's Tennis Association Tour Players Association, played in the Virginia Slims "Legends" Tour, and represented the United States in the Federation Cup. She is a television commentator for Grand Slam tournaments and a leading speaker on the international lecture circuit. In 1996, Martina was awarded an honorary doctorate in public service from George Washington University.

Nanette K. Gartrell, MD, is a tap dancing tennis fan who hopes to play on the professional tour in her next lifetime. She was the architect of the Lesbian Mixed Doubles (Butch/Femme) Tennis Tournament that raised over $100,000 for Lyon Martin Women's Health Services.

Address correspondence to: Nanette K. Gartrell, 3570 Clay Street, San Francisco, CA 94118.

[Haworth co-indexing entry note]: "Rainbow Philanthropy." Navratilova, Martina, and Nanette K. Gartrell. Co-published simultaneously in *Journal of Lesbian Studies* (Harrington Park Press, an imprint of The Haworth Press, Inc.) Vol. 5, Number 3, 2001, pp. 137-140; and: *Everyday Mutinies: Funding Lesbian Activism* (ed: Nanette K. Gartrell, and Esther D. Rothblum) Harrington Park Press, an imprint of The Haworth Press, Inc., 2001, pp. 137-140. Single or multiple copies of this article are available for a fee from The Haworth Document Delivery Service [1-800-342-9678, 9:00 a.m. - 5:00 p.m. (EST). E-mail address: getinfo@haworthpressinc.com].

137

KEYWORDS. Lesbian, lesbian activism, fundraising

Martina Navratilova is considered the greatest women's tennis player in history. Her astounding mix of physical and mental agility earned her eighteen Grand Slam singles titles, 167 career singles titles (including a record nine Wimbledon titles), and 166 doubles titles (including 31 Grand Slam titles). She holds the record for 109 consecutive doubles wins (with Pam Shriver), and the longest continuous winning streak (seventy-four matches). In July of 2000, Martina was inducted into the International Tennis Hall of Fame.

SOCIAL ACTIVISM

Martina was the first professional athlete to proclaim her lesbianism, and the only 20th century sports legend to become an outspoken advocate of lesbian and gay rights. In 1992, she took an active role in overturning Colorado's Amendment Two, a law that would have severely curtailed civil rights for lesbians and gays. At the 1993 and 2000 Marches on Washington for Lesbian, Gay, Bisexual and Transgendered Rights, Martina was a keynote speaker. She spoke passionately about the importance of coming out and being visible.

> *I believe the biggest, strongest weapon of our movement for equality is visibility, and the best way to get it is to come out . . . being a lesbian . . . is what I am. Nothing more and nothing less.* (1993)

In 2000, Martina spoke about the importance of basic civil liberties for lesbian and gay families:

> *My youngest family member who is here today is two years old. She has two moms. She, as well as children like her, symbolize the need for basic legal rights and equal protection [for lesbian and gay families]. In retrospect, I left Czechoslovakia so that I could be free to live my life as a gay woman. It did not dawn on me back then that freedom [and] fairness and the most basic of equal rights are granted to–and legally protect–heterosexuals only! Until that changes, our work for equality and for fairness is far from over. I still believe that the key to having full inclusion and the exact same legal rights that all others have is to come out–and live your life every day–in every way, out of the closet!*

Even though Martina's honesty about her lesbianism has cost her millions of dollars in endorsements, Martina continues to advocate for civil rights.

Martina Navratilova
Photo by Greg Gorman. Used by permission.

LESBIAN PHILANTHROPY

Martina has donated auction items to many lesbian community fundraisers. Between 1991 and 1995, she contributed tennis rackets, clothing, and Wimbledon grass court shoes to the Lesbian Mixed Doubles Tennis Tournament that Nanette organized. Martina's donations provided much-needed healthcare for poor and working class lesbians at Lyon Martin Women's Health Services. Her Wimbledon grass court shoes, auctioned individually on the theory that her dominant foot was more valuable, brought in over $2000!

In 1995, Martina became the spokesperson for the Rainbow Endowment. The inspiration for the foundation came from the strength and unity that was shared by nearly a million people during the 1993 March on Washington. Martina, along with Nancy Becker and Pam Derderian, Principals of Do Tell, Inc., a lesbian owned agency that specializes in marketing to the lesbigay community, created the Rainbow Card program. *"We were determined to find a way to harness the economic power of the lesbian and gay community to achieve humanitarian goals,"* said Martina.

The Rainbow Card was introduced as a fundraising tool for the Rainbow Endowment, a nonprofit organization that distributes corporate funds and revenue generated from the Rainbow Card program. The Rainbow Card program has raised over $1 million for lesbigay arts, cultural, and civil rights organizations. Derderian attributes the success of the program to the lesbigay community's economic strength (estimated at over $500 billion in aggregate income) and its responsiveness to programs which benefit lesbians and gay men personally as well as politically. Derderian also acknowledges the generous support of the Rainbow Card program's corporate sponsors–Subaru (the founding sponsor) and British Airways. Among the many organizations benefiting from the program are Astraea National Lesbian Action Foundation; the Gay, Lesbian, Straight Education Network; Lambda Legal Defense and Education Fund, Inc.; the National Breast Cancer Coalition; the National Center for Lesbian Rights; the National Lesbian & Gay Journalists Association; and the National Lesbian & Gay Health Association.

My Roots as an Activist

Caitlin Ryan

SUMMARY. Caitlin Ryan describes her early activist experiences, highlighting her work coordinating the 2nd National Gay Health Conference in 1979, publishing the first national lesbian and gay health directory, organizing the National Lesbian and Gay Health Foundation, and initiating and serving as co-investigator of the National Lesbian Health Care Survey. She describes the challenges of funding these and other projects, and of integrating lesbian activism into her life. An early AIDS activist, Ryan was the first director of AID Atlanta, a member of the Federation of AIDS Related Organizations, a founder of the National Association of People with AIDS, and a convener of the minority AIDS working group that became the National Minority AIDS Council. Drawing on her extensive experience, Ryan discusses the challenges facing lesbian research today. She believes that research and training infrastructure are sorely needed, particularly funding for policy and applied research to address longstanding gaps in understanding our rapidly evolving communities. Noting that our diversity and our evolving needs require more varied funding approaches that do not fit the narrow scope

Caitlin Ryan, MSW, ACSW, a clinical social worker who has worked on lesbian and gay issues for the past 25 years, is Director of Policy Studies at the Research Institute on Sexuality, Social Inequality and Health at San Francisco State University. She was a founder of the National Lesbian and Gay Health Foundation and initiator and co-investigator of the National Lesbian Health Care Survey. Her work has been acknowledged by many groups, including the National Association of Social Workers, who in 1988 awarded her the profession's highest honor, "National Social Worker of the Year," for her contributions to the AIDS epidemic and social change.

[Haworth co-indexing entry note]: "My Roots as an Activist." Ryan, Caitlin. Co-published simultaneously in *Journal of Lesbian Studies* (Harrington Park Press, an imprint of The Haworth Press, Inc.) Vol. 5, Number 3, 2001, pp. 141-149; and: *Everyday Mutinies: Funding Lesbian Activism* (ed: Nanette K. Gartrell, and Esther D. Rothblum) Harrington Park Press, an imprint of The Haworth Press, Inc., 2001, pp. 141-149. Single or multiple copies of this article are available for a fee from The Haworth Document Delivery Service [1-800-342-9678, 9:00 a.m. - 5:00 p.m. (EST). E-mail address: getinfo@haworthpressinc.com].

141

or "disease model" focus of government agencies, she urges lesbian activists to advocate for these issues. *[Article copies available for a fee from The Haworth Document Delivery Service: 1-800-342-9678. E-mail address: <getinfo@haworthpressinc.com> Website: <http://www.HaworthPress.com>* © *2001 by The Haworth Press, Inc. All rights reserved.]*

KEYWORDS. Lesbian, lesbian activism, fundraising

My roots as an activist were firmly planted in childhood. I inherited a keen sense of social justice from a family of Irish immigrants. My great-uncle was smuggled out of County Cork in a piece of furniture with a price on his head after the Easter Uprising, when the English Black and Tans routed their village and broke all my great grandmother's crockery. Twenty years later, during World War II, Grannie came out (as they said in those days) to America. I wasn't born yet, but my grandmother told me that Grannie would say her rosary in front of the radio, listening to Winston Churchill. After each decade of the rosary, she would drop her beads and say, "Damn the British!" Then she would pick them up again and move on.

For me, the most relevant part of that idiosyncratic Irish Catholicism was its commitment to social justice. My brother tells me that I used to lead the kids in demonstrations around the neighborhood with carefully lettered signs, and that I would beat up the local bullies when they preyed on the weaker kids. I can't remember what I was demonstrating against, but I carried that commitment into adulthood and became an activist in my late teens. During the late '60s, I worked with the tinkers (Irish gypsies) in Ireland; became a Vista volunteer at a coal camp in a West Virginia holler; and demonstrated in solidarity with Selma, for women's rights, and against the Vietnam War.

It was only natural that I would become an activist for nascent gay and later lesbian rights. And that's exactly what I did when I came out in New York in the 1970s–a celebratory time for a young lesbian–when we were learning about our emerging identities and forming the organizations that created parallel communities, enabling lesbians and gay men to live openly and with pride.

I started participating in lesbian events when few organizations actually used the "L" word–most subsumed lesbians under "gay." Activism was funded out of our pockets, and lesbian organizations and events were all in serious need of financial help, a trend that continues for many groups today. That was certainly the case for early lesbian and gay health activities.

The National Gay Health Coalition (NGHC), founded in 1976 by Walter Lear and representatives from lesbian and gay caucuses and committees of the

Caitlin Ryan

major professional associations (e.g., APA, APHA), was funded by coalition members, who also subsidized the first National Gay Health Conference held in the basement of All Souls Church in Washington, D.C., in 1978. Lesbians played a central role in early lesbian and gay health organizing activities, volunteering their time as members of their profession's newly founded committees on lesbian and gay issues, organizing early lesbian health services, coordinating health advocacy efforts through the NGHC and planning the first National Gay Health Conference. I volunteered to help organize the second conference held in New York in 1979, and–as often happened in those days when there were few volunteers and even fewer "out" health professionals–I ended up becoming the conference coordinator.

I had just returned to school to finish my undergraduate degree after taking a ten-year hiatus to work as an artist, musician and photographer and to figure out my career path. I was working as a waitress at Le Figaro Café in Greenwich Village and living in a loft in the flower district off Sixth Avenue in Manhattan. I had enrolled in a program at Hunter College that allowed me to plan my own curriculum. I majored in human sexuality and made the National Gay Health Conference the centerpiece of my academic program. This was the first major national lesbian and gay event I coordinated, and it set a pattern for the rest of my life of integrating lesbian activism into my work, relationships, and daily life.

My organizing approach at the time was purely functional, using my own personal resources to expand the conference geographically and programmatically. Since I had incorporated the conference into my undergraduate curriculum, I received academic credit for planning and coordinating it. As a member of the Hunter College Student Health Society, I was able to ask Joyce Hunter, then director of the Student Health Society, to use the school as a conference site and to coordinate student volunteers. I used my loft as a staging area, conference office, and meeting space for the conference steering committee and 13 subcommittees ranging from program to housing. And, in the days before beepers and cellular phones, when I worked night shift at the Figaro Café I generally chose the back waitress station near the pay phone, which served as a field office for follow-up calls to committee members and volunteers.

I had earned my stripes as a community organizer in Ireland and Appalachia during the late '60s, and put them to use mobilizing local and regional volunteers. With no real operating budget and no paid staff, volunteer labor produced a National Gay Health Conference in 1979 that attracted 800 participants from more than 35 states and included production and distribution of the first National Gay Health Directory. We sold ads in the directory to generate income, and many community members contributed in-kind services and skills, such as graphic design from Lee McCabe or baked goods for conference fundraisers (in my loft!) from Deanna Fleisher's High Tea bakery. This turned out to be the largest Lesbian and Gay Health Conference until 1987, when the 8th National Lesbian and Gay Health Conference and 5th National AIDS Forum convened in Los Angeles. It was also my first experience working with lesbian health.

The 1979 conference included sessions on lesbian health and mental health, though at the time no one was quite sure what lesbian health actually entailed. I began talking with Bernice Goodman (a social worker who had introduced the first policy statement on lesbian mothers and care of lesbian and gay clients to the National Association of Social Workers Delegate Assembly in 1978) about the need for a national lesbian health survey. During 1979, the first booklet on lesbian health *(Lesbian Health Matters!)* was published by Mary O'Donnell and the Santa Cruz Women's Health Collective, with partial funding from the Ms. Foundation. Focusing primarily on gynecological care, reproductive health, and sexuality, the booklet underscored the urgent need for lesbian health research.

After coordinating the 1979 conference, I suggested to Paul Paroski and Walter Lear (physicians and gay health pioneers who had helped plan the 1978 conference) that we start a national multidisciplinary organization that would focus on lesbian and gay health issues, conduct educational programs, and sponsor research. They asked me to develop bylaws, and I found an attorney to help incorporate what would become the National Lesbian & Gay Health Foundation (NLGHF). I spent the rest of the year in Central America and started working on a graduate degree in clinical social work when I returned. By then, NLGHF had been established, and Bernice and I decided to do a national lesbian health survey.

While finishing my graduate program in 1981 and 1982, I started framing the questionnaire by talking with various lesbians, individually and in small groups, from different races, backgrounds and occupations in different parts of the U.S. about how they viewed lesbian health. I used my personal resources to fund my activism, supporting outreach activities with money from my student loans and my salary as a supermarket checker. (I worked an evening shift after training at a child inpatient unit during the day.) Bernice talked to the Ms. Foundation, which expressed interest in the survey. In 1983 I wrote the first grant for the study ($10,000), and we hired Dot Parkel, a sociologist and survey researcher in Atlanta, where I was living at the time, to help design and draft the questionnaire. The funding covered printing and mailing the questionnaire, pre-paid postage for respondents, and some travel, but only part of Dot's time. I continued to search for someone with an institutional affiliation who could oversee the coding and analysis to offset funds we wouldn't be able to raise. I knew that this would be the hardest part of doing the National Lesbian Health Care Survey (NLHCS), since so many people were closeted at the time, particularly researchers and other professionals.

To try to find recruits who could help with the survey, we decided to include a session at the 1984 National Lesbian and Gay Health Conference in New York, where we were pretesting the first draft of the questionnaire. That's where I met Judy Bradford, a graduate student at Virginia Commonwealth University (VCU) who was getting ready to take a job at their survey research lab. Judy agreed to coordinate the analysis, and I focused on getting the rest of the funding, developing the sample and distribution network around the country based on my earlier lesbian and gay health organizing, and helping with revisions of the questionnaire. I knew that $10,000 was not enough money to complete the survey, but it would help us get started. What I didn't know was that the AIDS epidemic would absorb most of the limited community resources, so raising funds to finish the survey would become a greater challenge than initiating it. I was turned away by many foundations, including women's funders, so I began to solicit donations from individuals around the country, who sent several hundred contributions that ranged from $5 to $100.

By 1984, I had become director of AID Atlanta and routinely interacted with local, state and federal health officials. In 1986, I approached Juan Ramos at the National Institute of Mental Health (NIMH) whom I had met through my work in AIDS. I asked Juan for funding to analyze the NLHCS data in exchange for a report on lesbian mental health based on our findings, and NIMH gave me a grant for $8,000 to complete the analysis that Judy did at VCU. Other grants from the Chicago Resource Center and the Sophia Fund also contributed to the survey, but we funded distribution of the final report largely from our pockets and, in part, by charging a minimal fee for printing and postage.

During 1984, I decided to coordinate the first Southeastern Lesbian and Gay Health Conference, which was held in Atlanta at Emory University Medical School and was co-sponsored by the Emory School of Nursing and the Georgia Psychological Association. If you didn't live in the South more than 15 years ago, it might be hard to imagine, but holding this conference at the medical school and offering its CME's and CEU's (continuing medical education credits) was quite an accomplishment at the time. (I've sometimes equated it with holding an abortion conference at the parish hall of St. Patrick's Cathedral.) I funded the conference with some seed money from NLGHF, but, like other lesbian and gay health events, it was volunteer driven, supported by in-kind services and community groups.

In 1982, I graduated from social-work school with a newly minted MSW. I was living in Atlanta, where I did my clinical training as an intern at Smith College School for Social Work. I had applied there openly as a lesbian and worked to make the curriculum more responsive to the needs of lesbian and gay clients. That year, I began working to develop AIDS services when I saw an overwhelming need and too few people turning to help. Not surprisingly, lesbians provided key leadership in local AIDS efforts throughout the country, although many of us experienced hostility from some gay men and even some lesbians who perceived our AIDS activism as turning away from lesbian needs and concerns. As I see it, lesbian activism is anything a lesbian activist decides to do.

I helped develop AID Atlanta, the largest AIDS service organization in the Southeast, and became its first director. As part of the first national network to share community responses to AIDS–the Federation of AIDS Related Organizations (FARO)–I met people with AIDS from major cities around the country. Two early activists–Bobby Campbell and Bobby Reynolds, both from San Francisco–were especially concerned with the lack of information and resources for people with AIDS in second- and third-tier cities. So Bernice Goodman (who was then president of NLGHF) and I agreed to help develop the National Association of People with AIDS (NAPWA). We talked with people with AIDS from around the country, and I wrote a $10,000 start-up grant application to the Chicago Resource Center in 1983. NLGHF would provide staffing support for NAPWA until people with AIDS had sufficient capacity to run the organization themselves. Because there were so few people with AIDS who were able to serve as visible spokespersons early in the epidemic, especially outside of New York, Los Angeles, and San Francisco, this did not occur until 1986. So, for nearly 2 years, I helped coordinate networking activities through NLGHF, wrote the newsletter, and provided referrals for people with AIDS who contacted me from around the country. I donated my time, while the grant provided support for an office, phone calls, supplies, and coordination activities for people with AIDS.

Networking provided me with a bird's eye view of needs and gaps in AIDS programs. By 1985, Manual Fimbres (a social worker and then NLGHF board member) and I decided to convene a meeting of minority AIDS providers from around the country to conduct a special session on the care needs of people of color with AIDS at the 1986 National Lesbian and Gay Health Conference and AIDS Forum in Washington, D.C. We thought it was critical to bring minority AIDS providers together for several days so that they could identify gaps in care and work together to lobby their elected officials to provide services for minority communities affected by AIDS. So we wrote a grant to NIMH to fund a session on care delivery to people of color with AIDS, to explore barriers, challenges, and models of care, inviting minority AIDS leaders from around the country. Participants included Rev. Carl Bean, Art Brewer, Eunice Diaz, Don Edwards, Gil Gerald, Craig Harris, Paul Kawaka, Calu Lester, Diego Lopez, and Gloria Rodriguez, among others. In addition to the conference sessions, we audiotaped two days of meetings at NIMH, and I prepared a final report on mental health issues facing people of color with AIDS based on the invitees' recommendations. The meeting provided an important grounding for minority AIDS providers to network, share strategies, and interact with public officials. In fact, it was so successful that participants decided to establish the National Minority AIDS Council.

From 1978 until the present, I've been involved with coordinating many lesbian and lesbian/gay health activities and events. I have funded them all through a variety of grants from public and private sources, including in-kind donations and community contributions. I've donated my time by integrating activism into my daily life, and have managed to find resources when community funding was extremely limited and taxed by pressing health and social needs. In this paper, I've only written about the early days of funding lesbian health activism, rather than more recent events, in order to focus on a time when we overcame the greatest obstacles–lack of visibility, limited numbers, more intense homophobia and hostility, and lack of economic and organizational resources.

I'm excited and inspired by the changes in our communities and society that enable us to address long-standing concerns, raise adequate funds to meet a variety of needs, and network quickly, widely, and effectively. We've come a long way and have made great gains since the 1970s, when I first experienced the promise of lesbian activism. Since then, I've continued to work in lesbian research, to push for needed services and for essential infrastructure and organizational capacity. As far as we've come, however, we're facing new and substantive obstacles in mobilizing lesbian activism to fund essential community research projects that will enable us to identify changing trends and emerging needs and to fill gaps that have never been appropriately addressed.

Our communities are changing and evolving faster than we can identify and document those changes. Early work to document developments, needs, and concerns was generally funded out of our pockets, and many of us did this research as graduate students. As a result, there are major gaps in basic areas where we have little or limited information (such as the experience of lesbians of color, bisexuals, and transgendered persons). Our communities are evolving rapidly and their needs are changing. New challenges are emerging, but we lack basic information to provide important services–for example–for a growing population of lesbian, gay, and bisexual seniors.

Although the federal government and a few major foundations that fund research have begun to recognize the need for funding research on lesbians, our community foundations, many of which have substantial endowments as a result of economic gains, are reluctant to fund research, policy research, or even needs assessments, limiting their support to services and community development. Their commitment to supporting services is important and has helped our communities grow, but our diversity and growing needs require more diverse funding approaches, particularly for policy and applied research and community projects that do not fit the narrow scope or "disease model" focus of government agencies.

Lesbian activists need to continue advocating for research funds, this time appealing to community foundations to support the important projects that can help us to document and improve the quality of our lives. As an activist, it's hard to let this opportunity pass without making a pitch to my activist readers. I know Grannie would expect me to rise to the occasion, and I couldn't disappoint her, now could I?

Enhancing and Inspiring
Lesbian Philanthropy

Diane Sabin
Jessica F. Morris

SUMMARY. Diane Sabin has a long history of Lesbian activism and philanthropy while supporting herself in full-time non-activist jobs. In 1997, Diane joined with her friend, Andrea Gillespie, who had envisioned a unique organization entitled 100 Lesbians and our Friends. Its goal is to enhance and inspire Lesbian philanthropy for social change

Diane Sabin considers herself one lucky Lesbian. She has been fortunate to be active in the Lesbian community since the early 1970s. Starting with Artemis Productions in Boston, she has been involved in producing women's music as a vehicle for social change and personal growth. In addition, she served on the board of the National Center for Lesbian Rights and has worked with her friend Andrea Gillespie since 1997 on the amazing project "100 Lesbians and our Friends." She has funded her life and her Lesbian activism by contributing to the health of the community as a licensed chiropractor with a privately owned public clinic in San Francisco.

Jessica F. Morris is a licensed psychologist with an independent practice in Western Massachusetts. She received a PhD in Clinical Psychology from the University of Vermont and is a graduate of Vassar College. Her research and publications focus on the psychology of lesbians, including the coming out process, mental health, and ethnicity. For her clinical work, Jessica concentrates on psychological testing and forensic assessment; she teaches psychology at the graduate level. In graduate school, Jessica received a Distinguished Student Contribution Award from the Society for the Psychological Study of Lesbian, Gay, and Bisexual Issues, Division 44 of the American Psychological Association.

Address correspondence to: Diane Sabin, 281 Noe Street, San Francisco, CA 94114 (E-mail: dianesabin@hotmail.com).

[Haworth co-indexing entry note]: "Enhancing and Inspiring Lesbian Philanthropy." Sabin, Diane, and Jessica F. Morris. Co-published simultaneously in *Journal of Lesbian Studies* (Harrington Park Press, an imprint of The Haworth Press, Inc.) Vol. 5, Number 3, 2001, pp. 151-159; and: *Everyday Mutinies: Funding Lesbian Activism* (ed: Nanette K. Gartrell, and Esther D. Rothblum) Harrington Park Press, an imprint of The Haworth Press, Inc., 2001, pp. 151-159. Single or multiple copies of this article are available for a fee from The Haworth Document Delivery Service [1-800-342-9678, 9:00 a.m. - 5:00 p.m. (EST). E-mail address: getinfo@haworthpressinc. com].

151

and cultural memory. 100 Lesbians and our Friends is a grassroots initiative developed by San Francisco Bay Area Lesbians who share information about and a passion for Lesbian projects, organizations, and individuals in need of funding. 100 Lesbians and our Friends is the vehicle through which Diane encourages Lesbians to live examined lives, to stretch our generosity, and to develop our strength as individuals and as a community. *[Article copies available for a fee from The Haworth Document Delivery Service: 1-800-342-9678. E-mail address: <getinfo@haworthpressinc. com> Website: <http://www.HaworthPress.com> © 2001 by The Haworth Press, Inc. All rights reserved.]*

KEYWORDS. Lesbian, lesbian activism, fundraising

Lesbians, says Diane Sabin, are very giving of resources and time. Talking with each other about giving, however, is a different issue.

During the late 1980s and early 1990s, Diane served as a board member of the National Center for Lesbian Rights. She saw it as a way to put profits from her job into Lesbian community activism. It was a major accomplishment in Diane's life when she was able to donate $1000 a year to NCLR. After serving on the NCLR board, Diane began exploring other ways to channel her activist energy. Professionally, she had become quite successful, and therefore able to increase her own philanthropic contributions.

FOUNDING 100 LESBIANS AND OUR FRIENDS

In 1997, Andrea Gillespie shared her inspiration and vision for 100 Lesbians and our Friends. Diane became excited about Andrea's idea for creating a way to make personal donations and simultaneously encourage Lesbian philanthropy. For about two years, Andrea and Diane strategized about this endeavor. Initially, they had planned to raise $1000 from 100 Lesbians and donate the $100,000 to one Lesbian organization. This strategy was designed to have a substantial impact on the recipient organization. They had also intended to target Lesbians who had substantial financial resources, especially those who were interested in but not yet giving to Lesbian causes. As their thinking evolved, they realized that they needed to modify these goals.

Diane realized that 100 Lesbians and our Friends would not be consistent with her own values if the focus on Lesbians able to make donations of $1000 excluded other Lesbians with more limited means. At an early meeting of in-

Diane Sabin
Photo by Jewelle Gomez. Used by permission.

Jessica F. Morris

terested and experienced Lesbian community activists, these issues were discussed in depth. They explored the complexities of class, feminism, and philanthropy in our capitalist culture. As a result of these discussions, the group eventually opened itself to donations of any amount. Diane identifies with and primarily solicits those whom she thinks of as the "working well-to-do," a phrase she coined to describe employed Lesbians who have discretionary income. Diane places herself in that category, and hopes to stretch the consciousness and contributions of other gainfully employed women. She sees 100 Lesbians and our Friends as a vehicle for empowering such Lesbians to think and act expansively.

The idea of donating a large sum of money to a single Lesbian organization was also short lived. As Diane began to promote 100 Lesbians and our Friends, there was considerable disagreement about the "most worthy" organization. Diane realized that limiting the focus to a single organization was counterproductive to the goals of the group. She wanted to increase Lesbian giving, without generating disagreements about worthiness.

One of Diane's most meaningful experiences occurred when a group of about 30 Lesbians sat in her living room, took out their checkbooks and wrote checks for 100 Lesbians and our Friends' first round of funding. Many of those present announced how much money they were contributing, and discussed their decision-making process. For almost everyone, this was the first disclosure of detailed financial information to anyone other than an intimate. There was no pressure to give or to reveal, but the feeling of sisterhood generated considerable momentum. Diane described that meeting as an incredible opportunity to discuss the development of consciousness and community, and the dynamics of money and power.

The goal of 100 Lesbians and our Friends is to enhance and inspire Lesbian philanthropy for social change and cultural memory. 100 Lesbians and our Friends is a grassroots initiative. It is not a non-profit organization; it doesn't have a board of directors, a budget, or a bank account. Thus far, donations have ranged from $10 to $9000, reflecting the women's own resources. Within its first year, the group raised over $100,000 for Lesbian causes.

No check is ever actually written to 100 Lesbians and our Friends, only to the organizations, projects, foundations, or individuals to whom a Lesbian wishes to donate. However, the checks are sent, individually or collectively, with a cover letter from 100 Lesbians and our Friends. The cover letter describes the group and explains its goal of increasing philanthropy for Lesbian causes. In some cases, the group forwards a donation to a non-Lesbian organization that a Lesbian wants to fund. In these instances, the cover letter details that the donation is being made to fund Lesbian-specific projects. This gives 100 Lesbians and our Friends the opportunity to educate organizations about

Lesbian issues and Lesbian giving, and challenges organizations to create something within their structure that acknowledges and serves Lesbians. Non-Lesbian organizations are sent a cover letter that requests the board discuss how it can use the donation to fund a Lesbian project.

AN OPPORTUNITY TO DEFINE LESBIAN

Growing up in the fertile Cambridge Lesbian feminist community of the 1970s has given Diane a strong political consciousness and an understanding of the power and importance of everyday decisions. This includes a commitment to honoring self definition. Bringing together those who want to donate to Lesbian causes has provided her with an opportunity to add to the ongoing public dialogue about what it means to be a Lesbian. Diane's honoring of self definition has been enhanced and complicated by her realization that her own thinking might lead her to disagree with another's self definition. Figuring out a way to disagree respectfully was an important step in Diane's evolution. It is a step that has taken the group to the public discussion of who is a Lesbian.

Acknowledging and adding to the variety of definitions currently used, 100 Lesbians and our Friends defines a "Lesbian" as a woman who is born a girl, raised a girl, and is now a woman who is relating, or hoping to relate to a woman who was born and raised a girl. The name of the group includes "friends" in the title (a term preferred over "ally"), with the intent of welcoming the participation of those who are not Lesbians. This is a deliberate strategy since Lesbians have made considerable contributions to non-lesbian communities. Reciprocally, 100 Lesbians and our Friends hopes to foster contributions from non-lesbians to the Lesbian community. Therefore, *all* financial donations are welcome. The group also wants to create space for women to gather together, so the public events are *for women*. And certainly, the group wants to create time for Lesbians to meet and discuss ideas, so the every-other-month gatherings are specifically *for lesbians*. Diane and the group believe that this 3-tiered approach reflects their commitment to our diverse movement/community. It creates many opportunities to participate and honors the unique spaces needed to cultivate growth. 100 Lesbians and our Friends thinks this is vital, and hopes it is understood and respected.

Diane and a core planning group organize the various gatherings, meetings and celebrations for 100 Lesbians and our Friends. As they enter their second year, having *surpassed* their original goal of raising $100,000 for Lesbian organizations, projects and individuals, many new ideas have emerged. They will now have four different types of regular gatherings, rather than one catch-all meeting. Diane has proposed to the group that they have general introductory meetings at different sites in the Bay Area to increase access for those living in outlying areas. In addition, she suggested regular meetings devoted to feisty feminist conversation about the issues of money and power and how these issues affect us personally and politically. Invariably, there would be an administrative meeting for those interested in creating and refining the methods of operation for this rambunctious endeavor. And finally, 100 Lesbians and our Friends would sponsor seasonal presentations–bringing together executive directors and administrators of organizations, as well as artists and musicians, visionaries and developers–giving them the space to present their projects to an audience of dedicated donor dykes. Diane hopes that such opportunities for Lesbians to get to know each other would strengthen the bonds of our community.

Diane has a number of Lesbian friends who have a strong tradition of financial giving along with participation in the Lesbian community. However, when they have examined their patterns of giving, they found that only a small percentage of the donations were to Lesbian causes. The 100 Lesbians and our Friends gatherings provide the opportunity to encourage Lesbians to examine their charitable donations and to share information about Lesbian organizations in need. Lesbians who are committed to furthering Lesbian activism can reflect that choice in their giving. Diane's personal philanthropy has always included a component of supporting individuals who are contributing to our community. For example, in the late 1970s, Diane, Andrea Gillespie, and another friend pooled their funds to enable their friend Emily Culpepper to complete her Lesbian feminist doctoral dissertation at Harvard University. More recently, Diane and other members of 100 Lesbians and our Friends have sustained the Angel Fund for Del Martin and Phyllis Lyon. Del and Phyllis are heroines of Diane's because of their incredible bravery, their groundbreaking work, their tenacity, and their insistence on creating a better world. Del and Phyllis have more than a century of activism between them. Diane feels honored that 100 Lesbians and our Friends provides a public vehicle for contributions to the Angel Fund.

PERSONAL AND PROFESSIONAL COMMITMENT TO ACTIVISM

The development of 100 Lesbians and our Friends comes out of Diane's own history of Lesbian activism. In 1972, Diane moved to Cambridge, Massachusetts, to take a year off from her undergraduate education. After coming out to her parents, she had been cut off financially and needed to support herself. Although she later reestablished a positive relationship with her parents, this move to Cambridge set her life on an exciting course. Diane describes her background as Jewish middle class, growing up on Long Island, New York, with two working parents.

The Cambridge feminist community of the early 1970s was vibrant; Diane described it as a wonderful incubator of Lesbian activism. Diane first experienced a large group of Lesbians at a Daughter of Bilitis (D.O.B.) meeting. She became active on a Lesbian softball league, and later in the women's music community. After attending the first Boston Women's Music Festival (which inspired the ongoing Michigan Womyn's Music Festival), Diane decided to produce cultural events. She joined the group that organized the Boston festival, Artemis Productions. While this was mostly volunteer work, the staff tried to pay themselves when they could, since money was scarce.

During this time, Diane was working full time as an administrator for a university. This position gave her a steady salary, health benefits, and the flexibility to work at Artemis. Unofficially she had the resources of her office–a copier, telephone, and supplies–which allowed her to do things such as use her phone number as a contact for events. Diane achieved a degree of financial security that allowed her to work as much as she wanted with Artemis Productions, producing Lesbian cultural events, even though there was rarely money for salaries for producers. The Artemis staff even funded some concerts with their own money. This was a time when providing Lesbians with cultural and community activities was relatively new. Diane remembers that time as exhilarating, intense, and important. When there was extra profit from an Artemis Productions event, Diane and her co-workers created the Boston Women's Fund, which still exists today.

Seeking a change, Diane moved to San Francisco. Through friends in San Francisco, Diane got a day job moving boxes and began to produce concerts and the main stage at the annual Lesbian and Gay pride event. She then obtained an administrative job at a university similar to her job in Massachusetts. The actual tasks of her job took a small proportion of her time and left her with plenty of time for her activism. Although she had enough money to support herself, her resources were too limited to make philanthropic donations.

One evening, when Diane and some colleagues were packing up a truck after a Gay pride event they had produced, she was hit by a car and injured. This accident interrupted her daily life for almost half a year and provided her with an opportunity to reexamine her choices. As part of her treatment, Diane went to a chiropractor, something she had not done before. Diane had previously been skeptical of chiropractic treatments–believing them to be more nonsense than medically helpful. But, through her own experience as a patient, she was drawn to this method of healing and inspired to think about a career change.

The deciding factor in Diane's decision to become a chiropractor was that she would be able to bring in a salary that would allow her to fund Lesbian activism and donate to Lesbian causes. Diane realized that it would take a number of years before she would be financially stable as a chiropractor, but she was willing to make the change. In 1987, Diane opened her own chiropractic practice. She finds it a rewarding career. While it was the car accident that prompted Diane to make a major life change, it was her commitment to activism that finalized the decision.

ADVICE FOR FUTURE ACTIVISTS

Diane encourages all Lesbians to be engaged and interested in the greater world and creating our place within it. She advises us to be inventive, imaginative, and persistent. She believes that all Lesbians can be active community members. Diane sees her own philanthropy as an important part of her personal fulfillment. Diane knows that all of us invariably make mistakes. She encourages us to be accepting of those mistakes, both those we make and those made by others. She considers mistakes to be part of the lively and messy process of invention. Diane encourages Lesbians to recognize and acknowledge our achievements, to talk about money and power, to stretch our generosity, and to develop our strength as individuals and as a community.

(For information about 100 Lesbians and our Friends, the Angel Fund for Del Martin and Phyllis Lyon, or for any other reference in this article, please contact: <dianesabin@hotmail.com>.)

The Sound of Activism:
A Personal Journey

Boden Sandstrom
Charlene Vetter

SUMMARY. A longtime advocate for female empowerment and equality, Boden Sandstrom has worked for political change in many arenas. In the 1960s, she began a career as a librarian, but soon made activism her full-time job, working for feminist, leftist and socialist causes. In the 1970s, she found a way to turn her lifelong passion for music into a career as a sound engineer. Once established in that profession, she began donating her services to political events, marches, demonstrations, and rallies. After thirteen years of running her own company, called Woman Sound, Inc. (later City Sound Productions, Inc.), she turned to the study of ethnomusicology. She is now Program Manager and Lecturer for the

Boden Sandstrom lives in Takoma Park, Maryland, and is currently Program Manager and Lecturer for the Ethnomusicology Program at the University of Maryland, where she is earning a doctorate in that subject. She holds a Master's degree in Audio Technology from American University, Washington, DC, and one in Library Science from the University of Michigan. She is a former musician, librarian, and disc jockey, and is currently a sound engineer and technical producer.

Charlene Vetter lives in Buffalo, New York, where she works as a project director for the State University of New York Research Foundation. She holds a Bachelor's degree in psychology from the State University of New York at Buffalo, and a Master's degree in counseling from Canisius College.

Address correspondence to: Boden Sandstrom, 3110B Clarice Smith Performing Arts Center, School of Music, University of Maryland, College Park, MD 20742.

[Haworth co-indexing entry note]: "The Sound of Activism: A Personal Journey." Sandstrom, Boden, and Charlene Vetter. Co-published simultaneously in *Journal of Lesbian Studies* (Harrington Park Press, an imprint of The Haworth Press, Inc.) Vol. 5, Number 3, 2001, pp. 161-167; and: *Everyday Mutinies: Funding Lesbian Activism* (ed: Nanette K. Gartrell, and Esther D. Rothblum) Harrington Park Press, an imprint of The Haworth Press, Inc., 2001, pp. 161-167. Single or multiple copies of this article are available for a fee from The Haworth Document Delivery Service [1-800-342-9678, 9:00 a.m. - 5:00 p.m. (EST). E-mail address: getinfo@haworthpressinc.com].

Ethnomusicology Program at the University of Maryland, where she is also working on her doctorate in that subject. She continues to freelance as a sound engineer and serve as a technical producer for major events. *[Article copies available for a fee from The Haworth Document Delivery Service: 1-800-342-9678. E-mail address: <getinfo@haworthpressinc.com> Website: <http://www.HaworthPress.com> © 2001 by The Haworth Press, Inc. All rights reserved.]*

KEYWORDS. Lesbian, lesbian activism, fundraising, women's music

Music has always been my first passion, but activism has also played an important role in my life. The ways in which I have fought for change have varied greatly over the years. There was a time in my life when all my waking hours were spent working for political causes, but my love for music eventually led me into a career as a sound engineer. As I became established in that profession, I began to support political causes by donating my talents at rallies, marches, and fundraisers.

In the late 1960s, while working as a librarian at Dodge Library at Northeastern University, I began to get involved in political organizations in Boston. I held memberships in several feminist, leftist, and socialist organizations, including Female Liberation and the Young Socialist Alliance (YSA). My income helped to support both myself and my former husband, Rogelio Reyes, a political activist working for such causes as the Puerto Rican Independence Movement and the Farmworkers' struggle. In 1971, I resigned from Dodge Library and made political activism my full-time career. I began working as the office manager for the Boston Greater Peace Action Coalition, and briefly held the position of organizer for the Boston YSA. During that time, I was very active in the anti-war movement, and supported the struggles for freedom in many countries in South and Central America and the Middle East. My daily activities largely consisted of organizing demonstrations and protests, attending meetings, and writing and handing out literature. It was an all-consuming endeavor, with usually only one half-day off per week. Any extra money I had went right back into the causes.

In the early 1970s, I decided to leave organized politics. Sacrificing myself on a daily basis left me with very little time and energy to develop as an individual. From my political life, I had gained priceless memories and invaluable leadership and organization skills, but I decided it was time for me to grow emotionally and intellectually. I needed to begin exploring who I was as a woman. As a feminist, I strongly believed that I had to become a complete per-

Boden Sandsrom
Photo by Deborah Jenkins. Used by permission.

Charlene Vetter

son in order to bring about lasting change in the world. Since my childhood, when I first started playing an instrument (the trumpet followed by the French horn), I yearned to make music an ever greater part of my life. I played the French horn every day of my life throughout graduate school but never thought I could make a living pursuing this interest. I was brought up to find fulfillment in marriage and was not encouraged to pursue my musical ability; in fact, my instrument choice caused much harassment by the boys I played with. I consequently had a liberal arts education and became a librarian. In 1972, I moved to Washington, D.C., and became a librarian at Martin Luther King Library. I found the work fulfilling, but I still wanted to find a way to turn my passion for music into a livelihood. As it turned out, a chance encounter at a concert afforded me the opportunity to fulfill my lifelong dream of working in the music industry.

While attending my first women's music concert, a farewell concert for the women of Olivia Records, the first women's record company, I saw a woman mixing the concert. In that instant, I knew what I wanted to do. As a French horn player I had learned how to hear and fit in with all kinds of musical groups. Another strong academic interest was math and science. I instinctively knew that the role of an engineer would combine these two skills as well as serve as an outlet for musical expression that was missing in my life at that time. I felt empowered by the women's music–music by women written for women–I heard that night.

I struck up a conversation with Judy Dlugacz, the woman who was mixing the sound for the show (Judy is one of the founders of Olivia Records and its current president). I expressed to her my interest in learning her profession. She told me she knew a musician, Casse Culver, who was looking for a woman to train as a sound engineer. That serendipitous meeting changed my career path forever. I had discovered a way to work on a daily basis at something about which I felt passionate. My new career would provide me with countless opportunities to use music to contribute to the causes in which I believed. The concert also had a profound impact on my personal life. Listening to female artists sing love songs about women confirmed my identity as a lesbian.

I was still working as a librarian when Casse asked me to be the assistant sound engineer on her first album in 1976. When my employer denied me a five-week leave to work on the project, I decided to resign from my position. Fortunately, Washington's unemployment laws provided for career transitions, and I was granted full benefits. This gave me enough money to live on and provided some extra funds to help Casse and me start our own sound company, Woman Sound. From then on, all our financial resources went into Woman Sound. We never turned a profit because we constantly had to buy new equipment to keep up with the demands of the musicians that were hiring us. With no corporate sponsors, we had to become experts in creative financing. We sought out female investors, and eventually incorporated and sold stock in the company. A loan from the Feminist Credit Union also helped us stay afloat.

Competing with other sound companies for business often turned into a battle of the sexes, as many rival companies were run by males who were not above giving each other inside information to underbid us for government contracts. Fortunately, two of our lesbian supporters informed us of these deceptive business practices, and afterwards we were able to bid successfully on these contracts.

The wild ride of running Woman Sound lasted thirteen years. Casse and I dissolved our business partnership in 1978, but I carried on as sole owner and operator until 1988. During that time, I cultivated many friendships with people in the political community. I mixed sound at feminist and gay pride rallies, offering my services at a considerable discount. I also worked within the women's music network, and worked events showcasing female artists, such as The Michigan Womyn's Music Festival and SisterFire. I had finally found my niche as a woman, a professional, and an activist. Through my art, I contributed to the struggle for freedom and equality for lesbians, for all women and people. I would not trade the experience of running Woman Sound for anything. It allowed me to achieve creative and personal fulfillment, and I was able to inspire many women to join a male-dominated profession.

Unfortunately, but perhaps not surprisingly, I had to make many personal sacrifices during that time. I barely made enough money to survive because of the capital needed to upgrade equipment. Free time and vacations were nonexistent. I worked constantly, and had neither the time nor energy for a personal life. At the same time, I earned a Master's degree in Audio Technology. When we started Woman Sound, I had no idea how expensive and time consuming it would be. By 1988, I realized that I could no longer afford to run the business, and it was time to sell out. My one regret, looking back at that time, is that I did not let go sooner and become a freelance engineer so that I could seek out other meaningful sound engineering jobs. In the time since I sold my business, I've continued to work at gaining expertise in sound engineering. I pursue my love of music within the field of ethnomusicology, the study of music in and as culture.

I am currently Program Manager for the Ethnomusicology Program at the University of Maryland, where I am also studying for a doctorate in ethnomusicology. In this field I utilize all of my skills: sound engineering, archival research, and teaching. As part of my work, I am engaged in preserving the history that many of us have lived. At the moment, I am collaborating on a film entitled *Radical Harmonies: The History of Women's Music* with my friend Dee Mosbacher, whom I met during my political organizing days. Dee was one of the generous supporters of Woman Sound and we could not have done without her contributions.

I have also been working as a technical producer, which encompasses sound, staging, stage management, lighting, security, etc., for musical events. I supplement my teaching income by freelancing as a technical producer, and I work as the sound engineer at Robert F. Kennedy Stadium. My academic pursuits currently take center stage in my life, but many political issues are personally important to me. There are so many changes left to be made. There's the fight for female equality, of course, and the fight against the military's policy on gays and lesbians, as well as the need for hate-crimes legislation. On a global scale, we face overpopulation and the need for environmental conservation.

Once I have completed my doctoral dissertation, I intend to return to my activist beginnings by devoting more time and energy to these causes. I hope that, after my journey of self-discovery, my activism will be more focused now, and perhaps more personally satisfying. My advice to activists is that they first come to know themselves as individuals, and, in doing so, discover what issues are most meaningful to them personally. By listening to their inner voice, they can learn what truly moves them. The more personally invested in an issue one is, the more productive and personally fulfilled one will be as an activist.

Caring Deeply, Changing the World:
A Profile of Sherry Thomas

Sherry Thomas
Marcia Perlstein

SUMMARY. Sherry Thomas's history of activism and fundraising in the lesbian feminist community, told in her own words, offers us a point of view of periods of our evolving culture and knowledge that will both inspire and teach. From the rural reaches of Northern California and the nascent consciousness raising and country women's movement, to the burgeoning publishing and women's bookstore culture, Sherry was on the frontlines. Then in the larger lesbigay community, first for San Francisco's Main Library fundraising campaign and currently for Lambda

Sherry Thomas is currently national Director of Development for Lambda Legal Defense and Education Fund. She has been publisher of Spinsters/Aunt Lute Book Company and Country Women, part of the collective that ran Old Wives' Tales Bookstore in San Francisco, and Executive Director of San Francisco's New Main Library capital campaign.

Marcia Perlstein has been a practicing psychotherapist in Berkeley and San Francisco, California, since 1967. She was Director of the Alternative Family Project, San Francisco, California, and Founder and Director of the East Bay Volunteer Therapist AIDS Project. She offers Aspirations workshops for women and girls across the country and diversity training for businesses, schools and non profits; trains virgin and veteran psychotherapists; and, as a former Associate for National Commission on Resources for Youth and high school principal, consults with school districts and parents in organizing with young people to be providers of services rather than recipients.

Address correspondence to: Sherry Thomas and Marcia Perlstein, 1806 Martin Luther King Jr. Way, Berkeley, CA 94709 (E-mail: scraggs3@ncal.verio.com).

[Haworth co-indexing entry note]: "Caring Deeply, Changing the World: A Profile of Sherry Thomas." Thomas, Sherry, and Marcia Perlstein. Co-published simultaneously in *Journal of Lesbian Studies* (Harrington Park Press, an imprint of The Haworth Press, Inc.) Vol. 5, Number 3, 2001, pp. 169-178; and: *Everyday Mutinies: Funding Lesbian Activism* (ed: Nanette K. Gartrell, and Esther D. Rothblum) Harrington Park Press, an imprint of The Haworth Press, Inc., 2001, pp. 169-178. Single or multiple copies of this article are available for a fee from The Haworth Document Delivery Service [1-800-342-9678, 9:00 a.m. - 5:00 p.m. (EST). E-mail address: getinfo@haworthpressinc.com].

Legal Defense, Sherry teaches us how inextricably related organizing and funding are. *[Article copies available for a fee from The Haworth Document Delivery Service: 1-800-342-9678. E-mail address: <getinfo@ haworthpressinc.com> Website: <http://www.HaworthPress.com> © 2001 by The Haworth Press, Inc. All rights reserved.]*

KEYWORDS. Lesbian, lesbian activism, fundraising

I'd known Sherry Thomas by reputation for many years. About ten years ago, I attended a workshop she was presenting on publishing and writing for lesbians. I expected her to be articulate and informative, and she certainly was. She was also wise, warm and generous. I carried from that workshop the feeling that, as busy as she was, if any one of us needed help in the future with our work in the lesbian community, she'd respond and either help us herself, or point us to someone who could. So when I was asked if I wanted to be interviewed for this book on lesbian activism, I opted instead to interview Sherry. I felt that although we were of the same generation of activists, I still had much I could learn from her, especially about fundraising. The following illustrates that she more than met my expectations.

There are incalculable benefits that come from being an activist: community, pride, fulfillment, the knowledge that you're changing the world for the better. I don't see how anybody can live without being an activist. I believe we shouldn't settle for less.

EVOLVING ACTIVISM

Like many people, Sherry Thomas's activism started during the Vietnam War era. In 1968, she was studying political science at Brown University, but found the contradictions between learning how to manage mass movements in a very academic setting and what was going on in the streets were too great for her.

Activism is a funny word. What is activism in one decade may not be seen as that at all in the next. Historical context matters. Then there's also the didactic of political overlay that's in all of our heads: activism means marching in the streets or direct political organizing.

I came of age in the anti-Vietnam War movement and the student revolutions of the late sixties; the quintessential old-style activism. I even earned a

Sherry Thomas
Photo by Alex Sabin. Used by permission.

living (paid for by the Ford Foundation) doing campus organizing in 1969, the perfect intersection of revolution and co-optation. That experience gave me the belief early on that I could survive economically, doing what I cared deeply about, changing the world, being an activist–something that stood me in good stead for many years.

Marcia Perlstein
Photo by Karen McLellan. Used by permission.

With the beginning of the women's movement and my own personal coming out during this period, my definition of activism changed dramatically. It is hard to even describe that time now–there were no words for what we were creating; there were no models, no roadmap. I was sleeping with women before I ever heard the word lesbian. Before the women's movement, there were no conversations about women's sexuality and women's health, about women and work, about violence against women. We had to create these conversations while re-inventing ourselves. Feminism and activism became, for me, one and the same.

COUNTRY WOMEN

Sherry packed her East Coast life into a Volkswagen bus and headed to California's North Coast to start a sheep ranch. She joined other women who had been out longer than she and who were starting a consciousness raising group. This was late '69; it was when she first remembered seeing the Furies.
We began organizing in that small town. Mendocino was an area much like Santa Fe or Woodstock where a number of counterculture people were moving. In those heady days, we began falling in love with each other. It's hard not to love someone who is struggling so honestly to re-invent herself. We had probably half the women in the town in consciousness raising groups. All of a sudden this town of mostly married women was a town of lesbians. It had a fascinating radicalizing effect on the town and the community. If the personal was political in consciousness raising, the political was really personal in a small, rural town.

PRINT POWER

I think it is because lesbians and feminists had no language for who we were and what we were creating that we gravitated so strongly towards publishing and writing. By the mid-seventies a large part of the women's movement was organized that way: there were newspapers, magazines, bookstores, presses, book publishers, and of course writers.
Where I was living, none of us had the remotest thought of being writers, although many of us had been to college. We created a magazine, *Country Women*, because we wanted to find other women like ourselves, and because we wanted something to do together after the consciousness raising groups broke up. But the interesting side effect of organizing a movement around print media was that it also became an economic endeavor. We found that we could

live our passions, that we could change the world, while at the same time earn a marginal living doing it. You have to keep in mind that money went a lot farther back then. I recently did a calculation, and $300 in 1972 is the same as $1,200 today. There's no way I could live in San Francisco on $1,200 monthly today.

Country Women was just the right thing at the right time. We started out typing issues on an IBM Selectric; by issue number 6 we had 17,000 subscribers from around the country. It was one of the biggest lesbian feminist publications of the time. And we found ourselves suddenly part of a much larger network and conversation going on around the country. New women were continually attracted to the area because of the magazine, so we had a pretty vibrant women's culture.

All the members of the Country Women collective also had some kind of other job. Sherry worked nights in the State Park and used to type the magazine on a portable typewriter in the Park's registration booth for campers. From the magazine they also created a book called Country Women. *Sherry describes it as the intersection of the feminist and the back-to-the-land movements that had very fortuitous timing, selling over 100,000 copies in just the first year.*

I don't think that I've ever seen quite another model where so much of a movement was organized around writing and publication as the lesbian feminist movement was. In that period of time so much activism was funneled into some form of that–everything from producing poetry chat books to newspapers to the network of bookstores to the nascent lesbian publishing movement that started.

WOMEN IN PRINT CONFERENCES

There were three national Women in Print conferences during that period between 1976 and the early 1980s, where all of the magazines, bookstores, book publishers, and printers got together. The first one was held in Omaha, Nebraska, a site chosen because it was halfway between the coasts, and therefore, we believed, more accessible to everyone; the second conference was held at the 4-H center in Washington D.C., and the last one took place in Oakland, California.

This was a movement. We all firmly believed that writing and publishing could help prompt social change. Tens of thousands of readers proved us right. The written word could reach a mass audience with a very personal politic. By meeting together at those national conferences, strong ties and relationships were built that changed the way the movement organized and transformed itself.

Along with the political component of what we were doing, the print move-ment also provided opportunities for me to grow my skills, both as a writer and an organizer. After publishing two books, I moved to San Francisco to join the Old Wives' Tales bookstore collective. Old Wives' Tales and the other hun-dred or so bookstores around the country functioned as community and cul-tural centers as well as the distribution point for books about and by women that were literally unavailable elsewhere. Old Wives' Tales was, like most of the women's stores, the front line for newcomers in town and the place where lesbians could discuss most of the cutting-edge issues of the time.

When the Old Wives' Tales collective fractured, I went back to my first love, publishing, taking over Spinsters Ink from two women I'd met at the Omaha Women in Print conference. With $3,000 that my grandmother gave me and a small grant from the California Arts Council, I published my first three books and supported myself while doing so. A few years later, Spinsters merged with Aunt Lute Books from Iowa City.

We would publish a non-fiction title and then the book would sell so much better a couple of years later. It wasn't that we were prescient, but it takes a time for a community to absorb new ideas. I believe print media can carve the way to another level of knowledge or acceptance. Publishing is never a very good economic proposition; you put up all the cash up front, and wait one hun-dred eighty days or more to get paid back. It became clear that we were just on the edge of survival every inch of the way. We'd get to where we had to pay royalties every six months and the bank account would be absolutely dry. We wouldn't know how we could make payroll; the partners didn't get paid if we had to pay the workers and it was rough. It worked; but it was rough. We de-cided after asking a lot of people for advice to split the press into a non-profit press and a for-profit press. We put the activist books and the movement books into the non-profit side of the press and did fundraising to support it.

FUNDRAISING AS NECESSITY

The attempt to raise money for the non-profit arm of Spinsters/Aunt Lute was Sherry's first official foray into fundraising and philanthropy. She re-ceived her first fundraising training from Marya Grambs, founder of the Women's Foundation, and Kim Klein, who had been training grassroots activ-ists to do fundraising for years. They mailed a fundraising appeal to the entire Spinsters/Aunt Lute mailing list. The response was extraordinary: one woman they'd never met mailed them $9,000, and another $80,000 was donated by or-dinary lesbians around the country who wanted to see the press continue.

I became interested in fundraising because of the whole Spinsters/Aunt Lute experience and realized that so many of our lesbian institutions had been crippled by lack of resources. At the time I rather naively thought if we only had enough resources, we could do anything in the world.

While still running Spinsters, Sherry volunteered for a couple of non-profit boards and got a little bit better at fundraising. And then she heard that a new main library was being built in San Francisco. The campaign pledged to be all inclusive of San Francisco's diverse communities, including the gay and lesbian community. Sherry thought it provided an unusual opportunity to create a great civic institution. Her passionate belief in the power of the printed word and the message of the campaign made the library a symbol for social change. Sherry believed if you could put free books in the hands of everyone, you could change an amazing amount of culture.

With this passion, Sherry went to the San Francisco Library Foundation in 1991 and said, "I want to be a part of your campaign." They weren't hiring. Undaunted, she offered to volunteer. The foundation director accepted her offer, and she soon went from being a volunteer fundraiser to being the half-time paid person in charge of the Gay and Lesbian Center. When the opportunity arose to become the Director of Special Gifts, Sherry started looking for a buyer for Spinsters. By the time the Major Donor Director position was offered to her the following year, Spinsters had been sold to Joan Drury, who moved the press to Minneapolis. By happenstance, the Executive Director position became available next. Sherry's career was set. She had found a new passion, not really so different from her old one: supporting the institutions and visions that allow us to create social change. In all, Sherry spent eight years with the Library Foundation, working with the Chinese, Latino, Philippino, gay and lesbian, environmental and other communities, helping to raise $36 million.

Now at Lambda Defense and Education Fund, Sherry is working in a national gay and lesbian civil rights organization. She credits all her previous experiences with leading to her current one.

FUNDRAISING AND ORGANIZING

My job as a fundraiser is to match plans and dreams with people who want to be a part of that. I sell visions of what is possible. For me, it's just another way, on a very big canvas, to facilitate change.

The experience of organizing the Gay and Lesbian Center at the San Francisco Library taught me two things: it taught me how hungry people were for community–people mailed us gifts from across the country–and it taught me how much we needed a history and culture. I began to understand that donors to gay and lesbian causes give because they want to be a part of a larger movement, because they want to actively be involved with change. Fundraising when it works best is about empowerment; if you don't have the volunteer time to be an activist, you can be an activist with your money. It means being really thoughtful; it means being proactive; it means doing your research and your homework. It means being strategic with your gift, maybe leveraging it for multiple purposes. You can do amazing things by giving money to organizations that have very concrete results.

The Gay and Lesbian Center in New York does an annual women's event; last year they asked people who could to add an extra hundred dollars to their ticket so that women of color and low income women could also attend the event. And at first I worried that it was patronizing to assume that women of color don't have any money. But in fact what happened was that it was the most culturally diverse event of women I'd seen in fifteen years. We can leverage new possibilities, we can build community, we can stimulate change and sometimes money is the way to do it. I think women are too afraid of money, too ashamed of money, too uncomfortable with money and we need to get over it. Because our movement needs us to, and when we do we'll be able to have profound impact.

FUNDRAISING FOR LESBIAN CAUSES:
COMPLEX OBSERVATIONS

When Sherry looks at fundraising efforts within the lesbian community, much like an older sister, she is outspoken and constructively critical in a context of advocacy and concern. She is not afraid to make some difficult observations about the way many of us, unless we are willing to be extremely mindful and vigilant, are still products of our acculturation. Thus, we may unconsciously act from messages we were taught as girls.

If there's a crying need for us as lesbians right now, it's to be clear. We need to address what a lesbian agenda is in a gay and lesbian world. There are places where support needs to be for women only but we're not very good about articulating those needs and we're not good at selling it as a movement.

If you choose to live in a lesbian-only world or a women's-only world, there is often a lack of resources. We also have a lot of issues about money and comfort with money. It's complicated and much harder to raise money from women only. I have found an amazing number of women don't know that they should give, don't know how to give, don't know where to give. I've met some extraordinarily talented women who know how to invest in the stock market, but who've said to me, "How do you get on a board? You know, I've always wanted to do a little bit more but I don't know how to do it." No one ever says something like, just give some money; you know, volunteer, get involved. I think that there's a real hunger to have more meaningful lives than just the day job, especially when the day job is demanding but not terribly fulfilling.

All this needs to be modeled and taught. I still don't think we're doing a great job at training those who follow us. One of our lesbian foundations has struggled for years to figure out what they should do with the money; they don't have a purpose. We have been bad about making breast cancer as important an issue as AIDS. We're getting better. And we need to work harder at giving women access points to social change movements or to activism even if it's only in their volunteer time.

TIPS FOR YOUNGER SISTERS

I think the wonderful legacy of the early women's movement was we really believed we had to invent it.

Follow your passion; take risks; don't assume it has to already be in place before you can get involved. Volunteer to be on a non-profit board. Create things from the ground up; there are lots of access points. Ask questions and try to figure out how to become a part of an organization that you really like, or figure out how to expand an organization's programs in a direction that you feel is missing. Movement jobs do exist, but there are many other ways to be an activist. If you choose to focus your life on social change, expect to work hard. Learn to manage, learn to write a good letter, learn the real value of money.

CONCLUSION

Sherry Thomas's journey indicates that she is about risking and reinventing; clarifying, creating, collaborating, and community. In conversation she is quite generous in crediting the community effort and others as well as herself. Our interview was peppered with "we" when describing the variety of threads in the movement in which she participated actively and, in many cases, propelled. She is positive and proactive; sees the personal in the political and the political in the personal. She acknowledges setbacks and fears when they occur, but moves through quickly reframing the inevitable difficulties to challenges, refusing to allow the women she works with to get stuck in a victim stance. Sherry Thomas doesn't miss a beat in going beyond "can we?" to "how can we?"

Out About Class:
Social Change Philanthropy

Léonie Walker

Ingrid Sell

SUMMARY. Lesbian activist Léonie Walker traces the evolution of her involvement in social change philanthropy and her work to bring together activists of diverse class and racial backgrounds. She shows how

Léonie Walker is a philanthropic activist and advisor, socially conscious investor and feminist philanthropist. She currently serves on the national Board of Directors of the Astraea Lesbian Action Foundation and is Co-chair of their $3.4 million Endowment Campaign. Léonie was a founding director of the Ms. Foundation's Women Managing Wealth program and held positions in the Development and Training departments of Equity Institute. She is a past member of the Board of Directors of the National Center for Lesbian Rights and The Lesbian and Gay Community Services Center in New York and the Community Funding Panel for the Astraea Lesbian Action Foundation. In 1997, she co-chaired the Gill Foundation's second OutGiving national conference for leading donors to the lesbian and gay community. In 1999, Léonie received the "Changing the Face of Philanthropy" award from the Women's Funding Network and was recognized as a "Women We Love" honoree by the Brothers for Sisters Auxiliary of the Astraea Foundation.

Ingrid Sell holds a PhD in Transpersonal Psychology with a Clinical Psychology specialization from the Institute of Transpersonal Psychology in Palo Alto, CA, where she is currently a Faculty Mentor in the Global Program. Her dissertation research on the experiences of individuals with intermediate (neither male nor female) gender identities received the 2001 Sidney Jourard Award of Division 32 of the American Psychological Association. A writer and artist, she holds a BFA in Media and Performing Arts, and has written for, among others, *Bay Windows*, *Sojourner*, and *New Directions for Women*. She lives in Cambridge, Massachusetts, and southern Vermont with her life partner, Sharon Boccelli.

Address correspondence to: Léonie Walker, Philanthropic Activist & Advisor, 40 Buckeye, Portola Valley, CA 94028-8015 (E-mail: LeFlies@aol.com).

The authors would like to thank Kate O'Hanlan, MD, for invaluable editorial assistance with this article.

[Haworth co-indexing entry note]: "Out About Class: Social Change Philanthropy." Walker, Léonie, and Ingrid Sell. Co-published simultaneously in *Journal of Lesbian Studies* (Harrington Park Press, an imprint of The Haworth Press, Inc.) Vol. 5, Number 3, 2001, pp. 179-187; and: *Everyday Mutinies: Funding Lesbian Activism* (ed: Nanette K. Gartrell, and Esther D. Rothblum) Harrington Park Press, an imprint of The Haworth Press, Inc., 2001, pp. 179-187. Single or multiple copies of this article are available for a fee from The Haworth Document Delivery Service [1-800-342-9678, 9:00 a.m. - 5:00 p.m. (EST). E-mail address: getinfo@haworthpressinc.com].

179

she was trained as an activist, discusses conscious and socially responsible ways to steward wealth, and gives voice to the seldom-heard experiences of LGBT people with inherited wealth. The co-founder of the Women Managing Wealth program at the Ms. Foundation and a board member of Astraea Lesbian Action Foundation, she has also developed and facilitated numerous Dismantling Classism workshops. In this article, she discusses the importance of, and ways of implementing, cross-class, cross-race dialogue that can further understanding among activists of different backgrounds. *[Article copies available for a fee from The Haworth Document Delivery Service: 1-800-342-9678. E-mail address: <getinfo@haworthpressinc.com> Website: <http://www.HaworthPress.com> © 2001 by The Haworth Press, Inc. All rights reserved.]*

KEYWORDS. Lesbian, lesbian activism, fundraising

My awakening as an activist began around the time of my coming out as a lesbian. There had been an undercurrent, for most of my childhood and adolescence, of feeling very much at odds with the privilege that I was born into and the role I was supposed to play. I was born and raised in New York City to a wealthy family, second generation wealth on both my parents' sides. Growing up Catholic and wealthy, a path was laid out for me, both in terms of class expectations and also as a girl child. My options were pretty limited in terms of what I could be. I was supposed to grow up, find a wealthy guy, get married, have kids, maybe do some volunteer work. I was not expected to work; I wasn't even really expected to go to college. I knew that I didn't quite fit the mold, but I didn't know what was awry for a long time, not seeing any models for me in my world. Part of that was about fitting in the female role, part of it was about being a lesbian, and part was about class around growing up wealthy, likely due to the strength of the already internalized messages about who I was supposed to be.

I was raised primarily by caregivers hired by my parents to take care of me. At any given time we had three full-time people working and living in our home: a cook, a maid, and a nanny. A variety of people went in and out of those roles, but a constant for me was often feeling like the warmest place in the house was the servants' quarters. From an early age I had close relationships and a warm bond with the working class folks in my house. From my relationships with our house staff, I got a glimmer that there were other ways of being than what I saw in my family and social milieu, but it was only a glimmer until much later.

Two things happened that significantly altered the course of my life. First, my father died of lung cancer in 1985. In addition to a trust fund that I had

Léonie Walker
Photo by Jill Posener. Used by permission.

Ingrid Sell
Photo by Sharon Boccelli. Used by permission.

come into when I was 21, I received an additional inheritance after he passed
away. He had been both gracious and generous in how he had set up our inheri-
tances, in that they were in our names and I didn't have to try to undo any
trusts. As long as he was alive, it was hard for me to take ownership of the
money he had given me, for many reasons. With his passing, I could finally
claim that money as my own on an emotional and psychological level.

Secondly, in 1986, I recognized that I was a lesbian. When I came out, I felt as though I had finally found myself, that I was coming home to my true self. While I was raised with a heavy dose of heterosexism, I didn't grow up with a lot of homophobia. With the exception of coming out to my family, my coming out was a very positive experience. I think because of that I jumped into activism without reservation, mostly around lesbian and gay and social justice issues. I was really coming "home." As I realized that I no longer had certain civil rights that I had previously taken for granted; my sense of privilege as wealthy, able-bodied, Gentile and white was severely undermined. This realization was a critical motivator for me in terms of taking up activism and philanthropy around LGBT issues.

After my father's death, my inheritance allowed me more choices than I'd had before. I could actually consider not working. Soon after, I read an interview with Tracy Gary in the alumnae bulletin of the prep school that I went to. Her childhood story was similar to mine. As an adult, however, she had struck out on her own in a strong way. She started a program in San Francisco called Managing Inherited Wealth. I thought, "Here is at least one other person in the world who's got the same story as I do. She's also a lesbian; she has inherited wealth and she's out and telling the truth about her money!" This was unheard of. You just didn't do or say that, but she was a dyke and she was doing it! I called her up immediately and said, "Help!" She told me, "Well, the first thing you should do is call Bread and Roses Community Foundation and get yourself into their Women and Money group. The second thing you should do is come out to our Managing Inherited Wealth semi-annual retreat in California. The next one's coming up soon, so come on out!"

I attended six successive retreats over the next three years. That's where I got my financial education. I learned how to choose and manage investment managers. I learned how to do a budget. Then I learned that I could give away money. This was my introduction to socially responsible investing and social change philanthropy. I began to steward my money in accordance with my most deeply held values. Through giving, sharing, lending and even spending with a socially conscious focus, I discovered I could contribute to a more just and sustainable world by how I used my money. I learned a lot, but more importantly, I joined a network of women who were dealing with these same issues. This was my training ground for becoming an activist. Getting my own house in order, as a woman with inherited wealth, was pivotal in preparing me to be an activist in the world.

My first act as a change agent was in my own community of wealthy women. I co-founded a program at the Ms. Foundation for Women, called Women Managing Wealth, and ran it from 1987-1990. It was a support and educational program for women with primarily inherited wealth, who had more than they needed and wanted to get educated around financial management issues, work choices, and philanthropy.

Being publicly associated with the Women Managing Wealth program put me in a position where people wanted to meet me, thinking they would have access to a group of wealthy women. As a result, opportunities came to me: for instance, I was invited to interview to serve on the board of the Lesbian and Gay Community Services Center in New York. Being elected to that board, and having the opportunity to work in a community organization as a volunteer, was another key part of my training/education as an activist.

It was at that time that I met Katherine Acey, the then-new executive director of Astraea Lesbian Action Foundation. As a new dyke I was very excited to find a lesbian foundation, so I made a donation to Astraea. That's how my relationship with many of the organizations that I've been affiliated with, as both donor and activist, starts. When you send an organization a significant contribution, you often get a call from them, wanting to meet with you. I started hooking up with what would become my new network of peers and colleagues in social justice work, which included gay and lesbian activism and philanthropy.

I was invited to apply to be on Astraea's Community Funding panel, their grant-making panel, in 1995, and served on the panel for 4 years. I was elected to their board in 1999, and am currently co-chairing Astraea's $3.4 million endowment campaign. As a board member and a philanthropic activist, I attend conferences such as the Women's Funding Network, OutGiving and the Women Donors Network. I attend, speak at and help organize conferences, events and activities that are related both to my work for Astraea and to my work as a donor-organizer and philanthropic activist. I fundraise for a number of organizations, although right now I am focused on Astraea. I also have a small practice as a philanthropic advisor, working with donors to direct their money, mostly to socially progressive, feminist and LGBTQ organizations. I am a member of the Women Donors Network, a national network of women philanthropists who have annual philanthropic budgets of $25,000 or more. I try to have a relationship with any organization that Kate, my spouse of 14 years, and I have supported in a major way. More often than not, in addition to giving them money, I will help them with fundraising.

One thing I have struggled with was some of the class dynamics in progressive social change organizations, specifically the chasm between wealthy people and others working for social justice. As I came into the progressive community, I became aware of a pretty harsh attitude towards wealthy people that was really disdainful. Although it wasn't personally targeted at me, I observed resentment in the way people regarded wealthy individuals. I came to understand that it wasn't helpful to collude with the perception that wealthy people are bad.

It has been my experience that in progressive circles, rich people are often the targets of misunderstanding and contempt. This does not encourage wealthy people to be partners in philanthropy or activism with their peers from different class backgrounds. There is isolation and shame at both ends of the socio-economic spectrum, and sharing power is something few of us have learned to do well. The result is a painful gap between otherwise potential allies and partners. There are many wealthy people who do progressive philanthropy, who are not out about their wealth. They might be out about being gay, but they are not out about their wealth. Part of my agenda is to bring more of my wealthy peers into social change philanthropy, which requires making it a more compassionate field. That means being able to have honest, but respectful, cross-class dialogue between wealthy, middle class, working class and poor people. It's not helpful for any of us to see each other as less than human, no matter what our class background is.

While working at the Ms. Foundation, I was introduced, and became a donor to, the Equity Institute, a national non-profit diversity training institute. They had a model of working on racism and classism that was inclusive and embracing. It was a place where I could be a wealthy, white lesbian and be respected for all of who I am. The founders of Equity had come out of the radical left civil rights movement of the '60s. Early on in their work, they had had an "eat the rich" attitude. They soon realized that they weren't going to be very successful raising money from wealthy people as long as they held that attitude, internally or externally. As a result, and as an integral part of their diversity curriculum, they developed an inclusive and respectful way of dealing with the difficulties of class difference. I engaged with them as a volunteer, and eventually I went to work for them. I formed a close friendship with one of the founders who was raised working class. An important aspect of our relationship was our conscious commitment to explore class issues in our relationship, and to use what we learned about each other in our lives to form a basis for developing a Dismantling Classism program. I became a trainer, helped to develop curriculum, and co-led trainings on class issues.

I come from a tradition, in my family, of wealth accumulation and preservation, and that doesn't feel right for me. Accumulating far more than one needs is not healthy for individuals, society or the planet. I think everybody should have as much as they need in order to have freedom, flexibility, security and choices. I have made a conscious choice not to give away all of my money. I have friends and colleagues, for whom I have a deep respect, who have given away most or all of their wealth, and some who have chosen more of a voluntarily simple way of life than I have. My spouse is a physician. She has a good income, and we live a comfortable life. We don't have a lot of stuff, but we have a beautiful home, two good cars that work, and we travel on our vacations, but neither of us likes to be burdened with the maintenance or administration of a lot of material things. We enjoy the freedom of financial security and the choices that that brings. We're also very generous philanthropically. It's a balancing act. We have a responsibility, and we hold a spiritual belief in the need to keep money moving among our beloved on the earth, and not just sit on it. Money is another form of energy really. I'm always happiest when I'm giving, spending, lending . . . trying to keep it dynamic. I feel good about these choices we have made, as long as we give to the world as well as to ourselves, and keep a balance that feels like it has integrity to it.

What has been wonderful about my relationship with Kate is that she was raised middle class, always knowing that she was going to have to work. She doesn't have any money coming to her from her family. She works really, really hard, and she has a very different sense of entitlement about the money that she earns than I ever will about the money that I inherited. When we were first looking at the beautiful house that we live in now, I had a really hard time thinking about buying it. I felt guilty. I felt like it was too much. I felt like there were too many discrepancies in the rest of the world, and that somehow we didn't deserve it. Very irrational, but there it was. Kate said to me, "I work really hard for my patients. We work very hard for our world. We deserve a beautiful place, a comfortable place to come home to and to live in. And it's OK for us to have this." She has really helped me to achieve balance and learn to enjoy some of the creature comforts that are possible when you have abundance.

Another important influence in my activism has been my nine-year friendship with two of the women that I met through my work at Equity Institute. We call ourselves the Troika. All three of us are lesbian, two of us are white, one is African American. We were all raised Catholic. I was raised wealthy, Betty was raised working/middle class, Carole was raised working-class/poor. When we met, Betty was on the board of Equity, Carole was co-founder of the organization, and I was a volunteer. Around the time that we were starting our Dismantling Classism program, we barely knew each other, and Carole said to Betty and me, "I really like you guys. What do you think about us going away for a weekend together? We could tell each other our life stories, talk about class and get to know each other more deeply." And I thought, "What an amazing opportunity to grow!"

We went to Provincetown and spent a weekend by the ocean, asking one another questions and getting to know one another. That was our first Troika. We have had 25 Troikas over 9 years. We formed a training team for the Dismantling Classism program at Equity, but more than that, we created a life-long commitment to this cross-cultural, cross-class, cross-race relationship that has been, on a personal level, profoundly important for each of us. The core of our commitment when we started getting together was to tell one another the truth, to talk about race and class, and to share culture.

We also play a lot, hang out, relax and have fun, but we have an agenda almost every time we get together. We take turns coming up with provocative questions. Inevitably, we do a lot of storytelling and sharing of information about the effects of class in our lives. We also manage money issues in the relationship with a lot of honesty and respect. As a training team, we used to do a panel where we would tell the participants about our Troika. We would talk about what we'd learned and share where we had conflicts and differences and how we worked them out. Then we'd let people just ask us questions. It was fascinating. People were hungry for this kind of honesty in relationships with each other, and specifically for the permission to ask those kinds of questions that we so rarely ask each other.

Two years ago I also became part of another cross-class, cross-race support group with seven other women. We get together once a month for 4 hours, and go away on retreat a couple of times a year. It's a very mixed group. We range in age from our early 40s to our late 50s; white women, women of color, Jewish women, poor women, working class women, middle class women, wealthy women, lesbian, straight, and bisexual women. We came together with a conscious intent to support one another as women, and a specific commitment to focus on issues of class.

In all areas of my life, I try to ensure that I have the kinds of cross-class, cross-race connections and relationships that I have found in my women's support group and in my Troika. Wealth is potentially very isolating. I live in an affluent area, and I'm aware of how easily and quickly I can get disconnected and be isolated from the realities of other people's lives. Part of my commitment is to staying connected. I've made a conscious decision to stay engaged, and I've had a ball. I have many wonderful personal and collegial relationships with diverse people because of the philanthropic opportunities that I've had, both as a donor and as someone who has been willing to step into the stream and work as a volunteer.

I feel blessed to have made the decision to come out, to engage with the money that I received, to be transparent about that and to be willing to talk about class issues. I have always known that my own survival as a human being depended on my connection to others. Some part of me knew to work to figure out how to make the best of all of my gifts. I don't feel bad about being rich. I feel it's a blessing and a great responsibility.

Index

For Product Safety Concerns and Information please contact our EU representative GPSR@taylorandfrancis.com Taylor & Francis Verlag GmbH, Kaufingerstraße 24, 80331 München, Germany

T - #0125 - 270225 - C0 - 212/152/12 - PB - 9781560232599 - Gloss Lamination